Katie King is a new voice to the saga market. She lives in Kent, and has worked in publishing. She has a keen interest in twentieth-century history and this novel was inspired by a period spent living in south-east London.

THE EVACUEE CHRISTMAS

Katie King

ONE PLACE. MANY STORIES

HQ
An imprint of HarperCollins*Publishers* Ltd
1 London Bridge Street
London SE1 9GF

This paperback edition 2017

5
First published in Great Britain by
HQ, an imprint of HarperCollins*Publishers* Ltd 2017

ISBN: 978-0-00-825754-5

MIX
Paper from
responsible sources
FSC™ C007454

This book is produced from independently certified FSC paper
to ensure responsible forest management.

For more information visit: www.harpercollins.co.uk/green

Printed and bound in Great Britain by
CPI Group (UK) Ltd, Croydon, CR0 4YY

THE EVACUEE CHRISTMAS

Chapter One

The shadows were starting to lengthen as twins Connie and Jessie made their way back home.

They felt quite grown up these days as a week earlier it had been their tenth birthday, and their mother Barbara had iced a cake and there'd been a raucous tea party at home for family and their close friends, with party games and paper hats. The party had ended in the parlour with Barbara bashing out songs on the old piano and everyone having a good old sing-song.

What a lot of fun it had been, even though by bedtime Connie felt queasy from eating too much cake, and Jessie had a sore throat the following morning from yelling out the words to 'The Lambeth Walk' with far too much vigour.

On the twins' iced Victoria sponge Barbara had carefully piped Connie's name in cerise icing with loopy lettering and delicately traced small yellow and baby-pink flowers above it.

Then Barbara had thoroughly washed out her metal icing gun and got to work writing Jessie's name below his sister's on the lower half of the cake.

This time Barbara chose to work in boxy dark blue capitals, with a sailboat on some choppy turquoise and deep-blue waves carefully worked in contrasting-coloured icing as the decoration below his name, Jessie being very sensitive about his name and the all-too-common assumption, for people who hadn't met him but only knew him by the name 'Jessie', that he was a girl.

If she cared to think about it, which she tried not to, Barbara heartily regretted that Ted had talked her into giving their only son as his Christian name the Ross family name of Jessie which, as tradition would have it, was passed down to the firstborn male in each new generation of Rosses.

It wasn't even spelt Jesse, as it usually was if naming a boy, because – Ross family tradition again – Jessie was on the earlier birth certificates of those other Jessies and in the family Bible that lay on the sideboard in the parlour at Ted's elder brother's house, and so Jessie was how it had to be for all the future Ross generations to come.

Ted had told Barbara what an honour it was to be called Jessie, and Barbara, still weak from the exertions of the birth, had allowed herself to be talked into believing her husband.

She must have still looked a little dubious, though, as then Ted pointed out that his own elder brother Jessie was a gruff-looking giant with huge arms and legs, and nobody had ever dared tease him about his name. It was going to be just the same for their newborn son, Ted promised.

Big Jessie (as Ted's brother had become known since the birth of his nephew) was in charge of the maintenance of several riverboats on the River Thames, Ted working alongside him, and Big Jessie, with his massive bulk, could single-handedly fill virtually all of the kitchen hearth in his and his wife Val's modest terraced house that backed on to the Bermondsey street where Ted and Barbara raised their children in their own, almost identical red-brick house.

Barbara could see why nobody in their right mind would mess with Big Jessie, even though those who knew him soon discovered that his bruiser looks belied his gentle nature as he was always mild of manner and slow to anger, with a surprisingly soft voice.

Sadly, it had proved to be a whole different story for young Jessie, who had turned out exactly as Barbara had suspected he would all those years ago when she lovingly gazed down at her newborn twins, with the hale and hearty Connie (named after Barbara's mother Constance) dwarfing her more delicate-framed brother as they lay length to length with their toes almost touching and their heads away from each other in the beautifully crafted wooden crib Ted had made for the babies to sleep in.

These days, Barbara could hardly bear to see how cruelly it all played out on the grubby streets on which the Ross family lived. To say it fair broke Barbara's heart was no exaggeration.

While Connie was tall, tomboyish and could easily pass for twelve, and very possibly older, Jessie was smaller and more introverted, often looking a lot younger than he was.

Barbara hated the way Jessie would shrink away from the bigger south-east London lads when they tussled him to the ground in their rough-house games. All the boys had their faces rubbed in the dirt by the other lads at one time or another – Barbara knew and readily accepted that that was part and parcel of a child's life in the tangle of narrow and dingy streets they knew so well – but very few people had to endure quite the punishing that Jessie did with such depressing regularity.

Connie would confront the vindictive lads on her brother's behalf, her chin stuck out defiantly as she dared them to take her on instead. If the boys didn't immediately back away from Jessie, she blasted in their direction an impressive slew of swear words that she'd learnt by dint of hanging around on the docks when she took Ted his lunch in the school holidays. (It was universally agreed amongst all the local boys that when Connie was in a strop, it was wisest to do what she wanted, or else it was simply asking for trouble.)

Meanwhile, as Connie berated all and sundry, Jessie would freeze with a cowed expression on his face, and look as if he wished he were anywhere else but there. Needless to say, it was with a ferocious regularity that he found himself at the mercy of these bigger, stronger rowdies.

Usually this duffing-up happened out of sight of any grown-ups and, ideally, Connie. But the times Barbara spied what was going on all she wanted to do was to run over and take Jessie in her arms to comfort him and promise him it would be all right, and then keep him close to her as she led him back inside their home at number five Jubilee Street. However, she knew that if she even once gave into this impulse, then kind and placid Jessie would never live it down, and he would remain the butt of everyone's poor behaviour for the rest of his childhood.

Barbara loved Connie, of course, as what mother wouldn't be proud of such a lively, proud, strong-minded daughter, with her distinctive and lustrous tawny hair, clear blue eyes and strawberry-coloured lips, and her constant stream of chatter? (Connie was well known in the Ross family for being rarely, if ever, caught short of something to say.)

Nevertheless, it was Jessie who seemed connected to the essence of Barbara's inner being, right to the very centre of her. If Barbara felt tired or anxious, it wouldn't be long before Jessie was at her side, shyly smiling up to comfort his mother with his warm, endearingly lopsided grin.

Barbara never really worried about Connie, who seemed pretty much to have been born with a slightly defiant jib to her chin, as if she already knew how to look after herself or how to get the best from just about any situation. But right from the start Jessie had been much slower to thrive and to walk, although he'd always been good with his sums and with reading, and he was very quick to pick up card games and puzzles.

If Barbara had to describe the twins, she would say that Connie was smart as a whip, but that Jessie was the real thinker of the family, with a curious mind underneath which still waters almost certainly ran very deep.

Unfortunately in Bermondsey during that dog-end of summer in 1939, the characteristics the other local children rated in one another were all to do with strength and cunning and stamina.

For the boys, being able to run faster than the girls when playing kiss chase was A Very Good Thing.

Jessie had never beaten any of the boys at running, and most of the girls could hare about faster than him too.

It was no surprise therefore, thought Barbara, that Jessie had these days to be more or less pushed out of the front door to go and play with the other children, while Connie would race to be the first of the gang outside and then she'd be amongst the last to return home in the evening.

Although only born five minutes apart, they were chalk and cheese, with Connie by far and away the best of any of the children at kiss chase, whether it be the hunting down of a likely target or the hurtling away from anyone brave enough to risk her wrath. Connie was also brilliant at two-ball, skipping, knock down ginger and hopscotch, and in fact just about any playground game anyone could suggest they play.

Jessie was better than Connie in one area – he excelled at conkers, he and Connie getting theirs from a special tree in Burgess Park that they had sworn each other to secrecy over and sealed with a blood pact, with the glossy brown conkers then being seasoned over a whole winter and spring above the kitchen range. Sadly, quite often Jessie would have to yield to bigger children who would demand with menace that his conkers be simply handed over to them, with or without the benefit of any sham game.

Ted never tried to stop Barbara being especially kind to Jessie within the privacy of their own home, provided the rest of the world had been firmly shut outside. But if – and this didn't happen very often, as Barbara already knew what would be said – she wanted to talk to her husband about Jessie and his woes, and how difficult it was for him to make proper friends, Ted would reply that he felt differently about their son than she.

'Barbara, love, it's doing 'im no favours if yer try to fight 'is battles for 'im. I was little at 'is age, an' yer jus' look a' me now' – Ted was well over six foot with tightly corded muscles on his arms and torso, and Barbara never tired of running her hands over his well-sculpted body when they were tucked up in their bed at night with the curtains drawn tight and the twins asleep – 'an' our Jessie'll be fine if we jus' 'elp 'im deal with the bullies. Connie's got the right idea, and in time 'e'll learn from 'er too. An' there'll be a time when our Jessie'll come into his own, jus' yer see if I'm not proved correct, love.'

Barbara really hoped that her husband was right. But she doubted it was going to happen any time soon. And until then she knew that inevitably sweet and open-hearted Jessie would be enduring a pretty torrid time of it.

Still, on this pleasant evening in the first week of September, as a played-out and shamefully grubby Connie and Jessie headed back towards their slightly battered blue front door in Jubilee Street, the only thing a stranger might note about them to suggest they were twins was the way their long socks had bunched in similar concertinas above their ankles, and that they had very similar grey smudges on their knees from where they had been kneeling in the dust of the yard in front of where the local dairy stabled the horses that would pull the milk carts with their daily deliveries to streets around Bermondsey and Peckham.

As the twins walked side by side, their shoulders occasionally bumping and two sets of jacks making clinking sounds as they jumbled against each other in the pockets of Jessie's grey twill shorts, the children agreed that their tea felt as if it had been a very long time ago. Although the bread and beef dripping yummily sprinkled with salt and pepper that they'd snaffled down before going out to play had been lovely, and despite Barbara having seemed quiet and snappy which was very unlike her, by now they were starving again and so they were hoping that they'd be allowed to have seconds when they got in.

They'd only been playing jacks this evening, but Connie had organised a knock-out tournament, and there'd been seven teams of four so it had turned into quite an epic battle. Connie had been the adjudicator and Jessie the scorekeeper, keeping his tally with a pencil-end scrounged from the dairy foreman who'd also then given Jessie a piece of paper to log the teams as Jessie had thanked him so nicely for the inch-long stub of pencil.

The reason the jacks tournament had turned into a hotly contested knock-out affair was that Connie had managed to cadge a bag of end-of-day broken biscuits from a kindly warehouseman at the Peek Freans biscuit factory over on Clements Road – the warehouseman being a regular at The Jolly Shoreman and therefore on nodding acquaintance with Ted and Big Jessie – as a prize for the winning team. These Connie had saved in their brown paper bag so that

Jessie could present them to the winning four, who turned out to be the self-named Thames Tinkers German Bashers.

As the game of jacks had gone on, every time Jessie had peeked over at the paper bag containing the biscuits that his sister had squirrelled close to her side (once, he fancied that he even caught a whiff of the enticing sugary aroma), his mouth had watered even though he knew the warehouseman had only given them to Connie as they were going a bit stale and had missed the day's run of broken biscuits being delivered to local shops so that thrifty, headscarved housewives would later be able to buy them at a knock-down rate.

Jessie knew that Connie had wanted him to present the biscuits to the winning team as a way of subtly ingratiating himself with the jacks players, without her having to say anything in support of her brother. She was a wonderful sister to have on one's side, Jessie knew, and he would have felt even more lost and put upon if he didn't have her in his corner.

Still, it had only been a couple of days since he had begged Connie to keep quiet on his behalf from now on, following an exceptionally unpleasant few minutes in the boys' lavatories at school when he had been taunted mercilessly by Larry, one of the biggest pupils in his class, who'd called Jessie a scaredy-cat and then some much worse names for letting his sister speak out for him.

Larry had then started to push Jessie about a bit, although Jessie had quite literally been saved by the bell. It had rung to signal the end of morning playtime and so with a final, well-aimed shove, Larry had screwed his face into a silent snarl to show his reluctance to stop his torment just at that moment, and at last he let Jessie go.

Jessie was left panting softly as he watched an indignant Larry leave, his dull-blond cowlick sticking up just as crossly as Larry was stomping away.

To comfort himself Jessie had remembered for a moment the time his father had spoken to him quietly but with a tremendous sense of purpose, looking deep into Jessie's eyes and speaking to him with the earnest tone that suggested he could almost be a grown-up. 'Son, you're a great lad, and I really mean it. Yer mam an' Connie know that too, and all three o' us can't be wrong, now, can we? And so all you's got to do now is believe it yerself, and those lads'll then quit their blatherin'. An' I promise you – I absolutely promise you – that'll be all it takes.'

Jessie had peered back at his father with a serious expression. He wanted to believe him, really he did. But it was very difficult and he couldn't ever seem able to work out quite what he should do or say to make things better.

Back at number five Jubilee Street following the jacks tournament, the twins wolfed down their second tea, egg-in-a-cup with buttered bread this time, and then Barbara told them to have a strip wash to deal with their filthy knees and grime-embedded knuckles.

Although she made sure their ablutions were up to scratch, Barbara was nowhere near as bright and breezy as she usually was.

Even Connie, not as a matter of course massively

10

observant of what her parents were up to, noticed that their mother seemed preoccupied and not as chatty as usual, and so more than once the twins caught the other's eye and shrugged or nodded almost imperceptibly at one another.

An hour later Connie's deep breathing from her bed on the other side of the small bedroom the twins shared let Jessie know that his sister had fallen asleep, and Jessie tried to allow his tense muscles to relax enough so that he could rest too, but the scary and dark feeling that was currently softly snarling deep down beneath his ribcage wouldn't quite be quelled.

He had this feeling a lot of the time, and sometimes it was so bad that he wouldn't be able to eat his breakfast or his dinner.

However, this particular bedtime Jessie wasn't quite sure why he felt so strongly like this, as actually he'd had a good day, with none of the lads cornering him or seeming to notice him much (which was fine with Jessie), and the game of jacks ended up being quite fun as he'd been able to make the odd pun that had made everyone laugh when he had come to read out the team names.

As he tried willing himself to sleep – counting sheep never having worked for him – Jessie could hear Ted and Barbara talking downstairs in low voices, and they sounded unusually serious even though Jessie could only hear the hum of their conversation rather than what they were actually saying.

Try as he might, Jessie couldn't pick out any mention of his own name, and so he guessed that for once his parents weren't talking about him and how useless he had turned out to be at standing up for himself. He supposed that this was all to the good, and after what seemed like an age he was able to let go of his usual worries so that at long last he could drift off.

Chapter Two

When the children had been smaller, Ted and Big Jessie had met a charismatic firebrand of a left-wing rabble-rouser called David, and eventually he had talked the brothers into going to several political meetings in the East End aimed at convincing the audience of the need for working-class men to band together to form a socialist uprising. A lot of the talk had been of fascists, and the political situation in Spain and Germany.

It wasn't long before Ted and Big Jessie had been persuaded to go with members of the group to protest against Oswald Mosley's Blackshirts' march through Cable Street in Whitechapel, although the brothers had retreated when the mood turned nasty and rocks were pelted about and there were running battles between the left- and right-wing supporters and the police.

Ted, naturally an easy-going sort, hadn't gone to another meeting of the socialists, and within a few months David had left to go to Spain to fight on the side of the Republicans.

Still, his tolerant nature didn't mean that Ted would always nod along down at The Jolly Shoreman whenever (and this had been happening quite often in recent months) a patron seven sheets to wind would suggest that any fascist supporters should be strung up high. He didn't like what fascists believed in but, deep down, Ted believed they were people too, and who really had the right to insist how other people thought?

But in recent weeks Ted had had to think more seriously about what he believed in, and how far he might be prepared to go to protect his beliefs, and his family.

As he was a docker, working alongside Big Jessie on the riverboats that spent a lot of their time moving cargo locally between the various docks and warehouses on either side of the Thames, Ted had witnessed first-hand that the government had been preparing for war for a while.

He'd seen an obvious stockpiling of munitions and other things a country going to war might need, such as medical supplies and various sorts of tinned or non-perishable foodstuffs that were now stacked waiting in warehouses. There'd also been a steady increase in new or reconditioned ships that were arriving at the docks and leaving soon afterwards with a variety of cargo.

And recently Prime Minister Neville Chamberlain had taken to the BBC radio to announce hostilities against Germany had been declared following their attack on Poland. His words had been followed within minutes by air-raid sirens sounding across London, causing an involuntary bolt of panic to shoot through ordinary Londoners. It was a false alarm but a timely suggestion of what was to come.

Understandably, the dark mood of desperation and foreboding as to what might be going to happen was hard to shake off, and during the evening of the day of Chamberlain's broadcast Ted and Barbara had knelt on the floor and clasped hands as they prayed together.

Scandalously, in these days when most people counted themselves as Church of England believers (or, as London was increasingly cosmopolitan, possibly of Jewish or Roman Catholic faiths), neither Ted nor Barbara, despite marrying in church and having had the twins christened when they were only a few months old, were regular churchgoers, and they had never done anything like this in their lives before.

But these were desperate times, and desperate measures were called for.

As they clambered up from their knees feeling as if the sound of the air-raid siren was still ringing in their ears, they took the decision not, just yet, to be wholly honest if either Connie or Jessie asked them a direct question about why all the grown-ups around them were looking so worried. They wouldn't yet disturb the children with talk of war and what that might mean.

The next day, when Connie mentioned the air-raid siren, Barbara explained away the sound of it by saying she wasn't absolutely certain but she thought it was almost definitely a dummy run for practising how to warn other boats to be careful if a large cargo ship ran aground on the tidal banks of the Thames, to which Connie nodded as if that was indeed very likely the case. Jessie didn't look so easily convinced but Barbara distracted him quickly by saying she wanted his help with a difficult crossword clue she'd not been able to fathom.

Although naturally both Ted and Barbara were very honest people, they could remember the Great War all too clearly, even though they had only been children when that war had been declared in 1914, and they could still recall vividly the terrible toll that had exacted on everyone, both those who had gone to fight and those who had remained at home.

This meant they felt that even though it would only be a matter of days, or maybe mere hours, before the twins had to be made aware of what was going on, the longer the innocence of childhood could be preserved for Connie and Jessie, as far as their parents were concerned, the kinder this would be.

Once Ted and Barbara started to speak with the children about Britain being at war, they knew there would be no going back.

Now that time was here.

Just before the children had arrived home from school, things had come to a head.

For schoolteacher Miss Pinkly had called at number five to deliver a typewritten note to Barbara and Ted from the headmaster at St Mark's Primary School.

When Barbara saw Susanne Pinkly at her door, immediately she felt an overpowering sense of despair.

Without the young woman having to say a word, Barbara knew precisely what was about to happen.

By the time that Ted came in after the twins had gone

to bed – Barbara not bringing up the topic of evacuation with Connie and Jessie beforehand as she wanted the children to be told only when Ted was present – Barbara was almost beside herself, having worked herself up into a real state.

Ted had just left a group of dockers carousing at The Jolly Shoreman. Ted wasn't much of a drinker, but he had gone over with Big Jessie for their usual two pints of best, which was a Thursday night ritual at 'the Jolly' for the brothers and their fellow dockers as the end of their hard-working week drew near.

Now that Ted saw Barbara standing lost and forlorn, looking whey-faced and somehow strangely pinched around the mouth, he felt sorry he hadn't headed home straight after he'd moored the last boat. No beer was worth more than being with his wife in a time of crisis, and to look at Barbara's tight shoulders, a crisis there was.

Barbara was standing in front of the kitchen sink slowly wrapping and unwrapping a damp tea towel around her left fist as she stared unseeing out of the window.

The debris of a half-prepared meal for her husband was strewn around the kitchen table, and it was the very first time in their married lives that Ted could ever remember Barbara not having cleared the table from the children's tea and then cooking him the proverbial meat and two veg that would be waiting ready for her to dish up the moment he got home. Normally Barbara would shuffle whatever she'd prepared onto a plate for him as he soaped and dried his hands, so that exactly as he came to sit down at the kitchen table she'd be placing his plate before him in a routine that had become well choreographed over the years since they had married.

'Barbara, love, whatever is the matter?' Ted said as he swiftly crossed the kitchen to stand by his wife. He tried to sound strong and calm, and very much as if he were the reliable backbone of the family, the sort of man that Barbara and the twins could depend on, no matter what.

Barbara's voice dissolved in pieces as she turned to look at her husband with quickly brimming eyes, and she croaked, 'Ted, read this,' as she waved in his direction the piece of paper that Miss Pinkly had left.

At least, that was what Ted thought she had said to him but Barbara's voice had been so faint and croaky that he wasn't completely sure.

Ted stared at it for a while before he was able to take in all that it said.

```
Dear Parent(s),

Please have your child(s) luggage ready
Monday morning, fully labelled. If you live
more than 15 minutes from the school, (s)he
must bring his case with him/her on Monday
morning.

EQUIPMENT (apart from clothes worn)
•  Washing things – soap, towel
•  Older clothes – trousers/skirt or dress
•  Gym vest, shorts/skirt and plimsolls
•  6 stamped postcards
```

- Socks or stockings
- Card games
- Gas mask
- School hymn book
- Shirts/blouse
- Pyjamas, nightdress or nightshirt
- Pullover/cardigan
- Strong walking shoes
- Story or reading book
- Blanket

<u>ALL TO BE PROPERLY MARKED</u>

<u>FOOD</u> (for 1 or 2 days)
- ¼lb cooked meat
- 2 hard-boiled eggs
- ¼lb biscuits (wholemeal)
- Butter (in container)
- Knife, fork, spoon
- ¼lb chocolate
- ¼lb raisins
- 12 prunes
- Apples, oranges
- Mug (unbreakable)

Yours sincerely,
DAVID W. JONES
Headmaster, St Mark's Primary School,
Bermondsey

The whole of Connie and Jessie's school was to be evacuated, and this looked set to happen in only four days' time.

Her voice stronger, Barbara added glumly, 'I see they've forgotten to put toothbrush on the list.'

After a pause, she said, 'Susanne Pinkly told me that not even the headmaster knows where they will all be going yet, although it looks as if the school will be kept together as much as possible. Some of the teachers are going – those with no relatives anyway – but Mr Jones isn't, apparently, as St Mark's will have to share a school and it's unlikely they'll want two headmasters, and Miss Pinkly's not going to go with them either as her mother is in hospital with some sort of hernia and so Susanne needs to look after the family bakery in her mother's absence now that her brother Reece has already been given his papers.

'But the dratted woman kept saying again and again that all the parents are strongly advised to evacuate their children, and I couldn't think of anything to say back to her. I know she's probably right, but I don't want to be parted from our Connie and Jessie. Susanne Pinkly had with her a bundle of posters she's to put up in the windows of the local shops saying MOTHERS – SEND THEM OUT OF LONDON, and she waved them at me, and so I had to take a couple to give to Mrs Truelove for her to put up in the window and on the shop door. While the talk in the shop a couple of days ago made me realise that a mass evacuation was likely, now that it's here it feels bad, and I don't like it at all.'

Ted drew Barbara close to him, and with his mouth

close to her ear said gently, 'I think we 'ave to let 'em go. The talk in the Jolly was that it's not goin' to be a picnic 'ere, and we 'ave to remember that we're right where those Germans are likely to want to bomb because the docks will be – as our Big Jessie says – "strategic".'

They were quiet for a few moments while they thought about the implications of 'strategic'.

'I know,' said Barbara eventually in a very small voice. 'You're right.'

Ted grasped her to him more tightly.

They listened to the tick-tocking of the old wooden kitchen clock on the mantelpiece for an age, each lost in their own thoughts.

And then Ted said resolutely, 'We'll tell our Connie and Jessie at breakfast in the mornin'. They need to hear it from us an' not from their classmates, an' so we'll need to get 'em up a bit earlier. We must look on the bright side – to let them go will keep them safe, and with a bit of luck it'll all be over by Christmas and we can 'ave them 'ome with us again. 'Ome in Jubilee Street, right beside us, where they belong.'

Barbara hugged Ted back and then pulled the top half of her body away a little so that she could look at her husband's dear and familiar face. 'There is one good thing, which is that as you work on the river, you're not going to have to go away and leave me, although I daresay they'll move you to working on the tugs seeing how much you know about the tides.'

There was another pause, and then Barbara leant against his chest once more, adding in a voice so faint that it was little more than the merest of murmurs, 'I'm scared, Ted, I'm really scared.'

'We all are, Barbara love, an' anyone who says they ain't is a damned liar,' Ted said with conviction, as he drew her more tightly against him.

Chapter Three

Three streets away Barbara's elder sister Peggy was having an equally dispiriting evening. Her husband Bill, a bus driver, had received his call-up papers earlier in the week, and he had to leave first thing in the morning.

All Bill knew so far was that Susanne Pinkly's brother Reece was going the same morning as he, and that after Bill and his fellow recruits gathered at the local church hall, all the conscripts would be taken to Victoria station and from there they would be allocated to various training camps in other parts of Britain, after which at some point he and the rest of them would leave Blighty for who knew where.

Bill was packed and ready to go, but he was worried about Peggy, who was four months pregnant and was having a pretty bad time of it, and so Bill wanted her to hotfoot it out of London as soon as she was able as part of the evacuation programme, as pregnant women as well as mothers with babies and/or toddlers were amongst the adults that the government advised to leave London.

'It's daft, you riskin' it 'ere in the interestin' condition you're in,' he told her.

'Interesting condition' was how they had taken to describing Peggy's pregnancy as they thought it quaintly old-fashioned and therefore a phrase full of charm.

'I want to go and fight for King and Country knowin' my little lad or lassie is out of 'arm's way, an' 'ow can I do that if I know you're still stuck 'ere in Bermondsey? Those docks will be a prime target for the Germans, you mark my words, Peg,' Bill added.

Deep down Peggy knew there was sound sense to Bill's argument. They had been childhood sweethearts and had married at twenty, and then had had to wait ten agonisingly long years before Barbara pointed out to her big sister that Peggy wasn't getting plump as she had just been complaining about, and that the fact that her waistband on her favourite skirt – a slender twenty-four inches – would no longer do up as easily as it once had was very likely because Peggy had in fact fallen pregnant.

Peggy was dumbfounded, and then thrilled.

A fortnight later Bill actually passed out, bumping his head quite badly, when Peggy showed him a chitty from the doctor that confirmed what they had spent so many years longing for, and which they – or Peggy at least – had completely given up hope of ever happening.

Until the doctor had confirmed all was well to Peggy, she hadn't dared say anything to Bill, knowing how many times he'd been cut to the quick when a missing or late period, or Peggy having a slight bulge in her normally flat tummy, hadn't gone on to lead to a baby. Perhaps now they could get their marriage back to the happy place it had once been.

Understandably, their relationship had struggled as the childless years had mounted, and as everyone around them had seemed to be able to have a baby every year with depressing ease. Peggy had often had to bite back bitter tears in public when she'd heard a woman complaining about being pregnant *again*.

She would have given anything to be pregnant just once, while Bill had sought solace in the bookies or the pub, and occasionally over the last year or two, Barbara had begun to wonder if he hadn't taken comfort in the arms of another, not that she ever dared raise the issue.

Being barren was bad enough, Peggy felt, but to be barren and alone, which could well be an inevitable consequence if Bill had found himself seeking a refuge from their worries elsewhere, was more than she felt she could cope with.

The doctor's confirmation that, as he put it, 'a happy event is in the pipeline', had felt to Peggy very much like the strong glue the couple needed to stick things back together again between them, and Bill had seemed to agree, not that he had ever said as much.

But this sense of optimism hadn't prevented Peggy's pregnancy being full of problems and worries, as she had continued to menstruate as if she weren't pregnant, she'd had terrible sickness from around virtually the very moment that Barbara had made the quip about the skirt waistband and more or less constantly since, until perhaps only a week or so previously.

This endless nausea had led to her losing a lot of weight, and so one day when Peggy was looking particularly blue,

Barbara had echoed the doctor with, 'That baby is going to take everything he or she needs from you – they are clever like that. And so although the very last thing you might feel like doing is eating or drinking, that is precisely what you must do, as you really do need to keep your strength up.'

Peggy was inclined to agree with her sister about the baby being quite selfish in getting what it needed. Right from the start her stomach had become very rounded – much more so, she was convinced, than other mothers-to-be she met who were roughly at the same stage as she – while her breasts were tender, with darkened and extended nipples that couldn't bear being touched.

While the baby seemed quite happy tucked away inside Peggy, the rapid weight loss from his or her mother's arms and legs and face had made her look very weary and drawn, while her extended belly and puffy ankles and fingers suggested that Peggy might be a lot less happy health-wise than her baby.

In fact, she had recently had to take off her wedding ring as her fingers had become too bloated for wearing it to be comfortable any longer. Now she wore the ring on a filigree gold chain around her neck that Bill had got from a jeweller's in Aldgate, Peggy saying that this was an even more special way for her to wear the ring as it held the precious wedding ring as close to her heart as it could possibly be.

The posters going up around London suggested it was going to be downright dangerous to stay in the city. Peggy knew

26

that Ted would be needed on the river and this meant that Barbara would stay by his side, no matter what.

'Peggy, I can't stay 'ere as I've got my papers,' Bill said as he sat on the other side of the kitchen table to her, 'an' I think you know that's true for you too, as it's likely that round 'ere it'll all be bombed to smithereens an' back.'

Peggy's breath juddered. Bill was right, but his blunt words rattled her, in part as she immediately thought of what Barbara and Ted might be going to have to face.

Bill's words were simple, but these were such big things he was saying. Of course she knew that she had a treasured new life growing inside – made all the more precious by the long time that she and Bill had had to wait for such a wondrous thing to occur – and so when push came to shove she would do what was best for their much-longed-for baby. And now that Bill had voiced his concerns about how dangerous London was very likely to be, she didn't want him to worry about her and the baby when he would have quite enough to fret about just looking out for himself while he was away fighting.

She would go, of course she would.

But she wasn't happy about it. She had never spent time away from Bermondsey before; it was a modest area, but it was *home*.

In terms of what needed to be done in order for her to go, it wasn't too bad. Peggy and Bill rented their house and it had been let to them along with the furniture they used. They didn't have many possessions and very few clothes, and so Peggy knew that with Bill away she could easily make use of Barbara's offer of storage space in the eaves

27

of her and Ted's roof, which was reached through a small trapdoor on their tiny landing, for Peggy to put their spare clothes and some of their wedding present crockery and so forth, if she did decide to be evacuated herself.

Peggy was sure that if she supervised the packing then Ted would actually do it for her, as she got so tired these days she couldn't face the idea of putting things in tea crates (of which Ted could get a ready supply at the docks) herself, and then Ted would borrow a handcart to lug everything over to his so that it could be safely stowed away.

'Go,' Bill urged once more, cutting across her thoughts. 'Go and stay somewhere that's safer – you'll be doing it for *our* baby, remember.'

Peggy understood what he was saying, but she could feel the ties of community entwined around her very tightly, and so she and Bill had to talk long into the night before she could find any sense of peace, and it was only after he had held her snugly for an hour once they had gone to bed that she was able properly to rest.

Chapter Four

The next morning at just gone seven Peggy kissed Bill long and hard in the privacy of their home, and then, after he'd swung his heavy canvas kitbag up and onto his shoulder, she walked at his side to the church hall, where there was already a heaving group of raw recruits and their loved ones saying goodbye as uniformed officers and civilian officials walked around and about with clipboards and organised those leaving into groups designated for particular buses to Victoria station.

During her pregnancy Peggy had discovered that tears were never far away, and this Friday morning was no exception. She also felt a bit dizzy after just a couple of minutes, standing on the edge of the melee alongside Bill, as there were so many people bustling this way and that that it made for the sort of constantly changing vista that led to travel sickness.

Bill smiled at her and said, 'Peg, don't wait around. You 'ead on to your Barbara's for a cup of tea. There's no point you stayin' 'ere just to wear yerself out. We said our goodbyes earlier and now your work is to look after our babbie. I see Reece Pinkly over there and so I'll 'ave someone to look after me, don't you fear, my love.'

It was too much for Peggy, and she found herself violently sobbing on Bill's shoulder.

Just for a moment, she wished she wasn't an expectant mother. It felt too much responsibility, and in any case, just what sort of world was it going to be that in a very few months she would be bringing a poor defenceless baby into? How would she be able to manage? What if the future were very dark for them all? There was no guarantee that the Germans wouldn't end the war victorious, and then where would they all be?

Bill held her close for a minute and then he took a step back and looked at her seriously. 'Peggy, it's time for you to go,' he said softly but firmly, and he stepped forward to give her back a final rub. 'I'd say I'll write, but you know that's not my strong point... Still, I'll do my best, Peg.'

With great reluctance Peggy edged away from him, not daring to look back as she knew that if she did, she wouldn't be able to let him leave.

Peggy made her way slowly out of the church hall and crossed the street to stand with some other wives as they gathered on the pavement outside the meeting point.

She was unable to say for certain if she had managed to grab a final glimpse of Bill as she craned her head this way and that to look through the open door to the church hall, trying to pick him out from the constantly moving mass of people. Unfortunately the men all looked similar in their dark wool suits and Homburg hats (most of them having dressed in their best clothes to go), while more and more wives and children were now cramming the pavements around her, squeezing close, and suddenly Peggy felt nauseous and unbearably oppressed.

She staggered slightly for the first few steps as she headed in the direction of her sister's house but then she felt calmer and a little more certain of herself as she moved along the pavement.

There was a thrumming engine noise behind her, and a horn blasted out as a gaily painted charabanc that looked so hideously at odds with Peggy's dark mood began to inch by.

With a whump of her heart, Peggy saw Bill standing up in front of his seat, with his face pressed sideways to the narrow sliding bit at the top of the window, and he was waving frantically at his wife. Peggy could see the shadow of Reece Pinkly alongside.

'Peggy Delbert, I love you!' was a shout Peggy thought she heard above the din as now some wives and kiddies were pushing past her to run right beside the moving vehicle, some even banging the charabanc's sides as it edged its way through the grimy street.

She hoped she had caught Bill's words – he clearly had been saying something to her – but she couldn't prevent a slither of concern that perhaps some little mite would take a fall as he or she ran beside the bus, slipping to a heinous end under the rear wheels, and so she felt thoroughly discombobulated, quite done in with her undulating feelings. Bill's declaration of what she hoped was love now felt tainted somehow by the worry of the children running beside the large vehicle.

'Bill, I'll look after our baby, I will, I will,' she shouted back, her hands either side of her mouth in an attempt to make her voice as loud as possible. She hoped against hope that her husband could feel the strength and resolution in her cry, even though she knew he was already out of earshot.

She hoped also that he knew she was feeling the pain of his absence almost as sharply as if she had lost one of her own limbs. She had married him for better or for worse, and they had had the 'for worse' for too long – she was now determined on the 'for better'.

Evacuation simply had to be for the better. Didn't it?

Chapter Five

'Yer better give Barbara ten minutes on 'er own with our Jessie and Connie,' advised Ted, when he ran into Peggy as she was trudging towards her sister's house just a couple of minutes later. 'We've jus' told 'em they're to be evacuated on Monday mornin' along with the rest of their school an' it didn't go down well.'

Peggy couldn't fail but notice how deep were etched the lines on the face of her brother-in-law all of a sudden. He was only in his early thirties, but just at that moment, as he stood half in a weak shaft of early-morning sunlight and half in heavy shadow, she could see exactly how Ted would look at age sixty. Then she hoped that he would make it to such advancing years, and not be cut down in his prime as many people would inevitably be during the war.

'How did they take it, the poor little mites?' she asked, swallowing her sad feelings down and trying to concentrate instead on Connie and Jessie. 'I really feel for them as they'll hate being apart from you and Barbara. And I've promised my Bill that I'm going to go out of London too.

I don't really want to, but if I stay and something happens to the baby, then I'll never forgive myself, and he won't either.'

Ted nodded to show his approval of Peggy's decision, and then he confessed that it had been very hard for him and Barbara to find the right words to break the news of the forthcoming evacuation to the children.

They had found it a difficult line to tread, he explained, as they wanted to make it sound as positive an experience as possible for Jessie and Connie, without there being any option for them *not* to go, but with it all being couched in a manner that wouldn't make the children worry too much once they had gone to their billets about Ted and Barbara remaining in London to face whatever might be going to happen.

'Connie seemed the most taken aback, which were a shock, but that could be because we're more used to seeing Jessie lookin' bothered an' so we didn't really notice it so much on 'im. Still, it were a few minutes I don't care to repeat any time soon, and Barbara were lookin' right tearful by the time I 'ad to go to work and so she'll be glad to 'ave you there, I'm sure,' Ted confided to his sister-in-law.

Peggy went to touch Ted on the arm in comfort, but then thought better of it. He looked too tightly wound for such an easy platitude.

She contented herself instead by saying she was sure that he and Barbara were doing the best thing and that they would have broken the news of evacuation to the children in exactly the right way.

Nearly everyone, she'd heard, was going to evacuate their children out of London and so it wouldn't be much fun for those that didn't go, she added, as they wouldn't have any playmates, while schooling would be a problem, too as the government was going to try and make sure that all state schooling was taken out of the city.

Peggy thought she saw the glint of a tear in the corner of one of Ted's eyes as she spoke, but then he cleared his throat sharply as he averted his head, and added quickly that he had to go or else his pay would be docked, and with that he walked away curtly before she could say anything else or bid him farewell.

Peggy remained where she was standing, wondering if Barbara had had long enough on her own with the children, or if she could go and call on her now. She felt she had been on her feet for quite some time already that morning and over the last few days she had grown a bit too large not to be having regular sit-downs.

Then she saw Susanne Pinkly hurrying in her direction, with a cheery sounding, 'Peggy, I need to talk to you but I'm late for school – can you walk over to St Mark's with me? I was going to come and see you at lunchtime, but this will save me an errand if you can spare me a couple of minutes now?'

Peggy and Susanne Pinkly were good friends, having been at school together from the age of five, and later in the same intake at teacher's training college before they finally simultaneously landed jobs at the local primary school where they had once been willing pupils.

They'd also spent an inordinate amount of time during their teenage years discussing the merits of various local lads and how they imagined their first kiss would be.

Susanne was fun to be with, and was never short of admirers who were drawn to her open face and joyful laugh. Peggy had often envied Susanne her bubbly nature that had the men flocking, as Peggy was naturally more serious and introverted, and so when Bill had made it clear he thought her a bit of all right, it was a huge relief as she had been fast coming to the conclusion that the opposite sex were hard to attract.

Although some schools wouldn't let married teachers work, fortunately this hadn't been the case at St Mark's Primary School. While Susanne was still an old maid, being positively spinsterish now at thirty-one, Peggy had married Bill just a term into her first job without much thought as to what this might mean for her in the working world. Luckily St Mark's didn't have a hard and fast policy as regards making married female employees give up work, as some schools did, which Peggy found herself very pleased about, and increasingly so when she didn't become pregnant for such a long time. She couldn't have borne being stuck at home on her own and without anything to do – she would have felt such a failure, she knew.

However, when she fell at last with the baby, Peggy had had to stop working at the end of the summer term as her nausea had got so bad, and since then she very much missed her lively pupils and the joshing camaraderie of the staffroom. Bill spent long hours at the bus depot, and he was rather fond of a tipple with the lads on a Friday and a Saturday night if he wasn't rostered on the weekend shifts. Barbara's time was taken every weekday by her job at the haberdashery, and so quite often the days felt to Peggy as if they were dragging by. She discovered all too quickly that there was only so much layette knitting an expectant mother could enjoy doing.

It was still up in the air whether Peggy would ever be able to return to work following the birth of the baby, as most employers didn't want a mother as an employee, and Peggy knew that if in time she did want to return to her classroom – after the war with Germany was over, of course – then she would have to make a special plea to the local education authority that she be allowed to go back to work.

Before that could happen, she and Bill would have to decide between themselves that she should resume her job, and then they would need to sort out somebody to look after the baby during the day, which might not be so easy to do.

Bill didn't earn much as a bus driver (his route was the busy number 12 between Peckham and Oxford Circus), and aside from the fact that Peggy missed her pupils, and she knew she had been a good teacher, she suspected too that one day she and Bill might well feel very happy if she could start to add once again to the family pot by bringing in a second wage.

Peggy turned around and, linking arms with her friend, she walked along with Susanne, who wanted to see if Peggy was going to evacuate herself.

When Peggy nodded, Susanne cried perhaps a trifle too gaily, 'Music to my ears! I'm having to stay behind to work at the bakery, as you know Ma's been taken poorly and Reece is leaving today with your Bill. But if you're choosing to be evacuated and are planning on going on Monday as most people round here seem to be, then St Mark's needs another responsible adult to help escort the children to wherever they are being sent to, and I couldn't help but think of you! So far there's Miss Crabbe and old Mr Hegarty to look after them – well, Mr Jones is going too, but he won't want to be bothered with the nitty-gritty, as it were, and in any case, he's coming back just about the next day. One-Eye Braxton will be there and the kiddies run rings round him – and so I thought you would be the perfect person to go and keep an eye on both pupils and teachers.'

There was definitely a logic to this despite the chirpy tone of Susanne's words, Peggy could see, as she was familiar with the children and they with her, and she knew the quite often crotchety Miss Crabbe ('Crabbe by name, and Crabby by nature' was Peggy and Susanne's private joke about her) and the ancient Mr Hegarty (who was increasingly doddery these days after teaching for over forty years) would make for dour overseers for the evacuation journey for the children, and with headmaster Mr Jones planning on not sticking around...

And if Peggy went with the children of St Mark's, then it would probably mean that she would end up being billeted near where Jessie and Connie would be, and this would be reassuring for Barbara and Ted; and for herself too, it had to be said.

They'd reached the school gates, and Susanne nodded and then smiled encouragement at Peggy, obviously willing her to say yes.

'Let me think about it overnight, and I'll let you know first thing in the morning as I'm not quite certain about the other options for the evacuation of expectant mothers,' Peggy said, trying to look resigned and as if she shouldn't be taken for granted, but failing to keep the corners of her mouth from turning up into the tiniest of smiles.

Then Peggy caught Susanne looking pointedly at her expanded girth so she added, 'I think it's probably fine for me to come with your lot, but I just want to consider it for a while as I don't want to promise you anything I can't actually do.'

Susanne was already nipping across the playground towards the steps up to the girls' entrance as she called over her shoulder, 'Honestly, Peggy, it's just to make sure they don't get up to too much mischief on the train – and that's just the teachers! And Mrs Ayres will be there too, and Mr Braxton, and so you won't be too heavily outnumbered by the kiddies.'

This latest comment wasn't necessarily as hugely reassuring to Peggy as Susanne probably meant it to be, because although as sweet-natured a widow as Mrs Ayres undoubtedly was, she was a gentle soul, and even the youngest children could boss her around with absolutely no trouble, while Mr Braxton, who had had such a severe facial injury in the Great War that meant he'd lost an eye and part of a cheekbone, and who now wore a not very convincing prosthetic contraption that attached to his spectacles, also had problems in keeping the children in line, in large part as they didn't really like looking directly at him.

Peggy sighed. She could already imagine how this was very probably going to work out for her.

Several minutes later, as Peggy made her way at long last over to Barbara's, Jessie and Connie were walking along the street to school in the opposite direction, and they were so deep in conversation that they didn't notice their auntie until they were almost level with her.

Peggy thought they both looked wan and anxious – the news of leaving their mother and father to head for pastures new with their classmates had obviously hit them hard.

'Hello, you two. You'd better look sharp or else you're going to be late,' she said. 'But first, I'll tell you a secret. If it helps cheer you up, I think I might be coming on the train with you and your fellow school pupils on Monday. Won't that be fun?'

They stared at each other with intent, serious expressions, and then they all laughed as Peggy had to add, 'Well, maybe "fun" is the wrong word, but I daresay you know what I mean. If I can get a billet near to you, then you'll know there's always me to come to if either of you feel a bit miserable. And I shall be able to come to you if I'm feeling a bit sad about being away from home too. Is that a deal?'

Judging by their nods, it looked as if a pact had been made.

Chapter Six

Barbara was standing on the doorstep looking out for Peggy while polishing the brass door knocker, door handle and house number.

'I've already told Mrs Truelove that I can't go in today as I've got to get things organised, and she wasn't thrilled but...' Barbara's voice drifted away as she'd already turned on her heel to stomp off towards the kitchen, her footsteps ringing out on the brown linoleum that floored the narrow hallway at number five Jubliee Street.

Peggy followed wearily in her younger sister's wake (there was only the one year between them), very much looking forward to sitting down and enjoying a restorative cup of tea. It wasn't yet half past eight but already Peggy was quite done in.

Half an hour later she felt much better, as Barbara had also made her eat some hot buttered toast while Barbara jotted down a long to-do list, and an equally lengthy shopping list.

'Ted and I decided before we got out of bed this morning that we're going to use our rainy-day money to send them away in new clothes. Let's see how much is in the biscuit tin,' said Barbara.

Peggy was surprised at this. Most families scrimped and saved to put a little by for emergencies, but now Barbara seemed happy to dip into this fund when actually, as far as Peggy could see, the children already had perfectly acceptable clothes that were always neatly pressed and mended, and that were nowhere near as threadbare as some that many other local children had no other option than to wear.

While Barbara and Peggy had been born and bred within the sound of church bells that they still lived within hearing distance of, their father had been a shopkeeper, and so they had grown up in relative comfort when compared to that of many of their contemporaries, Bermondsey being known throughout London as being a very poor borough. They had been allowed to stay at school past the age of fourteen, when a lot of their friends had been made to leave in order that they could go out to work to bring another wage in to add to the family's housekeeping.

Peggy and Barbara's mother had been very insistent that they had elocution lessons, and the result of this was that although without question they talked with a London accent, it wasn't the broad cockney spoken by Ted and Bill, who joked that their wives were 'very BBC'.

While this wasn't strictly true as the received pronunciation of the broadcaster's announcers was always distinctly more plummy (in fact, laughably so at times), nevertheless the sisters knew that their voices did sound posh when compared to most people in Bermondsey. Jessie and Connie had also been encouraged to speak properly by Barbara, another thing that hadn't endeared Jessie to Larry, who had the slightest of stammers.

Barbara was always very set on keeping up family standards, and this required her taking good care of Jessie and Connie's clothes, making sure they were always mended, clean and pressed, while Ted buffed and polished their leather T-bar sandals every evening. It gave both parents pleasure to see their children bathed and clean, and neatly turned out.

This sartorial attention was a whole lot more than many other local parents managed where either their children or themselves were concerned, although Peggy had some sympathy for why this might be as she could see it was very difficult for some families, who might have, perhaps, more than ten children to look after but with only a very scant income coming into the home each week.

Nevertheless, she suspected that when her and Bill's baby arrived, she would find herself equally as keen to keep up the standards already heralded by Barbara.

Now Peggy watched with slight concern as Barbara climbed precariously up onto a stool to lift off the high mantelpiece above the kitchen hearth a slightly battered and dented metal biscuit barrel that commemorated King George V coming to the throne in 1910.

Peggy remembered this biscuit barrel with fond thoughts, as it had sat in their parents' kitchen throughout her and Barbara's childhood. Although Peggy was the oldest daughter, and therefore in theory should have had the first dibs on their parents' possessions, when it came to closing up their house after they both died within months of each other, Peggy did a magnanimous act. It was just before Barbara and Ted's marriage, which meant it was a year after Peggy and Bill's own nuptials, when their mother succumbed to influenza and their father died not long after of, they liked to say, a broken heart. With only the slightest of pangs as she had always loved the biscuit barrel, Peggy had allowed her sister to stake, claim to the majority of their mother's possessions, including the biscuit barrel, as Barbara was poised to set up her own home and Peggy had just about got herself and Bill comfortably fitted out by then.

Now, Barbara clunked the barrel down and onto the table, the number of large pennies in it adding considerably to its apparently hefty weight. She loosened the lid with her nails until she was able to work it off, before tipping the contents onto the maroon chenille tablecloth that adorned the kitchen table.

Peggy had long teased Barbara about her beloved tablecloth that had to be removed whenever the family ate, or when anything mucky was being done on the table. Barbara could be very stubborn if she chose, and so she resolutely refused to accept the tablecloth, with its extravagant fringing, was anything less than practical. Now, at long last, it came into its own as it turned out to be a good place to sort the pile of money that had been in the tin as the chenille prevented the coins rolling around too much, and it cushioned too the several notes that had tumbled from the biscuit barrel.

Barbara counted out five pounds and replaced them in the barrel.

Then she totted up what was left. It was a small fortune: a whole £37 15s. 7½d. With a raise of her eyebrows Barbara put another £20 back in the kitty, and then a handful of silver half-crowns and florins, and then she clambered laboriously back onto the stool to return the biscuit barrel to its home on the mantelpiece.

'Goodness,' said Peggy enviously, as her and Bill's rainy-day money had never broken the £10 barrier. 'I had no idea.'

'Ted's been doing overtime, and of course I always try and put away all of my wages. But I won't deny that a lot of scrimping and saving has gone into that blessed tin,' said Barbara. 'We've been saving extra hard ever since the children started school and we had even been wondering about a proper holiday next year, and a mangle for the washing and a new bed for Jessie. But now I want Connie and Jessie to be evacuated looking as if they are loved and cared for, and as if we think nothing of sending them away in new clothes. I think that might help them get a better class of family at the other end, don't you think?'

Peggy wasn't certain that would be the case, but she decided to keep quiet.

Some Bermondsey families would be hard-pressed even to give their kiddies a bath or to send them off in clean clothes, she knew, and so it could be that some of the host families would take pity and choose those clearly less advantaged first. She knew too that some of the children were persistent bed-wetters, and so she hoped that wasn't going to cause too many problems further down the line.

Peggy made a decision not to ponder any further on

this just then, as it seemed too loaded with opportunity for fraught outcomes. Although, of course, she hoped that Barbara's view was the correct one, rather than hers.

After one last cup of tea and a final peruse of Barbara's list, the sisters decided they would head up to Elephant and Castle to see what they could buy.

Barbara carefully placed her to-do list in one pocket and her shopping list in the corresponding pocket on the other side of her coat front, and then she tucked her purse away out of sight at the bottom of her basket, hidden under a folded scarf.

Peggy took the opportunity to spend a final penny before slipping into her lightweight mackintosh, as these days with the baby pressing on her bladder she needed to go as often as possible.

And then the sisters left for the bus stop so that they could make the shortish ride to Elephant, as the area was known locally.

At school meanwhile, Susanne Pinkly was experiencing a rather trying first lesson of the day.

Understandably, none of the children had their minds on their timetabled lesson for first thing on a Friday, which was arithmetic; even at the best of times that was never an especially pleasant start to the final school day of the week.

This particular morning, all the whole school wanted to do was talk about the evacuation, and what their mothers and fathers had told them about it.

Susanne could completely understand this desire, but she wasn't utterly sure what she should say to the children as she didn't want to make a delicate situation worse, or to make any timid pupils feel even more fearful about the future than they would be already.

Susanne always kept an eye out at playtime for Jessie Ross, as she knew the bigger boys could be mean to him. She had a soft spot for Jessie as he was one of the few children who patently enjoyed their lessons (very obviously much more than his sister did, at any rate) and who would try very hard to please his teacher.

Jessie was lucky to have a sister like Connie to stand up for him, Susanne thought, although just before the Easter holidays Ted had requested to headmaster Mr Jones that Connie be moved to the other class for their forthcoming senior year at St Mark's as he and Barbara felt that Jessie was coming to depend too much on his twin sister fighting his battles for him.

Sure enough, at the start of this autumn term the twins had been separated and now were no longer taught in the same class. Susanne had suggested she keep Connie, and that Jessie would be moved in order that he could be taken out of Larry's daily orbit, but Mr Jones said that he thought that might make Jessie's weakness too obvious for all to see, and that the likely result would be that Larry's bullying would simply be replaced by another pupil becoming equally foul to Jessie.

Generally, the teachers didn't think Larry was an out-and-out bad lad as such, because when he forgot to act the Big I Am, he seemed perfectly able to get on well with the other children, Connie having been seen playing quite amiably with him on several occasions. The teachers believed that he had a troubled home life, as his park keeper father was well known for being a bit handy with his fists when he was in his cups, while Larry's mother bent over backward to pretend all was well, despite the occasional painful bruise suggesting otherwise. The days Larry came in to school looking a bit battered and with dried tear tracks under his eyes was when he was prone to go picking on someone smaller than him. It was rumoured that Larry's father had been dismissed from his job the previous spring, and Susanne was sorry to note that there had been a corresponding worsening of Larry's behaviour since then.

Having just spoken with Peggy made Susanne think afresh of Jessie, as she knew Peggy adored her niece and nephew, but that Peggy always wished that Jessie had an easier time in the playtimes and lunch breaks at school than in fact he did.

So Susanne had been intending to pay special attention today to see how he was faring now that he would be getting used to not having his sister nearby at all times. But now Susanne had to put that thought to the back of her mind as she had just had a brainwave.

She would acknowledge the forthcoming evacuation but in a more oblique way than discussing it openly. She would do this by talking about some London words and sayings that might not make much sense to people who came from outside the confines of Bermondsey.

After making sure Larry was sitting at his desk directly in her eyeline so that she could keep tabs on him, Susanne got up from her seat behind her desk at the front of the class, smoothing her second-best wool skirt over her generous hips and checking the buttons to her pretty floral blouse were correctly fastened (to her embarrassment, she'd had a mishap with a button slipping undone the day before, and had the chagrin of catching a smirking Larry and several others trying to sneak a sly glimpse of her petty).

Going to stand in front of the blackboard, Susanne began, 'Who knows what the word "slang" means?'

A bespectacled small girl called Angela Kennedy who sometimes played with Connie after school put her hand up in the air, and when Susanne nodded in her direction, she answered, 'Miss, is it a special word fer sumfin' that's all familiar, like?'

'Sort of, Angela. Well done,' said Susanne. 'Slang can vary from city to town to village, and might be different whether you live in the town or the country, or whether you are a lord or a lady, or you are just like us. Slang words are those that quite often people like us might use in everyday life, rather than when we could choose the more formal word we would find in the dictionary. And I know that following our lesson last week on dictionaries, you all know very well exactly how a dictionary is organised and all the special information you can find there!'

There were a few small titters from the pupils who didn't have the same confidence in their ability to find their way around a dictionary that their teacher apparently had in them.

Ignoring the sniggerers, Susanne went on, 'Now, can anybody here tell me an example of a word that is said around where we live in Bermondsey, but which might not be understood over in Buckingham Palace, say, which I'm sure we'd all agree is a whole world away from what you and I know in our everyday lives, even though the palace itself is close enough that we could all bicycle there if we wanted to?'

'Geezer,' yelled a boyish voice from the back of the class.

'Okay, geezer it is,' said Susanne. 'So, has anyone got another perhaps more polite or proper-sounding word that might be the same as geezer but that wherever you lived in the British Isles you would know that everybody who heard you say it would understand what you were talking about?'

She was hoping one of her pupils would have the nous to say 'man'.

'Bloke,' said Larry.

'Chap.'

'Guy.'

'Guv'ner.'

'Guv.'

'Anything else?' asked Susanne.

'Cove,' said Jessie thoughtfully, 'although I prefer dandy.'

Somebody gave a bark of laughter.

Jessie really didn't help himself sometimes, Susanne thought.

'Nancy boy,' Larry yelled as he wriggled in his chair, trying to turn around to look at Jessie. 'That's you, Jessie, er, Je… *Jessica* Ro—'

'Behave yourself, Larry, and keep your eyes turned to the front of the classroom at all times. Ahem. What I was hoping was that someone might say "man",' Susanne interrupted very sharply without pausing between her admonishment of Larry and voicing what the word was that she had been wishing a pupil would say. 'Now, what about one of you coming up with another slang word that you can think of where several others can be used?'

'Bog.'

'Thank you, Larry,' said Susanne in the sort of voice designed to shut Larry up, but that at the same time indicated to both Larry and the rest of the class that Larry wasn't really being thanked at all and that really it was high time that he buttoned his lip.

'Lavvy,' somebody shouted out before Susanne could say anything else to get the lesson back to where she wanted it to be.

The class was waking up now to what Susanne was wanting from them. Almost.

'Crapper.'

'WC.'

'Jakes.'

'Karzi!'

Susanne tried not to think of what any of the posher billets might think to language such as this as she attempted and failed to conceal a smile, although she supposed they would most likely all have to ask their way to the outhouse or the toilet in their new homes at some time or other.

'A polite term, children, remember,' she said encouragingly.

The following silence told Susanne that 'polite' was quite a hurdle for some to overcome.

'*Pissoir*,' Jessie called eventually, looking down quickly, although not quickly enough that Susanne couldn't see a cheeky cast to his eyes.

Their teacher had to turn to write on the blackboard so that her class couldn't see the lift of her eyebrows that indicated she was suppressing a feeling lying smack bang in the centre of exasperation and humour.

East Street market was only a ten-minute stroll from Elephant along the Walworth Road, and when Elephant failed to come up to Barbara's expectations as to the shopping opportunities, and as Peggy felt that she had a second wind as walking around was making her feel better, they decided to head towards Camberwell so that they could go to the market.

One purchase had been searched for in Elephant without success. Ted already had from his and Barbara's honeymoon a long time ago a smallish cardboard suitcase that had long been holding Jessie's large collection of painted lead soldiers in their colourful garb of Crimean War uniform (the softness of the metal having meant that Ted was forever straightening bent rifles or skew-whiff feather hackles on the headwear of the tiny fighters). Barbara had decided that Jessie could be sent off with his possessions carefully stowed in that suitcase, with the soldiers left behind in a drawer in his bedroom ready and waiting for him to play with after he returned from evacuation.

A second suitcase was needed, this time for Connie, as on the bus to Elephant Barbara had realised as she and Peggy talked about the evacuation that there wasn't a guarantee that both children would be kept together and so each child needed to be catered for and packed for quite separately.

There had already been a run on all the small cases, though, as presumably other parents had been quick to snap them up for the evacuation, and this meant that only the big cases were left and they were all too large for even Peggy to lug about.

Barbara cursed roundly when she realised this, and then Peggy sat down on a step to wait as Barbara darted in and out of several shops just to be certain, before she returned empty-handed and announced that they would have to head along the Walworth Road in the direction of Camberwell in order that they could go to East Street market.

'Barbara, I've been thinking,' said Peggy as they walked along. 'I've a spare cardi that Connie can take – it'll be a bit big, I know, but it's practically brand new, and she can roll up the cuffs, and actually she's grown so much over the summer holidays that I don't think it will totally swamp her. It's that one with the little buttons on that you liked when we took the children egg-hunting in the park at Easter.'

Her sister smiled her thanks, and promised that, her treat, they would stop for a bun and a hot drink after they had finished their shopping.

At the knitting shop, Barbara went to choose some four-ply to knit Jessie a pullover – she was a very fast knitter, and although she didn't think she'd have enough time before the children left on Monday to finish the sleeves to make Jessie a long-sleeved winter jumper, she thought she could manage a pullover in the time she had.

'Peg, help me choose the colour that is closest to that of the cardi you're thinking of for our Connie,' asked Barbara.

When Peggy said it was quite a bright green, Barbara then put down the skein of pale grey wool she had been holding, and chose the one that most approximated the green of the cardi for Jessie's woolly, so that the twins' new knitwear would more or less match.

Peggy bought some dark yellow wool, as she thought she could make Connie a woollen hat, as if they were going to be out in the far reaches of a country area where they'd be exposed to the elements, it would be perishingly cold in a couple of months, and Peggy knew for a fact (although she doubted Barbara did) that Connie's hat from the previous winter was lying somewhere on top of one of the warehouse roofs on the docks. Peggy knew this because she had seen Connie throw it up there when she was showing off to Larry and his chums as to her hurling prowess on the last day of the spring term just after the school had broken up for the holidays.

When Connie realised her aunt had seen her wondrous overarm lob, Connie begged Peggy not to say anything to her mother, and Peggy had agreed, as Connie's hat had had a tough winter, having often been used to carry marbles and all sorts of other things, many of them filthy and sharply barbed, and it had got distinctly scruffy to the point that it wouldn't in any case meet Barbara's exacting standards as to what 'would do' for another winter.

Peggy knew that Jessie had a grey worsted peaked cap that she didn't doubt that he would be taking on his evacuation. It wouldn't be of very much use in the keeping-warm sense when the harsh winter weather really set in, but she couldn't imagine him wearing anything else that might be cosier (i.e., anything knitted) in case this led to a new and possibly more vicious spate of teasing.

As they were about to leave the wool shop, Barbara saw some homemade knitted toys that were piled in a large wicker basket close to the shop door, and so she chose a small grey teddy for Jessie and a black and white panda for Connie. 'I know they're too big really for toys like this, but if they're homesick they can take these into their beds for a quick cuddle,' Barbara explained.

'That's a good idea. And why don't you give the toys a dab of your best scent too and wrap them tightly in paper to keep the pong in, and then there'll be a smell of you when they unwrap them?' said Peggy, to which her sister nodded agreement.

Then she reminded Barbara that the children would need new scarves and so Barbara bought some thick navy wool to knit them some, and some thinner wool in the same colour to make them both some gloves, saying luckily the weather was still summery and so she could get to this knitting once the children had left, as she was sure they'd love to receive a parcel from home.

Just then Peggy spied a machine in the corner, clattering away nineteen to the dozen – she knew what it was: a name-tape maker.

The headmaster had requested that all the children's clothing was labelled with their names, and although at first the shopkeeper said his wife was too busy with other children's names, he then looked at all that Peggy and Barbara were just about to buy from him and, with a sigh of defeat, he said that as a special favour the name tapes could be ready first thing in the morning if Barbara wanted to pay the 'premium rate' for a special service.

For a moment Barbara baulked as she didn't approve of anyone taking advantage of a situation where a customer had no choice, simply for a shopkeeper to earn themselves an extra few pennies when they had their customers over a barrel. But then she relented as the name tapes would save her so much time, otherwise she would have to embroider the children's initials on each garment.

With only the smallest discernible huff of irritation, Barbara looked the shopkeeper in the eye and said she would be happy to pay the premium rate, at which point Peggy turned her head sharply towards her sister as an indication of how unusual an acquiescence this was. The shopkeeper had the grace to look a bit uncomfortable in the glare of Barbara's unnerving stare as carefully he jotted down the names of Jessie and Connie. Peggy didn't like to think what would happen if he made a mistake in the spelling.

A little further down the market, there was a luggage stall that had lots of bags and cases piled up. It too had run out of the small cardboard suitcases that Barbara really wanted, but fortunately it did have a wide collection of holdalls and so Barbara chose a sturdy blue one for Connie's things to be stowed away inside.

Another stall was selling children's clothing and from here Barbara bought the children new vests, pants and socks, and a couple of shirts for Jessie (one grey and one blue) and a pretty sky-blue checked dress for Connie as well as a smart woollen red herringbone coat for her too.

'Jessie had a new mackintosh last year that's still got plenty of room for him, and although this red coat is going to be big on Connie, at least she'll be able to grow into it,' said Barbara, as she asked the stallholder to wrap the coat in brown paper, which he tied up with string, while all the other new purchases were carefully folded and placed in the holdall after it had had a good shake-out upside down with its zip opened, just to make sure there was no dust lurking inside. 'And they have their school blazers that they can wear under their coats if it gets frosty or snowy. We're so lucky being able to make sure they go with everything they need – I know some families are having to penny-pinch to send them away with even one decent set of clothes, let alone enough to keep them warm if they are away long enough for the bad winter weather to come.'

Peggy looked up at the clear and sunny sky that had only the smallest and fluffiest of clouds dotted here and there, and thought it was very hard to imagine that it might be snowing before too long.

Before she could get too lost in her thoughts, Peggy made herself rally and concentrate on what extra she might need to take for her own needs. She bought herself some new underwear, three pairs of natural tan fully fashioned Du Pont stockings (her favourite) and a pair of smart new gloves, and these too were placed into Connie's holdall. Luckily it turned out to be a very forgiving bag as it seemed able to contain much more than it looked as if it could, which was just as well considering that Peggy had forgotten her own shopping basket, she had been so caught up in the drama of seeing Bill off.

The sisters felt as if they had earned their toasted teacake and Camp coffee, and so they went into a small café on the way to the bus stop.

As they sat down, Peggy felt once more that she was about to cry.

Barbara saw immediately that it had all got a bit much for her, and so she said, 'Let it out, Peg, nobody's going to mind. It must have been very difficult for you to watch Bill go off.'

Being given permission to have a quick sob did the trick, Peggy realised a minute later, as she'd been able after all to keep her tears in check.

In fact, she was now smiling as she told Barbara for the second time how daft Bill had looked as he had angled his head so that he could shout to her as he was driven by in the charabanc with Reece Pinkly chuckling along beside him.

There was a call from behind the counter, and as Barbara stood up to go and get their teacakes, she opened her hand-bag to retrieve something, and then pushed a small white paper bag in her sister's direction. This was a surprise to Peggy, and she couldn't prevent a cry of pleasure when inside she saw a brand-new Coty lipstick in her favourite Cardinal Red.

'I nipped into the chemist's while you were having a rest on that step at Elephant,' said Barbara as she passed Peggy her teacake. 'Pregnant or not, we can't have you letting the side down outside London, and showing them we don't know how to make ourselves presentable, now, can we?'

Chapter Seven

The hours raced by over the weekend as everybody did their best to get ready for Monday morning.

Connie had to be drafted in to help Barbara sew the last few name tapes in discreet places on the various items of clothing for herself and her brother as this turned out to be a much more fiddly job than anyone had anticipated, or at least it was at the speed they were trying to attach them.

Barbara, while a good knitter, was impatient when sewing at the best of times, which wasn't helpful in a situation like this when they were working against the clock.

Often when standing behind the counter at Mrs Truelove's haberdasher's, when local women were asking advice on the merits of one thread over another for particular fabrics, she could barely withhold a private ironic grimace at the thought of her not practising what she preached, which was nearly always 'feel your way into it, and go slowly until you are used to how much the thread and the fabric like one another'.

Luckily Connie wasn't a bad seamstress in spite of being so young. In fact, for the previous Christmas, she had designed and made Barbara a cloth carry-all that had various pockets and compartments for her mother to keep her knitting needles and patterns tidy in. The quality of both the design and the stitching was so good that Barbara felt a sudden flip of envy as she knew her daughter's skills with cotton and needle had now surpassed her own by far, and Connie was very quick and rhythmical too in her sewing, which meant that all the stitches were a uniform size that already looked to be verging on the professional.

The men of the Ross family weren't getting away with sitting around idly either over the weekend, Barbara was making sure, as from the Friday afternoon there seemed a never-ending list of things that she wanted either Ted or Jessie, or sometimes both, to go and get from the shops or round about.

It was the first time the children had gone a whole weekend without being let out to play, and they felt very grown up.

They also wanted to stay close to Ted and Barbara, now that it was beginning to sink in that they really were going to be evacuated first thing on Monday morning, and by that evening they would be spending their very first night in beds other than at number five Jubilee Street.

When the twins caught a moment together they couldn't help but try to guess what it might be like, wherever they were going. Connie said she rather hoped their billet would have a dog for them to play with, while Jessie said he wished there'd be lots of food and not too many rules. Then they'd grow quiet, thinking of all the things they loved about their home and Bermondsey.

According to Barbara, the purchases of the various things they needed to buy were to be allocated as follows:

Toothbrushes and tubes of toothpaste for each child: Jessie

Soap, ditto: Jessie

Shoe polish, plus soft yellow dusters to shine the shoes, ditto (they hadn't been asked to take this, but Barbara insisted a shoe-cleaning kit was 'an essential'): Jessie

Notebooks and pencils, ditto (again, not on the list, but Barbara was firm): Ted

New combs, ditto: Jessie

Postcards and stamps, ditto: Ted

Knives, forks, spoons and tin mugs, ditto: Ted and Jessie

Raisins and prunes, ditto: Ted and Jessie

Large labels with string for their names and schools to be written on, along with their destination, ditto: Connie

Two containers for the butter, ditto: Connie

And so on, with Barbara's list ending up quite possibly four times as long.

Barbara and Ted, and Connie and Jessie were heartily sick and tired of it all well before they had sorted everything out that needed doing.

Barbara and Ted felt especially snappish and worn out, although they tried very hard to mask this and to put on a cheerful and brave face for the children, so that the twins would have nice memories of their last weekend in Jubilee Street.

Barbara was tetchy because she had been up well into the small hours on the Friday evening as she tried to finish knitting Jessie's green pullover, which was a hideous colour to knit with by electric light, she'd been irked to discover, and so she regretted not getting after all the dove-grey wool as that would have been much easier on her eyes.

Even later that Friday night, after stowing her knitting needles away in Connie's Christmas present, Barbara didn't go straight to bed but instead she spent a while agonising over writing a note for whoever would be taking in Connie and Jessie, as she set down a little about each child, with their likes and dislikes, and giving her and Ted's fulsome thanks to the unknown hosts for the billeting of their children.

As she finally lay down in bed, Ted's soft snores not breaking their rhythm, she had worn him out so with her myriad errands, she could hear the first chirps of the wild birds' dawn chorus and see a faint lightening of the sky over to the east of the city, and Barbara realised the last time this had happened to her was when she was still breastfeeding the twins. The pang in her chest was for the hopes she had had as she nursed her babies, and the loss of innocence that Jessie and Connie were almost definitely about to face.

Ted was just as frazzled when he woke up, although probably a bit better-tempered about it than his wife, as he found it very difficult to get cross or frustrated about anything, being one of those perpetually sunny and even-tempered sort of chaps, a trait that Barbara found could be most infuriating if she were feeling niggled herself and all Ted could do was smile about whatever was aggravating her.

Anyway, once poor Ted had finished doing all of Barbara's not inconsiderable bidding, he then had to trot over to Peggy's house early on the Saturday afternoon to do all that she wanted as regards what should be packed up of her and Bill's possessions for storage, and what should be put to one side for her to take away for her own evacuation, as well as what should be given away to those more needy.

Peggy looked tired and jowly, with dry skin and a heavy footfall, and so once he saw her diminished state, Ted was eager to help her as much as possible. However, he could have done without forgetting the large suitcase he'd asked to borrow from Big Jessie to pack some of the bits and pieces into, and so no sooner had he arrived at Peggy's than he had to leave immediately in order to head over to Big Jessie's to collect the case. All the houses were almost within spitting distance of one another, but still...

Worse came a little over thirty minutes later, just when Ted was looking forward fervently to the time when he could have a few minutes to relax after he had completed his tasks. He longed for the moment he would sink into his favourite chair and put his feet up for a quiet hour (accompanied by a glass of stout from the hole in the wall at the Jolly, he fantasised).

It was just at this moment that Peggy reminded her brother-in-law he needed to rustle up a handcart from somewhere to transport all the stuff over to his and Barbara's, and also that he had to make a further trip to the church hall as the local vicar was making a collection of bric-a-brac to keep in case people got bombed out and needed things when their houses came tumbling down, and so she had put aside a pile of possessions that needed to be transported over there too.

Ted groaned; after his silly schoolboy error with his memory failure concerning Big Jessie's big suitcase, he could barely credit it that he'd also forgotten about the damn handcart. He blamed Barbara for his oversight, although he thought this prudent not to share with Peggy, as he knew how close the sisters were. Barbara had most surely sent him on too many errands, Ted decided, and his day had been so busy that now he could hardly remember where his backside and his elbow were.

Then, the moment he had done the running hither and thither – and he had worked up quite a sweat getting all of Peggy and Bill's stuff for storage piled in the parlour at Jubilee Street, after which he had to return the handcart to its owner (who, Ted discovered, had a couple of people standing outside the yard where the handcart was kept as they were waiting to borrow it too, as Peggy wasn't the only local resident busy packing up a house for the duration and who needed various possessions moving around) – he set off on his return home clutching his longed-for jug of stout only to find Barbara insisting that before he sat down, Ted should take all of Peggy's possessions for storage upstairs as she couldn't have them cluttering up the (rarely used) parlour for a moment longer.

Somehow the stack of Peggy and Bill's possessions seemed to have multiplied in size, Ted thought, as he plodded up and down the stairs, and then, with Jessie's help, hoicked everything up the stepladder and from there hoisted it all into the spot in the roof space where (Barbara's instructions again) it had to be stacked neatly and finally covered with an old sheet tucked in all around to keep the dust off.

Ted closed the trapdoor to the roof space with a sigh of relief… after which Barbara pointed out that he had to return the suitcase to Big Jessie as his brother had promised the loan of it to somebody else and that if Ted had had his wits about him he'd have taken it with him when he took the handcart back.

Just for a second Ted felt the mildest of swear words almost bubble up, but he bit it back down, telling himself that his stout was going to be extra special when he could finally sit down to sup it.

All in all, it was a very tiresome weekend at number five – nobody could remember a more trying couple of days, not even when Barbara's parents had died. In fact, all of the Rosses were all kept so busy that Ted bought them fish and chips on both Friday and Saturday teatimes, which also had never happened before, although Barbara was quick to remind Jessie and Connie that this out-of-character behaviour was for a special treat only, and they weren't to get used to this sort of extravagance.

Chapter Eight

On the Saturday teatime, Peggy arrived just before they sat down to eat, with droplets of perspiration beading her top lip as she clunked her hand case down in the hallway, but luckily Ted had already got in an extra portion of fish and chips for her, as well as some raw fish scraps for somebody else.

This 'somebody else' was Peggy and Bill's tabby puss Fishy, now unhappily corralled into a sturdy cat basket Barbara had borrowed from a neighbour. Fishy was frankly livid about the whole thing and she arrived at Jubilee Street making her presence felt by creating the devil of a racket, mewling loudly as she clawed at the opening to the cat basket that Peggy had lovingly placed her in.

Fishy was being evacuated too, although in nothing like as drastic a manner as Peggy and the children. She was going to be seeing the war out billeted with Ted and Barbara.

The government had requested recently that pet owners have their dogs, cats and other animals put to sleep, and the London vets had been furiously busy since the edict as their waiting rooms had been crammed with tearful owners not wanting to destroy their beloved pets but feeling they were in an impossible situation and that this was the only thing they could do.

Although it was Bill who was the real softie where cats were concerned, in recent months Peggy had become very fond of Fishy, the more so since Fishy would alternate some squeaky upper tones with deep bass purrs as on the marital bed they snuggled close together during their afternoon naps once Peggy had stopped work.

Peggy had made Ted and Barbara promise that they would do all that they could to avoid such an unnecessary end for the little tabby as she couldn't bear the thought of putting down such a healthy animal so long before her natural time, and especially when she was such an affectionate creature as well as being an exceptionally good mouser.

'Don't worry, Peggy, we'll look after 'er fer yer. An' if anyone official asks about 'er, I'll take 'er with me to the docks, as they always need ratters and mousers at the warehouses, and she can 'ave a fine ol' time there as a working cat. I'll do my best for 'er,' Ted promised, 'and it'll be our way of thanking you for keepin' an eye out for our Jessie and Connie.'

Peggy found Ted's words very comforting.

She was worn out. Once Ted had lugged away the stuff for storage or passing on, Peggy had spent the rest of the Saturday afternoon cleaning the house that Bill and she had rented from top to bottom, making sure everything was left spick and span and so clean that any new tenant could quite literally have eaten their food straight off the floor if they were so inclined. Then Peggy had to deliver the keys back to her and Bill's landlord before returning to collect Fishy who was basketed up and waiting on the doorstep to go to Jubilee Street, with Peggy's packed hand case alongside.

And so by the time the Ross family was pulling up chairs to Barbara's kitchen table on the Saturday teatime, with slices of bread already buttered and large pieces of hot battered cod and chips in newspaper waiting to be divvied up between them, Peggy was feeling tuckered out and pretty much at the end of her tether.

She was going to spend the Saturday and Sunday nights in Jessie's bed, while across the bedroom Jessie was going to top-and-tail with his sister. Peggy urged Barbara not to bother about putting clean sheets on Jessie's bed for her just for the two nights, but Barbara insisted and Peggy felt too exhausted to argue about it any further, and the moment she had given Fishy the fish scraps for supper she had an early night.

Fishy proved to be an excellent distraction for Connie and Jessie, who were growing increasingly fretful and tense as the enormity of what was about to happen to them – separation from all that they knew – was feeling very real now.

Ted tied some feathers to a bit of twine and showed the children how to get Fishy chasing after it. Fishy seemed to have boundless energy and was quite happy to play for a long while, the children encouraging her to run up and down the stairs with them. It proved a very good way for them all to let off steam, although possibly quite noisy for Peggy and her early night, and the result was the twins went to bed feeling a whole lot better than they had done before Fishy arrived, with the puss proving to have strong nerves after having had the chance to explore everywhere at number five.

Try as they might, Jessie and Connie couldn't remember anyone ever sleeping over in their house, and once they were in their bedroom it felt very strange having somebody else under their roof for the night, even though of course they knew their Aunt Peggy well already.

The twins agreed, though, that it wasn't as much fun as they had hoped it would be, as Barbara had strictly forbidden the twins from talking to each other in their bedroom, saying that Peggy needed her sleep and they were to wake her on pain of death only, and so they had to content themselves with making a great show of creeping about as they got ready to climb into bed.

They couldn't help pressing their feet on each other's when Fishy, now snuggled into Peggy's back and feeling content with a full belly of the fish scraps that Ted had brought back for her, began to purr her squeaky purr more loudly than some people could snore.

In the morning, Jessie found Fishy sitting on his pillow staring intently at his face, presumably willing him to wake up.

Jessie looked back in silence at the tabby, and then carefully lifted in invitation the sheet and blanket that were covering him, to which Fishy gave Jessie a look as if to say, *At last – I was really wondering what I was going to have to do to make you understand The Rules!* as she sidled off the pillow and past his face to sneak under the bedclothes to nestle in a furry curl against Jessie's ribcage, before they both fell asleep once more.

Just as Jessie drifted off he thought that it was like having a small and very comforting hot-water bottle pressed close to his chest.

In fact, everyone was still so all-in that by the time Monday morning came around every single person at number five Jubilee Street overslept. Such a thing had never happened before.

'Barbara. Barbara! 'Ave you seen the time?' said Ted in a muffled, dozy voice. The sun was already quite a way up, and the birds' dawn chorus had quietened down to little more than an occasional chirp.

It was the clink of the glass milk bottles being delivered and the sound of the muffled feet of the horse pulling the milk cart that had roused Ted from his sound sleep.

His wife had been snoozing very deeply and clearly she hadn't fully come to as she inched closer to Ted under the protective arm he had over her.

Ted thought about putting the war on hold and letting them all sleep in; it was very tempting.

But then he realised that if he allowed that to happen, Barbara would never forgive him, and so he whispered, 'Barbara, it's getting on – it's not far off seven thirty.'

Seven thirty! A whole hour later than when Barbara had planned she would get up.

With a start of comical proportions, Barbara catapulted herself out of bed and ran from the room to bang loudly on the other bedroom door. 'We're late. WE'RE LATE!!' she shouted.

Fishy was terrified by the unexpected cacophony in a still-strange environment, and she shot out of the bedcovers at the opposite end of the bed to where she had gone in, which unfortunately was right beside Connie's face, as she sought refuge hiding in the furthest and darkest corner under the bed.

Connie felt a surge of panic and she heard herself giving an anguished squeal at the sight of something furry, grey and stripy shooting out of her bed at the rate of knots a mere inch or so in front of her nose.

Jessie sat bolt upright, and it took him a second or two to work out why, while it clearly was his familiar bedroom, it all looked so different and a bit like looking at something in reverse in a mirror, before he remembered that he was sleeping for the very first time across the room from where he normally slept, in Connie's bed. He felt for Fishy beside him, and then he realised that perhaps it was Fishy's hasty exit that had led to Connie making such a noise.

The twins looked at each other and then across at Peggy, but she didn't so much as break the rhythm of her stentorious breathing, she was still so soundly asleep.

So much for he and Connie having to creep around in case they woke her unnecessarily, Jessie thought as he sat up, stretched loudly and wildly, and then slipped his feet to the floor.

Barbara had planned a lavish breakfast spread of bacon, eggs and fried bread for everyone so that at least she knew they'd all be well set up for the day.

Needless to say, their late start meant that by the time everyone was dressed and downstairs, and Fishy was giving a cry that was definitely announcing it was high time for *her* breakfast, it was already ten to eight. And so the best Barbara could hurriedly prepare was tea and toast, and as they ate she made everyone cheese and pickle sandwiches for lunch that she hurriedly slapped together before she wrapped the sandwiches more carefully in waxed paper. Then they all got ready to walk together over to St Mark's Primary School, Ted announcing that he'd go to work once he had seen the children were safely delivered to the school and had everything they needed.

'And you've got to say goodbye to us, Daddy,' Connie reminded him, her small voice a far cry from how she spoke ordinarily; it made both of her parents recall when she had been a tiny girl. Connie added, 'We couldn't go away with the school if you hadn't said goodbye to us properly, could we, Jessie?'

Both Ted and Barbara felt a lump rising to their throats. Connie had inadvertently touched a raw nerve.

'Look sharp, you two – but before we leave, let's go through Mr Jones's list one last time,' said Peggy to the twins as they all put on their coats, seeing their parents needed a moment or two to compose themselves.

Ted meanwhile pressed on Peggy two £5 notes, so that she could dole out some pocket money to the children if she found herself billeted near to them, plus, he said, she'd have plenty over if they – or Peggy – needed anything that nobody so far had thought of, Peggy promising without being asked that she would keep a detailed account of what she spent on Jessie and Connie, and that she would return the money unspent if she were billeted somewhere else that was too far from the children for her to have much contact. This really was a significant sum and Peggy knew that Ted and Barbara could ill afford to waste it.

At last the little cavalcade was ready to set off, with Fishy keeping watch on them from an upstairs window. Everyone was clutching their gas masks in their brand-new cardboard boxes that had twine attached ready for the mask's owner to loop over a shoulder, and after a little tussle with Peggy, Ted and Barbara manhandling between them the three items of luggage along the road.

As Jessie and Connie headed down Jubilee Street in the direction of school, the twins were reminded forcibly that it might be quite some time before they saw these familiar houses again.

Connie briefly slid her hand into Jessie's, and announced, 'I can't believe it but I feel homesick already, when I haven't yet gone. They are ugly old houses, I'm sure, but I know every one.'

Not one of them could think of what they should say back to Connie and so nobody said anything for a while, although Barbara made sure that she smiled comfortingly at Jessie to let him know that she realised that he'd also be finding the whole experience very strange even though he was keeping quiet.

As they walked along they saw families similarly

heading to the school, although with none of the boisterous behaviour or whoops of laughter that normally denoted south-east London family outings. The children gave minute half-smiles in the direction of their pals, while the adults accompanying them nodded sombrely at their opposite numbers.

When they got close to St Mark's, it was to see the unusual sight of four single-decker coaches already parked up in the road outside the playground, the drivers wearing matching peaked caps and standing together as they chatted, all the while taking deep drags on Senior Service unfiltered cigarettes.

'Peggy, you go and report to Susanne, who'll be most pleased to see you I don't doubt, seeing the scrum that's here already, and I'll look after your handbag and suitcase while you sort yourself out,' said Barbara, as she looked at those milling across the playground, and then indicated to her sister where she and Ted would be waiting with the children.

It wasn't long before Peggy threaded her way back to her sister across the now-heaving playground as in the time she had been gone the mass of people gathered squashily in its confines had doubled.

Peggy reported that she and Connie and Jessie were all designated to the final coach, and this meant that they weren't due to leave the school until eleven o'clock.

'Mr Jones is going to ask all the parents to go in a minute as he thinks the children will start getting upset if their mothers and fathers stay too long,' she told Barbara and Ted, followed by, 'and Ted, you need to put our luggage

74

over by the wall where that "4" has been chalked as this is the mark for those going in the last bus. It means our luggage will go on the same bus to the station that we also travel on. Then you both had better start saying your goodbyes, and after that the teachers and me shall take it from there.'

The schoolchildren of St Mark's, in general, whether they be small five-year-olds or old-timers of eleven years of age, took the actual leave-taking in a much more stoical manner than many of the parents managed, as they said their goodbyes and took their final hugs (or, in the case of some of the sons and fathers, contented themselves merely with a brusque downwards pump of the hand). Most mothers and one or two of the fathers too had hankies out, and many weren't at all embarrassed to be seen allowing the tears to flow freely.

Jessie and Connie kept the proverbial stiff upper lip, as Barbara leant down to tie to their coat buttonholes big parcel labels that matched the labels already attached to their luggage that had in large capital letters their name, their London address and the name of their school, and then she made sure that they each had a pencil stub in their pocket so that once they knew where they were going they could write that too in the space below Barbara's writing.

'Now, you take care of each other, an' remember to be 'onest and polite to the people you are going to meet,' said Ted. 'An' work 'ard at school, and don't shirk on any errands or odd jobs around the 'ouse the people lookin' after yer ask of yer both. Eat up everything they give you – there's to be no leavin' of anyfing or sayin' yer don't like it, mind.'

'Send us a note the very minute you know where you are, and me and your dad will write back,' added Barbara. 'And do try to stick together in order that you are billeted together, remember. Hold hands when people come in to look at you, and try very hard not to take no for an answer if anyone tries to say that you can't stay together. Have you understood, Connie and Jessie? It really is very important that you do.'

Connie and Jessie each gave their mother a look which implied that Barbara's last instruction would obviously go without saying.

'And remember that I've written letters for whoever takes you in, so don't forget to hand those over,' Barbara went on huskily, as she dabbed now beneath her eyes with a pressed and folded hanky.

The children were hugged tightly, as was Peggy, and when Barbara and Ted turned just before they headed out the school gate to the playground to give a final wave, it was to the reassuring sight that the twins were standing side by side, looking united and determined, their auntie standing behind them as she rested a hand on each of their shoulders.

'Look after Fishy,' called Connie. 'She can do our errands for you with us gone!'

'Do you think our Jessie has grown a little?' said Barbara, once she and Ted had got to the end of the street, and she had dried her eyes and put her handkerchief back in her handbag. 'For a moment, I fancied he was looking as if he has.'

Ted still didn't trust himself to speak, but he nodded and then crept a comforting arm around Barbara's waist for a few paces.

Chapter Nine

As it turned out, the children and teachers were squeezed onto one or other of the four coaches by about ten o'clock, following a lively debate between the drivers as to the best bridge to drive across the River Thames – New London Bridge or Tower Bridge – a decision made more complicated by the drivers discussing the likely amount of traffic on the other side. The vehicles belted out black exhaust fumes as they were then driven away from Bermondsey in what turned out to be an achingly slow convoy.

It seemed to Peggy as if all of London was jam-packed with traffic as the St Mark's buses crawled over Tower Bridge and northwards up to King's Cross railway station.

At the massive London terminus there was then a tremendous kerfuffle going on already as, quite literally, chaos was reigning.

There were thousands of people milling hither and thither, with those from various evacuation centres and the ordinary fare-paying passengers rubbing shoulders with one another as they attempted to find out where they were supposed to be and which platform was the one that they needed.

Amongst them bustled all manner of people in uniform, some of whom were walking around with clipboards as they tried to organise those awaiting evacuation (these clipboard-holders were the people looking most harassed), while others shouted instructions and directions to various parts of the station through handheld megaphones. There were crackling announcements over the station tannoy too, but it appeared that nobody could decipher anything that was being said by these announcers.

One of the first things that Connie saw was a rotund woman in an expensive fur-collared tweedy two-piece suit that was at least a size too small for her, but who looked nevertheless like an imperious head of an exclusive girls' school. She was standing on an upturned wooden beer crate while her quaking voice was veering towards the tone that the twins associated with an oncoming tantrum.

Grown-ups were feeling out of their depth, clearly, and tempers were being frayed in the noisy hubbub of the station. Connie whispered to Jessie with a nod towards the portly woman on the wooden box, whose cheeks were quickly taking on puce undertones, 'King's Cross... And it don't look as if the Queen's too happy either!'

Of course, everybody from St Mark's needed now to go to the toilet, and there was an almighty queue for the gents and a spectacularly huge one for the ladies that was snaking to and fro in great loops.

Miss Pinkly had come to King's Cross to help with making sure no one got lost at the station, although once they'd chugged out of the station finally she would be going home later by hopping on a number 63 bus. Connie heard her and Peggy joke to one another that at this rate the children could go to the lavatory and then rejoin the queue at the back, as by the time they'd get to the front once more it would be time for them to relieve themselves again. At least Connie thought they were making a joke, but after spending thirty minutes edging forward a couple of inches at a time and still not having made it into a cubicle, she wasn't so sure.

St Mark's headmaster Mr Jones huffed with obvious disapproval at the chaos and promptly disappeared into an office marked *Evacuation Orders* for what seemed an age. When, finally, he returned with his bristly moustache quivering in indignation to where the pupils and teachers were standing with their luggage, he announced that they were to get the next train that would come in at the furthermost platform on the far side of the station. The train had been specially commissioned and they would see B:71 in the driver's window at the end of the train closest to where they would get onto the platform; this meant, apparently, it wouldn't have any ordinary passengers, as some of the other school evacuee trains did.

It was going to take them to Leeds, after which they would be transferred to another train that would take them on to Harrogate which was, apparently, where the powers that be had decided the schoolchildren of St Mark's, and Peggy too, would be billeted.

At this news, Peggy's heart sank. She'd hoped they'd be heading for somewhere within – at the most – an hour of London by train. Kent, possibly, or Hertfordshire or Berkshire, or even, at a stretch, Bedfordshire.

Harrogate seemed without doubt a ridiculously long way for them all to go. It had to be close on two hundred miles between the two places.

In addition, it was already past one o'clock, and so with the best will in the world it would be late afternoon by the time they got to Leeds, and then they'd still have another train to take before their journey would be completed and before they would end up presumably at some sort of reception centre, and only at that point would they finally be allocated their billets.

It was hard to think that there wouldn't be tears before bedtime from most of the children, as this was a punishing timetable for them, and Peggy wondered too if she might also be faced with her own sobs before the day was out. Her ankles felt uncomfortable, and the baby seemed to have picked up on her own anxiety as now and then she had a stab beneath her skirt waistband of something that felt not too far away from pain.

However, the children were being told right now to make sure they had the right suitcase or bag, and that they should get into pairs and then form an orderly line, all of which was easier said than done on such a busy day at the station.

Peggy and Susanne embraced and said farewell. Then Peggy tried to concentrate on making sure she and the pupils were as organised as they could be rather than allowing herself to think of how peaky she was feeling personally.

Then, once some sort of order had been established, a nice woman with a megaphone and a small triangular red pennant held aloft on a bamboo stick walked with them to the platform they needed, with Miss Crabbe saying repeatedly, 'Children, follow that red flag and look sharp about it – no stragglers.'

When the party from St Mark's got to the right platform they discovered they were to share the train with a school from Camden that was apparently destined for somewhere over near Sheffield or Leeds. Apparently there was confusion as to where that school was going and so everyone from this other school had been told to go to Leeds and the local officials could sort it out from there.

Oh well, thought Peggy, thank heavens for small mercies, I suppose. At least we know what town we are destined for, which is more than can be said for those poor pupils and teachers from Camden.

Once the St Mark's group had shuffled past the other school to the far end of the platform as the lady with the flag had directed, and then put their cases and bags and gas masks down on the platform to wait for the train, which was being brought to them from a rail siding nearby, Peggy clapped her hands for attention.

'Right, St Mark's school pupils, please go and stand with your own classmates. And when we get on the train and have sat down, there will be a headcount and your names will be ticked off against each class register. While the teachers do that, I want you all to eat your packed lunches and then try to have a nap. It's going to be quite late by the time we get to Harrogate, and you will feel tired, and so you will definitely find it of benefit to have a snooze on the train if you can.'

'Do yer know where we're going, miss?'

''Ave yer been there yerself, miss?'

'Is it in the country, miss?'

'Is 'Arrowgate posh, miss?' were the questions the children wanted to know.

'All I know is that we are definitely going to Harrogate as that is what Mr Jones said to us just now,' said Peggy, 'and I don't know much about Harrogate other than that it is famous for its water spas and it was very popular with Victorian visitors, and that it is in Yorkshire. Aside from that, you all know as much as me, which isn't very much, is it? Won't it be fun having a whole new town to explore and find out about?'

Not many pupils agreed with her rather rash assertion, it seemed.

A loud whistle behind her made Peggy jump very obviously, which caused a few ribald comments, and she turned to a black puffing billy chuffing at walking pace along their platform. The driver brought the train to a halt, and a hissy screaming noise came from his cab's whistle before a gust of steam was released from somewhere near the large steel wheels.

Very few of the children had even been across the River Thames before, let alone on a train. And as they went to find their seats, the level of chatter intensified and sounded more cheerful, and suddenly it seemed quite an escapade they were all just about to start. Even Peggy's spirits felt raised as she climbed on board.

Their adventure was about to begin.

*

Unfortunately this sense of optimism wasn't a feeling that could last indefinitely, the St Mark's contingent discovered, as the delay between the change of trains at Leeds was lengthy, with the air distinctly chillier than in London and the sun well hidden behind a seething mass of battle-grey clouds.

The children had eaten their packed lunches a considerable time ago and everyone was tired and thirsty. Peggy hadn't seen anyone napping, although she had managed a crafty twenty-minute forty winks herself, even though it was well short of the hour she had found herself needing during the afternoon most days. And so it was with huge relief to all when some WVS ladies in uniform eventually bustled onto the train platform bearing trays of sandwiches and bumpy rock cakes, large jugs of lemon cordial and long stacks of melamine beakers.

Peggy was feeling distinctly wobbly despite her nap, even though actually the children had been very well behaved, all things considered.

She found herself worried all over again about having made the decision to leave London; if anything went wrong with the pregnancy now, or with the birth, she was going to be a very long way from Barbara. And she discovered that already she was badly missing Fishy's pretty little face and soft, soothingly strokable fur too, and suddenly it all felt a bit much, and the effort of not giving in to her shaking lower lip gave Peggy a sudden bolt of headache.

Seeing that the other adults from St Mark's were supervising the doling out of the sandwiches and the continual head-counting of the pupils, she sank onto a wooden bench on the platform, leant back and closed her eyes. She wished Bill were with her – he felt a very long way away, and this added to a crest of sadness trying to overwhelm her. Peggy screwed her eyes up tighter. She mustn't cry, she mustn't. To give in to tears when she was supposed to be looking after the children would be unforgivable, it really would.

She fought back these hard-to-bear feelings with a determined swallow and then she heard someone sit down beside her but then a new wave, this time of exhaustion, made the thought of opening her eyes seem impossible.

After a while Connie tried to sound very grown up as she said, 'Mummy said I was to look after you, Auntie Peggy, and so if you want to be quiet for a minute or two, I'll look out for your handbag and such.'

And right after that Jessie arrived with some sandwiches and tea for Peggy, and as soon as she had eaten she felt much better, the world looking just that little bit brighter.

A few minutes later, Peggy felt up to explaining to a curious Connie, and Angela Kennedy who was now sitting with them, that the WVS initials stood for Women's Voluntary Service, and that their motto was 'the WVS never says no'.

'Right, children, you tuck in,' she announced then to other children from St Mark's who had now come to sit cross-legged on the concrete of the platform near to their little group in order to eat their sandwiches. 'It will be quite late, I suspect, by the time we arrive at Harrogate, and so I've no idea when we will all be eating again.'

It was a whole hour and a half later before a train arrived

to take them to Harrogate. What a long day it felt, Peggy thought, as she shepherded the pupils from St Mark's on board, but at least the queues for the lavatories at Leeds station had been significantly shorter than at King's Cross that morning. Maybe every cloud really did have a silver lining.

Chapter Ten

The children's first view of Harrogate wasn't promising in the slightest, even Peggy had to concede that, although she tried to keep a cheerful enough expression firmly glued to her face.

First of all, the train had headed away from Leeds through an unruly-looking mix of open countryside and factories, which hadn't gone down well with the children, who were used to endless streets of terraced housing or the brown expanse of the River Thames – or, on a day out, perhaps the hilly parkland of Greenwich where a family might picnic on a very special occasion – and so they seemed of the opinion that this West Riding farmland looked distinctly suspicious and the sort of place still to have highwaymen. They'd been content to travel through open country when they knew they still had a long way to go, but now they felt they were on the home run, countryside of any sort seemed to be much less appealing.

Peggy tried to point out how many travellers new to the area would find the undulating ground of the countryside, the stone walls and the sturdy cottages they occasionally passed to be very pretty, but Larry seemed to sum up the general mood with, 'Where's the offy? An' 'ow's the rat-catcher going' to kill the vermin out 'ere?'

Peggy pointed out that some areas they were going through were built up, and then she added that in the more rural areas she expected that the wild foxes would keep the rodent population down – she wasn't sure about this actually, but she deemed it a sensible assumption – and that there would be public houses in the large villages and, of course, also in the towns.

Then she thought she probably shouldn't be encouraging the children to think about public houses right before meeting their host families, as if they were to mention them right away it wouldn't be a terribly good first impression of what the London children were used to. The reality was, however, that public houses or 'offies' would in fact be something many of them would be used to hearing about at home from their parents as so much of the socialising in Bermondsey would – for the adults, at least – centre on one public house or another, an evening often ending in a good old sing-song in the bar, and hopefully not a round of fisticuffs in the gutter outside.

By now the sound of the train chugging along couldn't disguise the fact that the wind had got up. There was a sudden rain shower buffeted around in a squall that battered the windows with sharp-sounding gusts and heavy raindrops, with some of the children claiming they could feel the train carriage rocking from side to side the wind was blowing so much. Even Peggy had to concede that just at that moment everything they could see out of the windows of the train carriage was looking forbiddingly bleak and threatening, with any farm animals out to grass looking wind-tossed and sorry for themselves.

Soon, dusk began to fall, and as they hit the final run to Harrogate station, they noticed that the grand stone buildings that were now on either side of the train looked shadowy and imposing, and not at all inviting. Occasionally hints that there might be wide roads in Harrogate, and formal parks and gardens, many of which had been planted with impressive-looking flower beds, could be glimpsed through the carriage windows.

It was all very different to what they were used to in Bermondsey, and not necessarily for the better seemed to be the general consensus.

'Posh,' Jessie muttered to Connie, 'very posh indeed. We'll all be minding our Ps and Qs.'

Silently but with a tight look on her face, Connie nodded her agreement, and the twins felt terribly shy all of a sudden and ill prepared for what might be about to come.

Peggy felt similarly too, although she didn't want the children to see her own faltering of spirit.

She tugged at the clasp to her handbag to seek out the Cardinal Red lipstick Barbara had bought her as she thought a slick of scarlet could only bolster her self-esteem.

As she replaced in her handbag her small mirror as well as the Coty lipstick and Revlon cake mascara she'd quickly buffed up her lashes and brows with, Peggy caught a glimpse of the yellow hat she had knitted Connie the previous Friday night. She had worked hard to finish it before moving over to Jubilee Street the next day, and since then she had completely forgotten to give it to her niece.

What a dunderhead – I'd forget my own head if it wasn't screwed on, Peggy thought, and then she hoped that once she was no longer pregnant she'd feel alert and quick-witted in the same way she had always prided herself on previously.

'Here you are, Connie. It was done in a bit of a rush and I had to use knitting needles that were a little bigger than I'd choose normally, and so it might not be as warm as your last hat. A winter hat that, as we know, is sitting on top of that warehouse roof you threw it onto! But I daresay you'll find this one useful for carrying something or other around in, if not for wearing when it gets cold,' Peggy tried to joke as she lifted the hat from her bag and passed it over to her niece.

'I love it, Auntie Peggy, thank you so much,' said Connie, as she took it and then turned it around in her hands as she inspected it from every angle. 'And thank you very much too for never letting on to Mummy what happened to my hat of last winter. She would have strung me up if she had found out, wouldn't she?'

They shared a smile, and Connie pulled the new hat on. It really suited her, being a rich, golden hue that matched the shining autumnal tones in her shoulder-length hair and being too an arresting contrast to her intelligent blue eyes. The jaunty pom-pom was the perfect finishing touch, quite obviously.

It was a titfer of personality, niece and aunt decided, just as a harsh squeal of their train's wheels on the metal rail tracks as the driver applied the brakes signalled that they were starting to slow down in order for them to pull into Harrogate station.

Before the train had quite come to a halt, Peggy found a moment to say to Jessie she was very sorry but she hadn't knitted him anything as there hadn't been time, but that she would make it up to him soon, and in the meantime Jessie was to let her know if there was anything he needed and she would do her best to get it for him, or to make it for him if that were more appropriate.

With that the train shuddered to a dead halt, heralded by a final couple of clanking sounds and another ear-piercing tangle of brakes on track, and it was time for everyone to stand up, find their suitcases and their gas masks, and then clamber stiffly from the carriage and down the steep steps from the carriage to drop onto the platform.

Immediately they were met by a really quite chilly gust of wind that whipped Peggy's skirt to slap sharply against her legs as it channelled itself through the station, announcing quite forcibly that the weather was going to be much brisker up in Yorkshire than they were used to in London. Luckily the rain seemed to have passed through, and although the air felt damp at least no ploppy drops were still falling.

Peggy thought the boys might well need to wear long trousers for the first time in their lives if the children had to spend all winter in the North of England, if this icy blast was anything to go by, although many of their parents would be too poor to be able to supply them and so goodness knows how that would all play out.

But before she could think further on this there was a shuffling forward of a motley line of several chilled-looking people with hunched shoulders who looked to have been waiting on the platform for just a bit too long to meet the contingent from Bermondsey.

After the adults had shaken hands and introduced themselves (although with neither side being able to make out exactly what it was that the other was saying, it seemed to Peggy), then after one last headcount to make sure that none of the children were missing, everybody was escorted quite smartly from the station as it was too nippy for everyone, even the infants of five years old, not to stride out.

Fortunately they didn't have to go very far, although some muffled childish screams and laughter followed by the reverberating sound of quickly running feet, and quite a lot of curtain-twitching in the windows they passed, suggested that more than a few local people and children were sneaking a surreptitious look at the new arrivals and then quickly scooting off to share what they had seen with friends, or else were turning to have a word with someone in the room behind.

The group from St Mark's were taken to a small building with its name proudly displayed above the entrance door: Odd Fellows Hall. This caused a few comments from teachers and pupils alike who made up the London party, and then it was explained that Odd Fellows was a charitable society from Victorian times aimed at helping the 'unfortunates of the world'.

Or at least that's what Peggy thought was being said, as there was distinctly room for doubt.

The Yorkshire accents their hosts spoke with seemed very strong and hard to navigate, although to judge by the confused expression on the faces of those in the welcoming committee, it seemed that the St Mark's cockney voices were just as impenetrable to the welcoming committee as they were finding theirs.

Peggy also thought she spied their hosts looking down their noses rather snootily at the garb of the teachers and children, but she wasn't sure if she was mainly tired and grumpy, and was really only ready therefore to find fault rather than look for the positive things in their situation. If she was, she doubted she would be alone in this feeling.

However, any snooty or disapproving looks seemed more understandable, Peggy realised, when she herself turned to consider more closely the now creased and rumpled outfits of herself and her travelling companions. Taken as one, they really did look like a dastardly bunch of individuals, but she supposed that a whole day getting to where they were going, and having yet to be allocated their billets, would inevitably result in most of them looking bedraggled and a bit raggle-taggle by this stage of the day, with the result that they all appeared to be distinctly 'unfortunate' and as such probably the epitome of the type of person who should walk through the door to Odd Fellows Hall.

In addition, virtually all of the children sported expressions that managed to combine a tinge of something hangdog with extremely wary, but again this was only to be expected, Peggy concluded, and she hoped fervently that it wouldn't put any of the host families off when it came to them choosing which children they would be inviting into their own homes.

While tea was poured into green china cups from a giant urn waiting on a side table for those who wanted it, the alternative being small glasses of icy, slightly brackish water, and everyone who needed to go to the lavatory was given the opportunity to head off to the cloakroom to spend a quick penny, the reception committee explained that in ten minutes or so people with spare beds would arrive to choose their evacuees.

All the teachers were going to be billeted together, and it had already been decided where they would stay (which was in a guest house, apparently, that was called Dunroamin), although Peggy was slightly taken aback when she learnt that these plans for the St Mark's teachers didn't include her. It also became clear that the reason headmaster Mr Jones wasn't going to stay up in Harrogate was because he'd been told that he wasn't needed, rather than that he'd chosen to go back to London as he'd allowed some of the adults connected with St Mark's to think up until then, and this seemed to unsettle several of the Bermondsey teachers, who were now looking about themselves anxiously, as if checking to see if they were also for the chop.

As Susanne Pinkly had already intimated to Peggy, there simply wasn't need for two headmasters at the school St Mark's would be sharing, and so once everyone had had a day or two to settle in, off Mr Jones would go back to London.

Peggy wasn't quite sure what she felt about not being bunked up with the other teachers. While not technically a teacher just at the moment, she realised she'd been assuming she almost certainly would be rooming wherever they were, or at the very least some sort of provision would have been made that she would stay somewhere very close to them. She had been happy to help with the evacuation, and for no pay, after all.

In a way, though, she didn't particularly mind having to strike out off her own bat, as now that Susanne wasn't part of the troop, none of the teachers were close friends or had much – if indeed any – fun. But still they were familiar faces, and it did feel peculiar for Peggy to realise that in only a matter of minutes she would be very alone as far as any adult company or support went.

Peggy supposed that this feeling of having been cast adrift from the others was exacerbated by the reminder that the St Mark's headmaster would be returning south very imminently. She had never been a huge fan of Mr Jones, but the fact he ran a fair and tight ship was undeniable.

Pupils from St Mark's tended to do well at the eleven-plus examination and regularly won places to go on to the local grammar school for the primary school's catchment area, and thereafter the school pupils from St Mark's tended to secure a range of better jobs than pupils from other schools in Bermondsey often did.

Peggy hoped the children wouldn't find themselves in a radically different regime, or one with lax academic standards, as lost time in their schooling was always very difficult to make up when the majority of the school children would be joining the working world at age fourteen.

To judge by the very little she had seen of Harrogate,

it looked to be a moneyed area full of people wearing good-quality clothing and smart shoes, and some might say that people like these might not need to be able to look out for themselves in quite the way the poor families of south-east London had to scrabble around for every single penny in order to do the best they could. How keen they might be on education in lieu of this was anybody's guess, she decided.

Peggy was a tremendous believer in the value of education and she hoped that when the war was over she would still feel similarly.

Right now, as Peggy looked about her, to judge by the haughty look on the faces of some of the reception committee, it seemed as if the general attitude of their Yorkshire hosts intimated that they believed they had everything to offer, and that there wasn't much possibility that the people from London had anything to teach them.

Peggy wondered if that was true – surely there would be good things on both sides that the others could learn from?

At last the children were asked to line up, and Connie and Jessie made sure to stand next to one another holding hands, and then Angela pushed in on Connie's other side, while Jessie, rather to his horror, found himself standing beside Larry, although neither of the boys gave the slightest hint they had noticed each other.

Peggy meanwhile noted the surreptitious looks some of the reception committee were casting at her, and she understood that they didn't know whether to ask her to line up alongside the children or not. And then she realised that she didn't very much care either way. Right now, if it meant she couldn't be found lodging, she would head back to Bermondsey with Mr Jones quite happily.

With a sigh she wearily took her place in the line-up, standing right beside Angela. Peggy glanced at Jessie and Connie and saw both children sporting determined and slightly defiant expressions that almost seemed to be daring any adults to suggest that they be split up.

As Peggy had feared, the billeting process turned out to be quite nightmarish.

The largest pupils, both boys and girls, were the first to be picked, with Larry being the very first child to be chosen. As he walked off beside a stern-faced man, Larry looked as if he didn't know whether to be pleased or upset he had been picked so early. Some of the Harrogate hosts who had just come in looked as if they were farmers, not least as they were saying they wanted strong lads who could help them out on the land, while other hosts, all women, although clearly from a variety of backgrounds, chose the bigger girls, saying they were going to be helping with housework and so forth.

Once a list of addresses had been made of where all those who had already been chosen were staying, the next wave of local folk came in, and generally the more handsome and prettier children, both boys and girls, were chosen by this batch of billets. Angela was one of these children, and as she was chivvied from the hall by a rather flurried woman Connie risked calling goodbye, to which Angela waved cheerily enough, although her face remained worried.

There was a shabby and straggly-haired woman at the billeting hall who looked so strange that everybody hoped that they weren't going to be picked by her. After all manner of people – big and small, old and young – had walked along the line of children who had been waiting for their billets, with few even looking towards where Jessie and Connie stood, this strange-looking person marched down the line only to stop abruptly in front of the twins.

She stuck her face forward to peer into theirs, blasting them with a whiff of rapidly expelled rancid breath, the force of which made a long and solitary grey whisker on her chin quiver nastily.

The woman snatched at Jessie's hand and he felt what could only be described as a claw clutch at him, the callouses on her hands were so thick. The woman reached for Connie's hand, but she and Jessie shrank away from her, their shoulders touching and lending each other strength, while their eyes, unblinking in horror, looked black as their pupils had become so large in their fear.

Then, with a tut that frothed spittle into the corners of her thin lips, the crone flung Jessie's hand away from her as if it were boiling hot, and then she shuffled on her way down the line, leaving Connie and Jessie behind. The twins looked at each other, unable to prevent their mirrored shudders of disgust, to leave unaccompanied by anybody. There was a palpable sigh of relief throughout the hall.

Eventually it got down to about six children who were left, including Jessie and Connie, their refusal to be separated being more of an issue than anyone had expected, seeing that they were a boy and a girl, as some hosts turned out to be worried about sleeping arrangements as they weren't sure about mixing the sexes in bedrooms, especially if they already had children at home.

It didn't help that Jessie was looking sickly by then as it had been such a long day and so he kept sniffing, while Connie had made her new dress quite grubby en route.

Peggy was feeling increasingly uncomfortable as most people avoided looking at her altogether, and those that did would smile at her and then catch sight of her belly and, with the smile dropping from their faces, move quickly on.

At last another three of the children had been allocated, which left Connie and Jessie, and a little girl called Maggie whose clothes were filthy and the holes in her shoes clearly obvious for anyone to see, as were her nits; and she'd had polio as a baby, so she had a leg in a bulky, squeaky calliper.

Peggy was taken aback to find that, without waiting to see what would happen to the billeting of the stragglers, the teachers from St Mark's headed off to their guest house as their landlady arrived to say she couldn't hold their food any longer. The Dunroamin landlady looked a right battleaxe, and so Peggy decided they deserved each other, as she thought that if she knew where she was going to be staying, she would have made sure that a pregnant former colleague was sorted before heading off to the lure of supper.

A tight-lipped and grumpy woman from the WVS seemed to be losing patience, and Peggy felt close to saying something snappish to her as she wasn't feeling at all patient herself by this point.

Fortunately things took a distinct turn for the better

when a rather rich-looking woman arrived who had a massive fox fur draped over her new-looking astrakhan coat, and Peggy thought that she would choose Connie and then Jessie will be upset. But to everyone's surprise, she didn't seem to mind the nits or the calliper that Maggie had, despite the WVS woman pointing them out very rudely, and so she marched Maggie away, saying she was going to dunk her straight into a hot bath and then dress Maggie in some of her daughter's old play clothes.

Nobody came in for a while, and the twins and Peggy were just starting to look anxiously at each other, when a kindly-looking man in a dog collar and his jolly wife arrived.

After he had apologised for being late (which was something to do with a crisis with one of his parishioners, apparently) the man in the dog collar said, 'How wonderful. I see that they've saved the best till last.'

And with that he invited Peggy and the twins to his home, although not before his wife had shaken Peggy's hand just as if she really were delighted to see them all, dishevelled and messy as they were, and then this jolly-looking woman gave each of the twins a quick hug.

Peggy could have cried simply because somebody was being kind, and as the children each snuck a hand into each of hers as they began down the road with their new billets, Peggy thought the twins probably felt just as emotional as she did.

Chapter Eleven

Nothing could describe how strange all of the three London evacuees felt as Roger and Mabel Braithwaite escorted them to Tall Trees, which Roger described as a rectory.

Peggy and the twins looked at each other – they had no idea what he meant, although they could see that he was obviously a clergyman.

Then Roger added, 'We don't stand on ceremony at Tall Trees. You must all call me Roger, and' – he pointed to his wife – 'this is Mabel. She's the one in charge. You'll see!'

Roger and Mabel began to laugh as if Roger had just told an amazing joke, but again the evacuees all just stared at one another, and then looked back to their hosts.

It seemed extraordinary that the rector was suggesting they use his Christian name to address him. Even Peggy had never heard the like before, and she couldn't think what to say. Jessie thought, along with his aunt, that Barbara would have something to say about this – his and Connie's mother prided herself that, although she was poor, that hadn't stopped her being as proper as the next person at the Women's Institute.

As they walked, Jessie and Connie discovered their hearts still beat uncomfortably fast if they thought about the lucky escape they had had from the witchy-looking woman.

Roger and Mabel kept up a cheerful prattle, but Peggy and the twins found themselves bone-weary and terribly homesick for the narrow streets of Bermondsey, with its cheek-by-jowl homes jostling beside each other, and the sounds of carousing coming from the bar of one or other of the several public houses nearby. Here it was very quiet, and they weren't used to this at all.

Soon Roger halted and then stood to one side, indicating that they should turn in at the propped-open white-painted gate he was standing next to. Their feet hit shingle, which made a crunchy noise as they walked up to the rectory.

It was a very imposing house, they could see in the moonlight, and there was a large building beside it. It was obvious immediately how the house had got its name as there were some tall evergreen trees to one side of the garden, and the Londoners could hear the swish of the wind rustling through the trees' branches.

'We're at t'side,' said Mabel, as she led the way round the house to a door that opened into a small stone-flagged courtyard.

She turned the handle to the door with a flourish, and shepherded everyone into a warm and inviting kitchen, where a giant wooden table already had plates set out, and knives and forks sparkling in the light.

Mabel pushed the door to, and immediately had to open it again as a large black and white cat insisted on coming into the kitchen, although when he saw how many people were inside already, he promptly demanded to go out with what sounded very much like a yowl of disapproval.

Jessie and Connie didn't share the cat's opinion. After they had all too clearly imagined what the home of the woman with the hair on her chin might be like (not good by any stretch of the imagination), this homely kitchen was a very welcoming sight, especially with its tempting smells of hot food that were wafting about.

Then they noticed, once everyone had taken off their coats and washed their hands, that it was a much less tidy place than they were used to at number five Jubilee Street, as everyone had to move things off their chairs before they could sit down. Mabel seemed quite oblivious to this, and so after they'd held whatever had been on their seat for a while, they all just plonked it down on another chair.

Peggy's wooden seat was hidden under a whole bunch of old woollies where somebody had started to unpick seams and wind the wool into balls, presumably for knitting into something else, while Connie's had a pile of hymn books with broken spines that presumably were waiting to be repaired.

Jessie's hid a wallet and some spectacles that were camouflaged the same colour as the dark wood, the sight of which in Jessie's small hands prompted Roger to say with delight, 'Excellent find – I've been searching all day, and you managed to do in a minute what I couldn't. Well done, young man.' Jessie went quite pink, but Connie didn't feel like teasing him as she might have another time.

Jacket potatoes were produced, and some creamy

butter, and salt and pepper, and some crumbly cheese that Mabel simply called Lancashire, and a big bowl of steamed cabbage with a giant knob of butter softly melting into it.

A ravenous Peggy didn't think she'd ever eaten anything so delicious. And then everyone was offered a second potato, which felt like a luxury beyond compare.

Once everyone had eaten as much as they were able, they were shown to their rooms.

Jessie gave his lopsided smile when he saw he'd be sleeping in a large room, in a bunk bed. The room was untidy, with clothes and books scattered about, all obviously belonging to a boy, although Roger said he wasn't back yet. Neither Roger nor Mabel seemed particularly concerned about this, although Barbara thought as it was dark, it was late for a youngster still to be outside, and especially on a school night.

It was Connie, though, who was the most excited by her room. It was tiny, hardly bigger than her bed.

'You're in 'ere, Connie, and you can do wi' it just what you want. I don't much 'old with tidying and t'like, and so it's up to you if you keep it organised or not,' Mabel told her.

'Really?' Connie breathed, her eyes shining. Her mother would never say this. How exciting!

'Really,' Mabel smiled back at Connie.

With that there was the unmistakable sound of a boy charging up the stairs, and a loudly shouted, "Ow do?'

'Ah,' said Roger, looking slightly surprised and almost as if he had forgotten for the minute that he had a son. 'Meet our Tommy. Always in one scrape or another.'

Tommy was a nice-looking lad, thought Peggy, strong and open-faced.

Ignoring Connie, Tommy went up to Jessie and gave him a playful push on the shoulder. 'London, eh?'

'Um, yes,' Jessie mumbled.

''Appen so,' Tommy replied. Peggy and Connie weren't sure what Tommy meant, and neither was Jessie. But Tommy went on, 'What's yer name?'

'Jessie.'

'Get much stick fer that, eh?'

'No!' Jessie's voice was defiant and strong, and Connie felt proud of him.

Tommy appraised Jessie with an expression that said he didn't believe him for a moment.

Connie wasn't sure, but to her mind there seemed something calculating in the manner in which Tommy then said once more, ''Appen!'

Jessie detected a distinct quaver of mischief in Tommy's voice. Tommy rather liked the fact he was making an impression, thought Jessie.

Roger chose that moment to ask if anyone liked ginger beer, and the next time either of the twins glanced at Tommy he seemed the model of an angelic schoolboy.

The minute the children had had their ginger beer, which was homemade and also delicious, Tommy took Jessie back to the room they were sharing.

There were bunk beds, and Tommy had said they must toss a coin, and the winner could choose which bunk they wanted.

This proved to be more complicated an experience than

Jessie had bargained for as he lost the first throw, to which Tommy said he'd meant best of three, and then when Jessie won those two throws, as Tommy had appeared to be so obviously trying to make him feel at home, Jessie had then to try to gauge which bunk Tommy really wanted to sleep on in order that he could choose the other one.

'I've never slept in a bunk before, and so I'd better have the bottom one so that I don't forget where I am and roll out of the top one on top of you,' Jessie suggested tentatively, and was rewarded with such a genuine smile back that he knew he'd made the right choice, even though really he had wanted to bag the top bunk.

'We need 'ouse rules,' said Tommy. 'No smelly fartin' in t'bedroom, all worn socks left outside t'room and only pees done in t'jerry.'

Jessie had no idea what a jerry was, but then Tommy waggled his foot, and when Jessie looked down he saw that Tommy was indicating a large chamber pot with a gilded handle.

'And no burpin' either,' said Jessie, feeling he had to add his own rule, even though it was a pretty feeble one, otherwise if he kept quiet at this juncture he felt that he would always be the underdog as far as Tommy was concerned. And he thought he might have to come up with a further rule as to how the smell, or not, of a fart could be denoted before it arrived, although he decided to ponder more on the intricacies of that later.

There was something he had to do first to establish his credentials. And with that Jessie let out a huge burp – he was very good at burping, but he thought this might be quite the loudest one he had ever done, and so he felt rather proud – and of course then what could Tommy do but burp back as loud as he could in reply (it wasn't as loud, but it had a pleasing timbre to it all the same, plus it rang out for a satisfyingly long time), and then Jessie did another one that sounded for all the world like a dog barking.

There was the sound of a tremendous, vibrating burp from the other side of the door, and then they heard Roger call cheerfully, 'Beat that, boys!' as he made his way downstairs.

The boys looked at each other wide-eyed for an instant and then began to laugh, with Tommy chucking a pillow softly at Jessie.

As the children explored their bedrooms, Peggy said she'd be back in a little while and they could all sit down to write their letters to Barbara and Ted.

'I'll pop them into the post box for you – we have one just outside our gate, handily. They'll go first thing in the morning,' said Roger.

Then Mabel lifted up Peggy's suitcase, and escorted Peggy over to where she would be sleeping. This turned out to be across the yard and above the stables, which were in the large building to the side of Tall Trees that the evacuees had noticed when they first arrived.

These days the stables were more likely to be garages, Peggy supposed as she laboriously climbed a wooden staircase that had been constructed externally to the building.

Before they got to the top of the stairs, a pretty girl with her hair in a gaily coloured crocheted snood stuck her head out of the door.

'I'm Gracie,' she said with a wide grin, 'an' I were told I migh' 'ave someone in wi' me. Sleepin' in my room is like sleeping wi' a badger, my ma says, I snore so much, so I's feels sorry fer you already!'

Peggy was exhausted, but there was something cheerful and energetic to Gracie that was most appealing and impossible not to respond to.

She laughed. 'Peggy,' she said, extending her hand. 'I'm deaf to badgers.'

'Nice lipstick,' said Gracie in reply, as she caught Peggy's hand and then drew her into the room, as Mabel turned away to clatter down the stairs to let them get acquainted. 'Good brows too.'

Chapter Twelve

Dear Mother and Father,

I hope you are well. We are to stay at a vickerage. The vicar is called Revv Braithwaite, but he says we're to call him Roger, and his wife Maud, I think he said. They have a boy called Tommy and I am to share his room. Connie has lucked out as she has her own room! Tommy says he has a big box of soldiers – all from the Napoleonic war – and so he says he might let me play with them when he is playing with them. But he will have to get to know me first.

Your affectionate son,
  Jessie Ross

Dear parints,

I got my room and I dont have to share as it is all to my own. I lik it. Our tea waz not nice tho. Well some of it waz but we had kabbage. They have a Cat, but it won't come in.
  Connie

11th September 1939

Dear Barbara and Ted,

Well, we're here, and all I can say is that it took a long, long day and masses of patience to get here. All of the St Mark's children were good, with only one travel-sick, and fortunately Miss Crabbe was the 'lucky' person who had to sort that out, and just to be sure it was her and not me, I made very certain I looked in a very deep doze!

We have all found a billet with a Reverend Braithwaite, although he wants the children and me to call him Roger – he calls himself 'progressive', whatever that means (he said it in a way as if I should know; I didn't!) – and his wife is Mabel, with a son called Tommy who's the same age as your two.

I'm to share above the stables with a young woman called Gracie, who is local and who has been there already for a couple of months. It's much nicer than it sounds, and it's where the lads used to live when there were horses below. Gracie tells me the Braithwaites are very nice, although without enough money as they are always doing Good Works. Gracie is quite happy to admit she is 'a fallen woman' – and then when I looked at her, I saw that she is also going to have a baby, just like me, only poor Gracie doesn't have the benefit of a ring on her finger.

I might have minded about sharing with someone like her once upon a time, but this evening I didn't at all, as she was so friendly and full of beans. She's only fifteen and her parents won't have her in the house since she came down with the baby, and she's lost her job at the farm where she was working while the father-to-be doesn't want to know, so goodness knows what would be happening to her if Roger and Mabel hadn't taken her in. Some of the women in his congregation complained about Gracie being at the rectory, she told me, but Roger's next sermon had him booming out about those without sin casting the first stone, and that was enough to shut everyone up.

Roger says if I want he can ask around to see if somebody else has a room for me, but to be honest I think I might rather like Gracie – she has a few rough edges and she's a bit brazen and I bet she can argue like an old fishwife if she's in the mood (although of course just yet we can't make out at all what the other is saying!). But Gracie smiles a lot, and after a day's travelling that counts for a lot, let me tell you. She was kind enough to go and get me some tea and toast, and then she went back over to the kitchen to fetch me a hot-water bottle as my back is achy – and so for now I'm happy enough, not least as it's lovely being so close to Connie and Jessie, who seem happy enough with their billet.

Very best wishes,
  Peggy

PS and a special kiss for Fishy. There's a large black and white cat here, a tom, called Nebuchadnezzar, or

Bucky for short, but he has refused to take any notice of me!

PPS I forgot to mention that, luxury, the Braithwaites have a telephone! Harrogate 4141 – I'm sure Mrs Truelove would let you telephone from hers if you pay her for the call, or else perhaps the Jolly would.

Chapter Thirteen

The next morning Connie woke, quite literally it felt, with the lark, to judge by the cacophony of birdsong what sounded like only inches from her bed. She sat up and pulled aside a flimsy cotton curtain to glance out of the window under which her bed was placed, and she saw that there was a large garden outside.

It needed some work doing in it as even Connie, who had never been in a house that had a garden big enough to have a lawn as this one did, could tell that the grass badly needed mowing and something doing in the flower beds (was it weeding or cutting or hoeing? Connie wasn't sure), as quite a lot of the plants looked to have flowered and gone past their best, and there were things sprouting she thought looked possibly like weeds, if she had any idea of what a weed really did look like. Across the garden there were bushes and trees dotted about in a higgledy-piggledy fashion, and from these the birdsong was hailing forth. And then Connie spied a plank of wood, with ropes suspending it from a low branch in one of the trees – it was a swing! Another tree looked heavy with fruit, and Connie sighed as they were apples that looked as juicy and red as the one Snow White had eaten.

She began to look forward to exploring the garden and she hoped that she and Jessie would be allowed to play on the swing.

If she listened hard, she could hear hens doing chickeny things in a pen that she could see at the far end of the garden, and as she knelt up to get a better view, a conker-coloured rooster with a greeny-black cascade of tail feathers jumped up on top of the chicken house and belted out to the world at large a huge cock-a-doodle-do.

Connie peered to either side of the garden, but couldn't see any other houses. How odd, she thought, as Harrogate had looked like it was most definitely a bustling town as the train pulled in last night, but maybe she was mistaken as it had been nearly dark.

There were no sounds from elsewhere inside the house and so Connie supposed it wasn't yet time to get up and she lay back down in bed, and stared around the room she'd been given.

It wasn't very much larger than the bed she was in, and the wallpaper on the wall looked old-fashioned and faded. But to Connie it was as grand as any a bedroom in the land. It was *hers*, and hers alone, and that's what made it special.

She'd always thought she'd never have her own room, as she would share with Jessie, and would probably only leave number five Jubilee Street in order to get married, after which she'd presumably be sharing a bedroom with her husband.

Connie thought back to when Mabel had told her that the little bedroom was hers to do with as she wished, and she could hardly believe her ears. She could put her clothes away in whatever way she wanted in the drawers of the tiny wooden bedside table (or not at all, if that was what she wanted, Mabel had added with a wink in Connie's direction), and nobody would enter her room without knocking first. She could even pin some drawings up on the walls if she wanted.

Connie hadn't known what to say, and so she hoped now she hadn't seemed ungrateful when Mabel was obviously trying to be kind. It was more that she had been so overwhelmed at the prospect of her very own room that she feared she would burst into tears of excitement if she opened her mouth to say anything, and so she had just stared back at Mabel and hoped that somehow she knew how thrilled Connie felt.

Connie longed to talk to Jessie, and to see his room. But she didn't dare to go looking for him, not least as he was sharing with Tommy, and she felt peculiar at the thought of going into a strange boy's bedroom.

She'd been so thrilled at the prospect of her own room that she hadn't paid too much attention to Tommy, who hadn't been there when they had arrived, coming back an hour or so after them.

Tommy looked okay, although possibly slightly on the sly side, Connie thought now as she tried to picture him. She had caught him appraising Jessie through half-closed eyes as he tilted his head back, and she hadn't much liked that look. But only an instant later he'd looked much more open-faced and affable, and so Connie doubted what she had just seen.

Certainly Tommy had seemed very friendly to Jessie, and the boys had talked happily for a long time about their collections of small toy soldiers.

Connie realised she was desperate to spend a penny, but she didn't think the house, which, although large and comfortable, was also distinctly on the shabby side, had an upstairs toilet, and so she put off going as long as she could, as the previous night she had been told to use a WC in an outhouse beside the kitchen door – meaning you had to walk outside and into the backyard – and she wasn't sure she would be able to find her way there.

Eventually she could wait no longer and so she stood up and went to put her shoes on, but when she leant down to tie her shoelaces she spied a huge Victorian china chamber pot with a cloth square with little weights in each corner draped over it that somebody had thoughtfully placed just under her bed, and it was with huge relief that she squatted over it, replacing the cloth square when she had finished and carefully sliding the chamber pot back to its spot under the bed.

What a puzzle, Connie thought, as she snuggled back under the bedclothes again. The Braithwaites lived in a much larger and, from the outside, grander looking house than the Rosses did, and yet they didn't seem nearly so house-proud as Barbara was. The previous evening Connie had seen quite a lot of dusting and tidying up that needed doing and that Barbara would never have gone to bed on, with dried mud from boots all around the inside of

116

the front door and fire grates with ash and fallen soot in front of them; and as she'd noted already, the sanitation arrangements were more basic than she was used to.

But there were simply masses and masses of books lying around in rickety bookcases or in haphazard piles on tables or on the floor, and Roger had quoted from both the Bible and Shakespeare last night, not that Jessie or Connie would have recognised this had Mabel not tipped them off with a comical waggle of her head and a mouthed 'Bible' or 'Shakespeare' in their direction as appropriate.

And there was a piano and a trumpet and a fiddle that all looked as if they were used regularly at one end of the huge kitchen, and a massive pile of music and song scores piled on the piano, and with an abandon that Barbara would never have allowed them, she and Jessie had been allowed to eat as much supper as they could cram into their chops.

Roger had explained to Connie and Jessie that Harrogate had made a lot of money in the past from nearby wool production, and also from Regency and Victorian visitors coming to the town on special jaunts to take dips and drink the 'efficacious' spa waters, and that it was still a popular spa destination – well, at least until war had been declared.

Jessie said to Connie on their way up the stairs to bed that before the week was out he was going to include the word 'efficacious' in one of his letters to their parents, to which Connie hissed back, 'They'll think you've gone soft in the head if you do.' Then Jessie had to admit he didn't know what it actually meant, to which Connie added that he shouldn't worry as she doubted that their parents would either.

Roger had also said something about the Yorkshire Dales ('Very 'illy. And very wet,' was Mabel's commentary), the Pennines ('Makes an ordinary 'ill look a 'illock' – Mabel again) and the Pump Rooms ('Very Jane Austen' – yes, still Mabel, although the children had no idea what or who she was alluding to).

By this time Jessie and Connie had cottoned on to the fact that Roger and Mabel saw themselves as something of a double act, although they quite often spoke across each other, or happily interrupted, which was something that Barbara and Ted would never do, as they would always politely let the other finish whatever it was that they were saying before they gave their answer or continued the conversation.

Connie couldn't understand a whole lot of what the Braithwaites were saying as she wasn't used to the Yorkshire accent yet, but also she wasn't used to people quoting playwrights in everyday conversation, and so it had all felt quite peculiar, which meant, by the time she had climbed into bed clutching her knitted panda, she was quite glad to have some time on her own to think about everything that had happened since they had all left London, a place which right now felt a very, very long way away indeed.

As she got back into bed and settled herself under the covers, she had a pang of homesickness when she caught a whiff of Barbara's cologne, normally only dabbed on for best occasions. But it was a pang that was quickly subsumed by the excitement of having the little box room all to herself.

Connie's ruminations were interrupted by a delicious

smell of baking wafting up the stairs to her room, and immediately she realised that in spite of eating so late the previous evening she was peckish once again. She hoped it was almost time to get up and have some breakfast.

Down the corridor Jessie had been awake for nearly as long as his sister, the cockerel having roused him. He too had been lying in bed, looking around at his bedroom.

It was a large room, and very untidy, with clothes and various bits and pieces strewn around willy-nilly. There were lots of comics, and some boys' adventure books. Jessie could see a cowboy hat and neckerchief, and poking out from beneath the neckerchief what looked as if it could be the barrel of a toy gun. There was a large magnifying glass lying on the floor right beside Jessie, in the middle of a slew of brightly coloured Dinky cars; in addition there were some boxing gloves chucked on a wooden chair that had a raffia base which was coming unravelled, and a chart on the wall that showed how to read a compass and track a variety of wild animals by being able to recognise their footprints.

It was obviously the bedroom of a boy as there was nothing girlish anywhere that he could spy, and Jessie realised that this was the first time he had slept in such a masculine environment – and that he liked it very much indeed.

Jessie had gone to sleep snuggled with his teddy bear, but now he propped it up on the pillow beside him, just in case Tommy woke suddenly and caught Jessie holding it. He didn't want to be seen as a namby-pamby.

He thought about his sister – this was the first time he could remember that he had woken up without her being in the room.

Connie was a strong personality and back home the boys would look up to her. But as far as Jessie was concerned, these qualities of his sister's only emphasised how lacking he was in the boyish skills. He'd often thought that if only he'd had more boys' things or that if Ted would have properly taught him cricket or rugger, then he might have had more of a chance in finding his place amongst the local children.

He looked up and stared at Tommy's foot poking out from under the covers. Jessie didn't know why but he fancied it looked very much like a foot that belonged to a boy.

He wondered how he and Tommy would get on. He'd always rather liked the idea of having a brother. Of course, Connie was a wonderful sister and she could beat many boys at their own games, but now that he was in a proper boy's bedroom with a real boy actually in it, he could see that what he had known up until now just wasn't the same as having a *brother*.

Might Tommy feel the same? He was an only child after all, and so it might be possible. Could Jessie maybe grow in time to think of Tommy as a brother, or would he and Connie be going back to London soon, making all of this merely a blip in time for each of them? Or, if they stayed, would he and Tommy perhaps not get on? And if he and Tommy did get on, how would that be when they had to be parted when Jessie and Connie had to go home? And how would Connie fit into all this?

Jessie tried to imagine what he would feel like if he had had to have a boy move into his bedroom back in Jubilee Street, and he realised that he would have felt quite strange. There would be opportunities for some fun, sure, but it would be odd to have somebody else on your patch, and to be demanding attention from your parents, and so Tommy would be feeling uncertain too, Jessie guessed.

At the thought of Jubilee Street, and Barbara and Ted, and even little Fishy, Jessie felt a wave of homesickness. He reached for the knitted teddy he had found hidden in his suitcase and, putting his head under the blankets as he tried to be as quiet as possible, he gave into a few shuddering sobs at his sudden sense of violently missing all that he knew and the unsettling feeling that his childhood was slowly slipping away from him, and there was nothing in the world that he could do to prevent this from happening.

Chapter Fourteen

Above the stables Peggy spent a restless and disturbed night, by far the worst night of the three evacuees, and so much so that Gracie had got up at one point and had fetched her a drink of warm milk from the rectory as well as several cushions to put under her feet as her ankles felt so tender.

Peggy couldn't get used to the different smells and sounds of Harrogate.

Bermondsey had a sooty waft about it that lurked in the background aroma always, and in warm weather this was punctuated by a rich and slightly putrid odour rising off the River Thames.

And Bermondsey was never really completely quiet. Whatever time of day, there seemed to be people about somewhere or other, and in the summer when it was hot, voices could be heard talking through their open windows or out in their yards. It was very difficult to keep any secrets in Bermondsey as around where the Rosses and the Delberts lived the houses were small two-up, two-downs that were very tightly packed together, and although this could feel claustrophobic and aggravating at times, right at this moment Peggy was incredibly homesick and longing to hear the familiar sounds of neighbours bickering or laughing.

Here it smelt fresher and *greener* somehow, with only an occasional slightly metallic tinge to the peaty air.

Roger and Mabel had been welcoming and very pleasant, that was for certain, and Peggy had absolutely no complaints about either them or the quality of the digs they could offer, and of course it was wonderful that she and the children could remain united.

In fact, Peggy couldn't imagine hosts who could have gone out of their way to be nicer to their new arrivals, even if much of what they were saying to each other came across to her as gobbledegook.

But everything felt so different, with even the tea tasting strange, and this had meant that Peggy had gone to bed feeling very disorientated.

Gracie proved indeed to be quite a snorer, and so Peggy had to content herself with listening to her alternating deep and high rumbles, which to Peggy's surprise worked quite well after a while as the regular rhythm proved surprisingly soporific, and eventually Peggy was able to drift off.

Still, it wasn't a restorative sleep as she had a mess of jumbled dreams, the most vivid of which was her trying to tell Roger the difference between vicarages and rectories, and he turning into Tommy, and then Tommy turning into Bill as she stood in a church with amnesia, with the pupils who had travelled with her in the rail carriage crying when she couldn't tell them about the Dissolution of the Monasteries.

She felt totally exhausted when she awoke to Gracie getting up when it was still not quite light, and Gracie whispering that Peggy wasn't to mind her but she was going 'to help Mabel with the bread', after which she was going somewhere (Peggy couldn't make that out) and Roger and Mabel were going to – was it Leeds?

Peggy was too half-asleep and groggy to do more than nod in Gracie's direction and settle back down for an hour or two, distracted and then soothed by a couple of fluttery movements deep within her bulging stomach.

The next time she woke the sun was blazing in through the window and Gracie was placing a cup of tea on her bedside table with, 'I'm off now, Peggy, to t'greengrocer's where I do a few 'ours. Mabel thought you should 'ave a lie-in, but it's now pas' ten and you need t'get kiddies t'church 'all fer 'leven.'

Peggy realised she could hear whoops of children's laughter coming from the garden, and when she hefted herself out of bed and looked out of the window as she brushed the sleep from her eyes and then rubbed the aching small of her back, it was to see the three children larking about on the swing.

They looked very happy playing together, Tommy obviously having been allowed an hour or two off school that morning in order to help Connie and Jessie get used to things where they were going to be living, and Peggy thought it seemed as if the youngsters were settling into the new regime much better than she.

After Peggy had hurriedly got herself dressed, she made her way down the steep and rickety stairs from the room above the stables and across the yard to the back door to the kitchen of the rectory, the delicate teacup that Gracie had brought over rattling rather precariously in its saucer in time to the rumbling of Peggy's tummy as she was feeling distinctly peckish. On entering the kitchen she found that it was deserted.

The breakfast plates were stacked neatly on the draining board but hadn't actually been washed up yet, while the used knives, forks and spoons were still lying haphazardly on the table accompanied by quite a lot of breadcrumbs scattered around.

There was a wet dishcloth lying in the butler's sink, some cracked eggshells in the sink, and a crumpled tea towel was lying carelessly on the floor, which Bucky, the cat, was gnawing at, at the same time as paddling it furiously with his hind feet as he pretended it was some poor defenceless animal he needed to punish.

Peggy made a shushing noise and Bucky scampered away with an indignant purp and an angrily twitching tail, actions clearly designed to admonish her for stopping his fun with the tea towel.

She decided not to take it personally – befriending Bucky might be a long-term project, but Peggy knew that he had met his match in her.

She was delighted to discover standing on the kitchen table a huge teapot, which still had hot tea inside that had been kept warm by an alarmingly cheery knitted tea cosy plonked over it that had a multitude of decorative many-coloured frills adorning it (Peggy betting to herself that this cosy had been a rather exuberant gift from a grateful parishioner as the clashing tones of the wool were a very bold – some might say garish – choice if Mabel had knitted it herself). Alongside the teapot, and a clean cup and saucer, was a loaf of bread upended on its cut end to stop it going stale that was sitting invitingly on a wooden board so used and worn that the corners went up and the top edge of the sides dipped down almost to the table. In a china dish nearby there was butter, and beside it a bowl containing a dollop of strawberry jam that had a muslin cloth over it to keep any flies off.

Peggy realised she was starving and so she set about tucking in with gusto as she thought about the possible mechanics of how the pupils of St Mark's would be integrated into the very probably quite limited confines of the other primary school.

The plan was, she thought, that all of the St Mark's evacuees, herself included, would meet up at the Odd Fellows Hall again at eleven, and then from there they would be walked over to their new primary school. The headmasters of the merging schools would have met first thing to discuss whether the class sizes should be doubled up, or whether one school should have the use of the school premises for the morning and the other for the afternoon. In fact, by now the decision would almost certainly have been taken as to how it was all going to work.

There weren't going to be any lessons today, Peggy knew, and so all the St Mark's children would be returning to their billets for their lunches and presumably would be allowed to play with one another after that.

She wondered how the children from London had fared overnight. Many, if not all of them, would never have slept away from their homes prior to then, let alone have spent a night without their parents nearby; and some of the children were only five and so it would surely have been a very big thing for them to get through, and actually many of the older children would also be feeling similarly, she was sure.

Without exception, the school pupils had looked very forlorn and down in the mouth when they were lined up at the reception centre the previous evening, she'd thought, while some of the host adults hadn't seemed at all keen either on having to provide billets, although others – like Roger and Mabel – had walked in with big smiles and had gone out of their way to be as nice and as pleasant as possible during what was a pretty soulless process.

Roger had explained that local people had been told they would be taken to court if they refused to take in evacuees if they had the space, and this strong-arming on the part of the authorities had led to some people's noses feeling very put out of joint, with them claiming that having to have strangers move into their houses was a step too far on the government's behalf.

Peggy had winced visibly, as she could very much sympathise with this point of view.

Seeing her response, Roger quickly added that this reaction had been by no means universal as plenty of other people had said to him that they were proud to be of service in whatever way they could be for the war effort, and so were extremely happy to be able to help those who needed to get out of London. Of course, they weren't going to sniff either at the money they would receive for each person billeted at their homes, which was 7s. 6d. each week for children, and a bit more for adults.

Roger then realised that this last comment might intimate that he and Mabel fell into *that* second category rather than the first – well, the second of the second category, and not the first of the first category, was what he wanted to say – and he dug himself even further into this bit of a tangle, saying next that of course he and his wife had to support their parishioners of all opinions to do with the evacuation, even though they were delighted to have living with them three members of such a lovely family as Connie, Jessie and Peggy were by all accounts, even though there may have been a plethora of good reasons that they hadn't been chosen by the time he and Mabel arrived, and it was really no trouble at all for the Braithwaites to take them in.

Peggy couldn't help laughing just as Mabel said, 'Roger, give over!' and it was to the relief of all when a visibly chastened Roger said nothing for a moment, before coming up perkily with, 'Parkin? And a hot cup of tea? Just the ticket after jacket potatoes I always think.'

This was a very sweet couple who had taken them in, Peggy decided, even though she had absolutely no idea what parkin was, although she assumed it was something nice to judge by the happy looks of anticipation on her hosts' faces.

She wanted the Braithwaites to know that tired and grumpy as she and Jessie and Connie were, they did appreciate what was being done for them.

And so Peggy said that it was herself and her niece and nephew who should be trying to make Roger and Mabel and Tommy feel at ease, as they were all very – no, extremely – grateful for their kind gesture in providing them with such a lovely place to stay, they really were. And what was parkin, by the way?

Feeling much chirpier this morning in spite of her irregular night, Peggy ate her breakfast quickly and then popped the bread, butter and jam she hadn't consumed into the larder. Next, she swiftly did the washing-up and then she stacked the clean and dried crockery and cutlery away in what she hoped were the correct cupboards and drawers – it was hard to tell as none of the cupboards seemed to be organised according to any system that Peggy could fathom, being cluttered with all manner of bric-a-brac – and just as she was wiping down the draining board, a large grandfather clock in the hall outside the kitchen door struck a quarter to, and Peggy put her head out of the back door to call the children in.

Sure enough, after Tommy had shown Jessie, Connie and Peggy how to retrace their footsteps back to Odd Fellows Hall, and he had bade them a hasty cheerio before trotting off into school himself, Peggy had a quick word with the children as they stood grouped together on the pavement, each watching Tommy's jaunty walk as he headed away with both hands in the pockets of his dark grey short trousers and whistling something a bit tuneless.

Peggy said that before they went inside the hall to say hello to everyone from St Mark's, she wanted to grab a private word with Jessie and Connie to see if they had each passed a good night.

Connie replied that she found her little box room to be very nice, and Mabel had told her she could leave her clothes untidy if she wanted, but she wasn't impressed with the cockerel; and then Jessie told his auntie about the no-farting rule and then the burping attempt to out do each other that Roger had joined in on.

'Ah. Well, thank you, Jessie – I don't think I need to hear any more on your and Tommy's bedroom rules just now, do you, particularly the letting-off bit? Connie, I'm very pleased that you like your room; I would have loved it too at your age but maybe we won't mention to Barbara about you not having to put your clothes away as, knowing your mother, she'll have something to say about that. I have got a nice bed too, and Gracie seems pleasant enough, and Roger and Mabel very welcoming, and so Tall Trees doesn't seem too bad as far as we all are concerned, does it?' said Peggy, and both Connie and Jessie nodded their agreement as their aunt added, 'I think we might just have landed on our feet.'

Chapter Fifteen

Peggy's cheerful mood wasn't to last for long, though, as immediately she was inside the hall and Connie and Jessie had drifted over to talk to Angela Kennedy about what their various billets had been like, and the breakfasts they had been given, she could see that some of the Bermondsey children looked to have had quite a testing time of it over the previous twenty-four hours, if their pale faces and baleful expressions were anything to go by, with one or two having obviously long ago that morning given in to snivels and teary cheeks.

Suddenly something caught Peggy's attention. She was shocked to see that Larry had an absolute shiner of a purple and magenta black eye, with him now sporting an eyelid that was so swollen the skin was shiny, half-shut and looking stretched almost to breaking point.

It had to be tender and extremely painful, and when she asked Larry in a concerned voice – he wasn't one of her favourite children as she knew how very mean he had been to Jessie over recent months, but no child deserved this sort of treatment – what on earth could have gone on for such an injury to have happened, Larry replied sullenly that he'd been told after his tea the night before to take a bucket with some scraps and potato peelings out to the compost heap. His billet was a small-holding and nobody had talked to him other than to tell him to get some firewood in and take the peelings out.

As he was finding his way to where the family had their compost heap, three local lads, who must have been lying in wait, immediately set upon Larry, first tripping him up and pushing him to the ground, and then shouting out things he couldn't understand and landing several hard punches on his face before spitting on him and running off.

The people he was staying with hadn't seemed concerned unduly, only indicating to Larry that it was to be expected and that it would probably happen to him several times more, and that if he didn't want it to keep on happening, he should punch back and make sure that he gave as good as he got, and this might mean that he needed to give them a kick as well, and if he got in hard and quickly enough, then these lads would leave him alone.

Larry tried to make a show to Peggy that he was all ready now, and indeed at any time to come, to punch back harder and shout louder than these violent boys, but Peggy saw that the knee closest to her poking out of his grey serge short trousers was trembling despite the bravado of his words, making the hem of the trouser leg above it shiver relentlessly. Then she saw that Larry's lips were chapped and sore-looking as if he had been worrying at them overnight, and so she thought poor Larry probably wasn't feeling very plucky at all.

Peggy really hoped Larry's experience wasn't a typical case. But she could understand that for the local children who had been born and bred in Harrogate who had probably only been told a day or two ago about the evacuation of the London school pupils onto their patch, it would be a very odd experience – and probably quite a daunting, not to say threatening, one too – to have a sudden influx of strange children arriving in their midst. She recognised that the Bermondsey youngsters might well to untutored eyes look (or sound, with their unfamiliar ways of speaking) as if they were squaring up to tramp over already established childhood stamping grounds that the Harrogate children would naturally be very protective of. Indeed, some of the London children could be harbouring plans for squaring up to the local kiddies.

It wasn't a welcome state of affairs, but Peggy supposed that human nature tended to inch always towards sorting out pecking orders and revealing who the top dogs were, and that some Yorkshire children would have decided to get in first with reinforcing the message that no liberties could be taken by the London lot.

Once everyone had got used to each other, presumably it would all calm down, Peggy hoped, but until then the chances were that Larry's skirmish with the local boys wouldn't be the only one.

Peggy told Larry where she was staying and then she scribbled it on a piece of paper for him, adding that if ever he was worried or needed a London grown-up to talk to, now he knew where to find her.

Larry nodded in a very grave way, and then he turned to go and talk to some of his cronies. Peggy was pleased, though, to see Larry carefully folding the piece of paper with her address on and placing it deep down in one of his short pockets.

One thing that made Peggy smile was that she'd been right about the landlady of the guest house that her former fellow teachers had been sent to, as she had proved to be something of a harridan.

As Mr Jones stood silently rereading his prepared notes on a hardboard clipboard before him, presumably collecting his ideas together for whatever he was about to announce, Miss Crabbe whispered to Peggy in an aside that although the guest house was comfortable enough in the practical sense, there was an extremely long set of rules that set out all the do's and don'ts of Dunroamin that the landlady had compiled into a list that she had displayed clearly in each of their bedrooms, making sure it was tacked to the back of their doors in a very obvious manner, about precisely what was permitted (not very much) and what wasn't (almost everything). Worse, their breakfast earlier that morning had been limited to just the one boiled egg each and half a slice of toast which, considering the landlady was going to get over a guinea a week for each of them as they were topping up the government allowance from their own money, was a pretty poor show, the teachers had all decided as a unified group, and so, 'Words are going to have to be said,' Miss Crabbe hissed in a stage whisper in Peggy's direction.

Peggy thought with a pang of guilt of the three giant doorstop slices of bread she'd snaffled down not an hour earlier, and the endless tea in the pot that she had so appreciated being left waiting for her, and she tried not to look as if she felt quite full at the minute, even though in fact she did.

Luckily, right at that moment headmaster Mr Jones clapped his hands together loudly, and without the teachers having to admonish any of the children, the chatter abruptly died away.

'Pupils of St Mark's, sit down on the floor with your legs crossed,' instructed the headmaster, who then had to wait for a while until everyone had settled themselves in the most comfortable positions they could find.

'I want you all to listen to me very carefully. The school you are joining isn't far away, and it is called – wait for it, pupils from St Mark's, wait for it – Cold Bath Road Elementary School!' Mr Jones paused dramatically, and the more easily entertained schoolchildren drew in their breath with a pantomime 'Oooh', even though Peggy knew they were responding more to the headmaster's tone than because of anything sensational or witty that he had just said.

'The plan is that on Mondays and Tuesdays you pupils from St Mark's are going to share classes and classrooms with the current pupils, although this will happen only if enough chairs can be found for everyone to be able to sit down at one time. And meanwhile on Wednesdays, Thursdays and Fridays, St Mark's and Cold Bath Road Elementary will divide the day into two, with lessons for one school taking place between eight in the morning until twelve thirty, and for the other school, taking place from twelve thirty until five o'clock at teatime. This means that one school has the use of the school buildings and the playgrounds in the morning of those last three days of each week, while the other school will use them in the afternoon. Most of you will continue to be taught by your teachers from St Mark's, although we have had to do a little shuffling around as teachers such as Miss Pinkly, and indeed myself, will not be with you in Yorkshire.'

Already Mr Jones's words were failing to hold the attention of the youngest or the more easily distracted pupils, Peggy noted.

Mr Jones seemed oblivious.

'The schools will alternate weekly on who has the early slot and who has the late slot, so that if these new times are difficult for some of your Harrogate hosts and guardians, at least it won't be for all the time. The lessons will be divided by one twenty-minute break during the morning session, and one twenty-minute break during the afternoon; and all pupils, be they from London or Harrogate, will eat their dinner in the middle of the day, either after school at home if it is an early week for them, or before, if it is a late week, although in that case they will still have to make sure that they are at school on the button for twelve thirty, as any lateness will be a big black mark against you and this simply will not be tolerated after a first occurrence.

'Notes will be sent today to all parents, guardians and host families in Harrogate, who either are looking after you, or who have pupils already at Cold Bath Road Elementary, to advise everyone of the new system.

'St Mark's will take the first shift at the school tomorrow, and so remember, children, it is an eight o'clock start for all of you tomorrow, and by that I mean that eight o'clock in the morning is the time you must be in your classrooms and at your desks. This means that you and your guardians must make sure that you are on the school premises about ten minutes earlier, which means in the school playground at ten to eight at the latest first thing tomorrow morning!'

Mr Jones paused to let this information sink in, but there was none of the excited 'oohing' that had characterised the previous time he had paused, very probably because only Jessie and one or two of the other pupils was still listening to him.

Miss Crabbe realised that times, or indeed much of what had just been outlined, didn't mean a whole lot to many of the children and so she chipped in with, 'Well done for being quiet and paying attention for such a long time as Mr Jones spoke, St Mark's. What he was trying to tell you was that this means a very early start, children, definitely earlier than we had in Bermondsey.'

Peggy had to pick some imaginary lint off her cardigan so that no pupils could see her amused reaction to Miss Crabbe's comments. While Miss Crabbe had obviously only been trying to help explain what was going on, she had managed also to sound more than a tad critical of her head teacher's way with words.

Mr Jones drew in his breath sharply, and then couldn't prevent himself giving a small frown of temper in Miss Crabbe's direction. His staff knew how very much he liked to hog the limelight to himself at every opportunity.

Mr Jones lowered his voice to an even firmer and more sombre tone. Miss Crabbe looked quite pale, and some of the elder pupils shuffled uneasily as they recognised from the manner in which they were been addressed that something important was being mooted.

'It is very possible that there will also be lessons at your new school on Saturdays too, although this is unlikely to happen immediately. Therefore my advice to you all is to work very, very hard when you are at school, and then if the school curriculum for each week of the term stays on track, it is highly unlikely that there will have to be any lessons on Saturdays. But – and this is a big but – if things start to slip, the Saturday lessons will definitely become part of your school week! Remember that the standards we kept up at St Mark's in Bermondsey meant that we didn't have school at the weekends, and if this has to happen here, then on your own heads be it,' Mr Jones said.

There was a communal intake of breath from his audience as this wasn't pleasant news, either for the school pupils or for their teachers.

Jessie and Connie couldn't help but cast a fleeting look at one another even though they knew that Mr Jones was very particular about his school pupils' eyes being kept looking towards the front of the room when he was speaking.

They were used to having the whole weekend to play outside during the warmer months, and now they saw a possibility whereby they could lose their Saturdays, and quite a lot of their Sundays too, as Peggy had pointed out to them before they went to bed that, seeing as Roger was a clergyman, it would very likely mean that they would all have to go to church at least once on a Sunday.

Ted and Barbara encouraged church for all the family

at Christmas, Palm Sunday and Easter, but as they weren't regular churchgoers otherwise, they had never even encouraged the children to attend Sunday school, and so this would be a new experience for Jessie and Connie too, and frankly it was something else they weren't much looking forward to.

The children didn't have time to think further about any of what their headmaster had just said to them for long, though, as they were immediately marshalled into lines and then marched in procession right away to their new school, Cold Bath Road Elementary.

There, in the large tarmacked playground, they were lined up according to classes, there being two classes to each school year at St Mark's, although as Miss Pinkly wasn't there all of the senior year pupils were told to group together as one.

As they stood in the playground wondering what would happen next, there was a sudden sharp bang as the imposing school doors were crashed back against the wall, and the Harrogate boys from Cold Bath Road Elementary poured from the boys' entrance at one side to the school, while the girls shot into the playground from the girls' entrance at the opposite end of the building.

Peggy gave a start at the dramatic sound of the school doors blasting open at either side of the school building. This wasn't the best way of introducing the pupils of the two schools to one another, she was sure.

And so it proved. Whatever the original idea had been, presumably it didn't really go to plan.

With a cacophony of yells and shouts from the pupils – despite someone, presumably a teacher, hastily calling in vain from somewhere deep inside the Cold Bath Road Elementary school building, behind the exiting hordes, 'Quietly and slowly, children – QUIETLY AND SLOWLY!' – a veritable avalanche of school pupils tumbled out of the Victorian school building and raced to surround those from St Mark's.

Bill was a big fan of Westerns and he had taken Peggy to see many such movies, so Peggy couldn't help thinking for a moment that for all the world the hapless St Mark's kiddies looked like a threatened wagon train, with the hollering Red Indians – the local children, that was – circling the wagons in a predatory way, clearly out for trouble.

Very quickly for the older children there was some pushing and shoving between the two factions (there proving to be more than a few outlaws in the St Mark's wagon train who were happy to give back as good as they got), followed immediately by a display of some rather unpleasant goose-stepping by the biggest of the Cold Bath Road pupils, which the St Mark's pupils rightly took as an insult aimed at them and they responded with some angry sticking up of the proverbial two fingers, accompanied by coarse jeers and some extremely vehement effing and blinding.

For a second it was bedlam, with Mr Jones stunned into inaction, although his face and neck had flushed so highly they were verging on indigo.

The Cold Bath Road headmaster, Mr Walton, had to blow very loudly on a whistle to restore order, with everybody suddenly stopping what they were doing, and with the clearly furious Yorkshire headmaster then giving a bell-owed promise of double detentions for anybody – 'and I mean anybody!' – caught goose-stepping or 'flicking the vees' on school grounds on this or any other day.

The London pupils and teachers looked to be all rather taken aback by such a blunt reception to their new surroundings, seemingly staggered by how quickly an aggressive response from the Harrogate children had led to a general free-for-all.

Although to judge by the expressions on the faces of some of the Harrogate pupils, the majority of them were pretty shaken too, not least by the swift willingness of the Bermondsey children to go on the offensive and treat them very rudely.

While no one from Bermondsey had exactly expected the bunting to have been strung up across the playground to signal a happy welcome and there to be a general mood of celebration at their arrival, neither had anyone thought the St Mark's pupils would have received quite such an inhospitable greeting, although the two-fingered response by their elder lads, quickly copied by the younger London schoolboys, was just as much a shock.

Hurriedly the children were separated, and as the Harrogate children were corralled at the far end of the playground, the London contingent were quickly pushed in through the boys' entrance to be swiftly shown round the classrooms and where the lavatories were, and then they were reminded that they had to be in the playground by ten to eight the next day, which was Wednesday, all ready to start their lessons immediately.

The older children, which included Jessie and Connie, were told also that they would be tested on spelling and tables, and so, Mr Walton said irritably, the St Mark's pupils might need to do a spot of revision during this coming afternoon, as their performance tomorrow would be used to gauge how far they were lagging behind the Yorkshire pupils in their learning.

Peggy saw Mr Jones bridle at Mr Walton's assumptions that the Bermondsey children would be found wanting in the academic sense. She discovered herself glad that she was no longer responsible for making sure educational standards were met as quite a high proportion of children in the St Mark's catchment area came from families with problems and reduced income, and Peggy knew how difficult it was for these children to keep up to scratch. She loved to teach and she had an optimistic view of human nature that led her to believe that all children's potential could be brought out, but she didn't really approve of teaching children simply to be better than their peers.

Their resulting expression on the faces of both Mr Jones and the St Mark's pupils suggested that Mr Walton was incorrect in what he had just said on rather a lot of levels, an expression which Mr Walton answered with a glare of his own of such ferocity in the direction of the London pupils and staff that it all felt a bit awkward.

As the London children exited the building, the Harrogate children were quickly bustled back inside the building at the opposite entrance to the school (the girls' entrance), although not before Peggy had seen some of them risking when they thought Mr Walton and any other Cold Bath

Road staff were looking elsewhere a couple of final and very rude gestures with pumped fists raised surreptitiously and deliberately snarly expressions on their faces of raised top lips and exposed upper teeth aimed in the direction of the new children coming out of the boys' entrance.

At least Tommy wasn't one of the troublemakers, Peggy was pleased to note, even though he hadn't rushed forward to make Connie and Jessie feel at home by standing up for them either.

Some billet hosts were already waiting outside the gates to escort the children in their care back to their homes for dinnertime, and so quickly Peggy gathered together everybody's postcards to their parents in London who would be waiting anxiously for news, carefully checking names and new addresses were written correctly.

As she did this, Mr Jones said to the children who weren't being collected that if there was a grown-up at their billets during the afternoon then the children could return there, but if there wasn't or the children weren't sure of who was going to be there, or else they weren't certain of the way to their billets, then the St Mark's pupils could go en masse on a walk out into the countryside. He didn't mention what the provisions for food for their lunch would be, or anything about Mr Walton's assertion that they should be doing some work that afternoon to prepare for the next day's test on their spelling and arithmetic.

Most of the children opted to stay together, even if there might not be much prospect of dinner – Peggy thinking of the saying 'safety in numbers' – and so she said to Jessie and Connie she would see them back at the rectory later for a late snack if they weren't given something to eat very soon, and she thought she would let Mr Jones and Miss Crabbe and the others sort out how the Bermondsey children should spend the afternoon.

With that, Peggy decided to explore Harrogate a little on her own, as she wanted to look around as well as find a post office to send off all the cards to the anxious parents back in London.

As she left, she heard two of the teachers behind her saying there must be 'a plan of action' drawn up, to ensure that the pupils of the merging schools quickly settled down and stopped any antagonism of the other.

This proposal seemed easy to suggest, Peggy thought, but would it be harder to effect than to say?

'What do you make of that?' Connie asked her brother as they brought up the rear of the snaking line of children twenty minutes later as they plodded towards the countryside around the town.

She saw that Jessie was rubbing his arm, and so she guessed that somebody had thrown a sly punch at him as they had rushed past.

'I'm not sure. It wasn't great. They don't really want us here at all, do they?' said Jessie in such a dispirited manner that even Connie understood that he felt the bullying treatment meted out to him in Bermondsey looked very set to continue in Yorkshire, and perhaps in an even worse way.

'No, I don't think they do,' Connie agreed. 'But I rather liked the look of that tall boy with the red hair – did you notice him?'

'I'm pretty certain he was the one that hit me,' said Jessie. 'Or it could have been that tall lad behind him. But I think it was the ginger one.'

'Ah,' said Connie.

And after they'd walked a little further, she added, 'What a nuisance.'

Chapter Sixteen

The sun shone brightly and Peggy enjoyed herself exploring the town, strolling up and down the streets of Harrogate in a happily wayward manner.

For what seemed like the first time in an age she didn't feel the pressure of having to do something specific or be somewhere she had to be, and as the sun swathed everything in a rich, orangey light, she enjoyed looking at the buildings set off to their best advantage in the sun and contrasting appealingly against a deep-blue, cloudless sky.

Harrogate was a grand and elegant town, she could see immediately. Compared to what they were all used to back home in Bermondsey, in many ways it looked a lot, a lot more... er, more... In the end 'comfortable' was the best word that Peggy could come up with that seemed appropriate for what she saw as she looked about her.

As she wandered, she spent a lot of time reading notices on church and school boards and trying to memorise where various important buildings such as the Pump Rooms and the library and the town hall and the train station were in relation to one another, and to Tall Trees.

Generally, she thought, people seemed to be more smartly dressed than she was used to seeing in Bermondsey on a weekday late morning, with lots of good-quality worsted clothing and some expensive-looking tweed skirts having been chosen for (presumably) everyday, as surely not everybody she saw could be heading off dressed up for important appointments? She saw that the houses were substantially bigger too, and quite often semi-detached, or even detached, and sometimes with large gardens in front *and* behind, which was something that just didn't happen in Bermondsey. There, the most anyone could wish for was a small yard or garden at the back of the house.

The grey stone that comprised the majority of the buildings she gazed upon now looked austere and even quite hostile at first sight, but then Peggy noticed in the sunshine how the grey of the stone was really a palette of softer colours, sometimes even including shades such as a glittery lavender or occasionally a rich teal.

As she looked about her it became obvious how well the stone, which was likely to have been quarried locally to judge by the amount of it that had been used in all manner of buildings, from the modest to the ostentatious, contrasted with the sharp- and clean-looking white paintwork of most people's window frames.

Nearly all the doorsteps she passed were neatly brushed too, with their brass door knockers and knobs highly polished, and many of the windowpanes were so clean and shiny that they acted as mirrors, reflecting back images of birds and trees and the occasional passing car.

Indeed, Peggy had never seen such a general gleam of windowpanes, even though here and there some people had started to apply tape crosses across the glass, presumably, as Ted had done, in order to keep any shattering of broken glass as safe as possible if a German bombing offensive were mounted.

All in all, there was a general impression of a very house-proud community. And the fact there were lots of flower beds and carefully mown grass that weren't part of people's gardens, and virtually no litter at all, suggested that Harrogate felt a strong sense of civic pride.

Peggy didn't see many women wearing the floral wrap-over pinnies that were such familiar weekday attire for the housewives in Bermondsey, and then she noted how substantial and prosperous-looking the houses were and so she thought she may be in one of the more affluent areas of the town.

She noticed that the men tended to greet each other with just a simple 'How do?', which sounded very odd to her, and as she began to listen more closely to what people were saying to their friends and acquaintances as she walked along, she thought that in general the natives of Harrogate very much liked the words 'reckon', 'love', ''appen' and 'thee' as she heard them all used several times as she meandered about. She realised that she had never heard the word 'thee' used in ordinary conversation in Bermondsey, and neither had she been acknowledged in the way that was frequently happening this morning because, as she walked along, almost every stranger she passed nodded their head at her in greeting, sometimes accompanied by a strangely tuneful-sounding 'Mornin'' that had an upwards inflection on the second syllable.

Although she assumed she'd post the pupils' letters in the post box beside Tall Trees, Peggy found a post box en route and so she was able to discharge her final duty to St Mark's until after her and Bill's baby was born. As she slipped the postcards into the gaping mouth of the red posting box, she sent with them a little wish of hope that all the mothers and fathers of the writers of the laboriously penned missives were well and safe, and were happy that their children were safely out of London.

She headed a bit further along the street in the rough direction of Tall Trees, but she then ground to a halt, realising she felt slightly at a loss. It really did feel very peculiar to be in a strange place without anything that she had to do.

Peggy turned involuntarily towards the ding of a bell above a door, and she decided to go into the pleasant-looking café that was served by the bell and the door.

A cheerful woman about Peggy's age who had a crisply starched and spotless frilled apron tied about her waist indicated that she should sit at a table in the window that gave a good view of the street, and when Peggy asked for a small pot of tea and a toasted teacake, the woman said with a wise nod at her protruding belly, 'Aye, yuill be wantin' yer snap.'

Peggy wasn't sure how to respond.

Then the woman smiled as she obviously could see that Peggy was new to the area and a bit confused by what had just been said, and she pointed at herself, enunciating clearly, 'June.'

'Peggy. Peggy Delbert. How do you do?' Phew. She could manage that.

'June Blenkinsop,' the other woman said. And the pair of them smiled at each other.

The café was quiet as the late morning rush looked to have been and gone, and so June fetched Peggy's tea and teacake, and then through a raise of a brow and her head inclined towards the empty seat opposite, asked if she might sit with her a while.

Peggy tried not to look taken aback. She couldn't imagine somebody behaving in this forward way in London, as down in Bermondsey strangers tended to keep themselves to themselves, and anyone being overfriendly on first acquaintance tended to be treated with suspicion. There, strangers were to be treated with caution, and people had to earn their stripes before the hand of friendship could be extended.

June had something very warm about her, though, and so Peggy smiled again and nodded.

As the two women began to chat, even though they had to speak very slowly to one another and sometimes try several words until the other one could give a nod of understanding, Peggy felt herself relax in the warm sunlight coming in through the sparkling window to the café, and as she stretched her neck from side to side with the cricks easing, she realised how very anxious and tense she had been feeling over the past week or two.

It was with some regret that she saw June stand up fifteen minutes later, saying it was time for her to get back to work as otherwise the cashing up would never get done, but if Peggy came in the next day a bit earlier then at least she wouldn't be quite as 'off-comed-un' as today and June would rustle her up a tea and toasted teacake right quickly, or some nerks if Peggy fancied.

Peggy hoped that June meant that by tomorrow she wouldn't look quite such a fish out of water in a strange area. Meanwhile, the nerks could wait for a day or two before she would worry herself about whatever they might be.

Chapter Seventeen

At Tall Trees, after tea that evening, Mabel had a brain-wave.

Those from Harrogate would learn a song that had London slang in the lyrics, and the task would be reciprocated as then those hailing from London could be taught a song that contained some typical Yorkshire dialect.

Mabel asked Tommy to choose a song, and he decided that in the Yorkshire Corner it would be 'On Ilkla Moor Baht 'At'.

Mabel smiled and claimed this an excellent musical opener as it was always a firm favourite with everybody.

Roger explained to the Londoners that it was a slightly saucy song about a man spotted returning from a lover's tryst without his hat. And with that, Roger (with a deep bass), Tommy (shouting) and Mabel (not very tunefully as regards her singing, but with a good tune and timing being kept on the piano) launched with a lusty enthusiasm into:

Wheere wor ta bahn when Ah saw thee?
On Ilkla Moor baht 'at
Tha's been a-courtin' Mary Jane
Tha's bahn ter get thi death o' cowd
Then we s'll 'a' ter bury thee
Then t'worms'll come ter eyt thee up
Then t'ducks'll come ter yet up t'worms
Then we s'll come ter yet up t'ducks
Then we sill all 'ave etten then
Then we s'll 'ave us ooan back!
On Ilkla Moor baht 'at!
On Ilkla Moor baht 'at!!
ON ILKLA MOOR BAHT 'AT!!!

After this rousing rendition, Roger explained in more detail what all of the words to the song meant, adding that it could be stretched out to last a very long time, with the refrain 'On Ilkla Moor baht 'at!' usually being bellowed out repetitively and in an increasingly lively manner.

Peggy and the London children shared surprised looks when they understood what the words actually meant.

They'd assumed that Roger would have encouraged them to learn a religious song, and so they'd been racking their brains without result to come up with something not too risqué or offensive, and yet that was a firm favourite when gathered round a piano in Bermondsey. Songs sung routinely in Bermondsey were often risqué *and* offensive, now they came to think of them.

But with the impish Tommy's choice of 'On Ilkla Moor Baht 'At', they felt the gloves had come off, which meant they could make a choice based purely on what they knew everyone would really enjoy singing.

'We'll sing our Yorkshire song again and this time you three join in with us, and after that we'll sing summat from your neck o' t'woods,' commanded Roger, and Mabel struck an even jauntier version of the tune on the keys of the piano and they all sang 'On Ilkla Moor Baht 'At' with, exactly as Roger had promised, the refrains becoming louder and more raucous each time.

Jessie and Connie quickly came to understand what Roger meant about the chorus being very boisterous, and soon everyone was laughing as they each tried to outdo their companions.

When it came to the turn of the Londoners to come up with something for them all to sing, Connie insisted that Jessie and Peggy follow her outside of the kitchen and into a coy huddle in the hall so that they could make their deliberations in private. Then she marched them back to where the Braithwaites were waiting, and announced in a voice that was deliberately more cockney-sounding than the one in which she would ordinarily speak (Barbara having been strict always about them speaking with as nice an accent as she could encourage from when they were wee tots, Connie proving herself to be quite the little actress, if she felt so inclined, which apparently right at this moment she very much did, signally by some extravagant arm-gesturing too), 'We're goin' to 'ave a ding-dong inspired by the Pearly Kings an' Queens of Lundun, with two popla songs, ladies an' gents. 'Old on to yer 'ats as there's gonna be a right ol' knees-up!'

And with that, Connie, Jessie and Peggy launched as one into:

Any ol' iron? Any ol' iron?
Any, any, any ol' iron?
You look neat
Talk about a treat
Looking so dapper
From yer napper to yer feet
Dressed in style
Brand new tile
An' yer father's ol' green tie on
But I wouldn't give yer tuppence fer yer ol' fob watch
Ol' iron, ol' iron!

The second time they sang it, Mabel was able to bash out a tune in accompaniment on the long-suffering piano, and Connie led what some might say passed for dancing with a series of moves that Peggy joked apologetically to Roger and Mabel wouldn't have looked out of place in a Victorian-era music hall in south London but weren't quite what she would ever have been encouraged to do back at number five Jubilee Street.

'An' if yer thought that were fun, hold on to yer 'olly'ocks once more, fer it's time fer "The Lambeth Walk",' shouted a clearly excited Jessie, who was panting and quite pink in the face. It was rare for him to be so forward, and especially with strangers, and so Peggy raised her eyebrows in encouragement.

Tommy obviously knew the song as he started to parade

around as if he were drumming his fingers on pretend lapels as he stuck his elbows out. No one could fail to laugh.

Any time yer're Lambeth way
Any evening, any day
Yer'll find us all
Doing the Lambeth Walk
Oi!

It was very loud and not very tuneful as by now everyone, except for Mabel on the piano, was parading around doing silly walks and lifting their knees up as high as they would go on the 'Oi!' bits, and after a brief pause for Peggy to explain the meaning of the word 'Lambeth', they yelled it out again, before the sing-song was opened out to other favourites such as 'Hands, Knees and a Bompsadaisy' and 'The Hokey Cokey'.

At this point Peggy had to sit down as by now the baby had woken up and was doing an energetic dance all of his or her own but with each move very uncomfortably choreographed in various parts of her tummy.

Meanwhile Gracie came over to the kitchen from across the yard to see what all the noise was about and she was soon busy teaching Jessie, Tommy and Connie the moves to the charleston, saying that nobody danced it these days, but her mother had taught it to her when she was about their age and it was time they knew what it was and how to dance it, even if they never did so again.

Peggy bit back a smile as Gracie was talking as if she were Old Mother Time passing on an honourable tradition, whereas in reality she was a mere five years older than the twins and Tommy, and probably she had spent much more of her time dancing the big apple or the jitterbug than she ever had done shimmying to the charleston.

Tommy relieved his mother of the stool at the piano and proved to be a very able pianist, singing as he played 'Happy Feet', 'Cheek to Cheek' and 'Yes Sir, That's My Baby'. Roger danced with Mabel as Tommy played, and then Roger carried into the kitchen the gramophone from the parlour, and made a return journey with a generous box of records.

Their musical soirée ended over an hour later with Tommy standing up and singing an unaccompanied 'Danny Boy'.

When he wasn't larking around, he showed himself to have a beautiful singing voice, the sort that any choir would be pleased to have, and Peggy found herself with a lump in her throat that throbbed in time to the sheer beauty of what she was listening to.

Mabel nodded at her to acknowledge she had seen and understood Peggy's welling up of emotion, and then she mouthed 'church choir' with a nod at Tommy.

'You must be very proud,' Peggy replied.

'He has his moments,' said Mabel, to which Tommy answered with an extravagant bow, sweeping his left arm right down to the floor.

That evening everyone went to bed in a much happier frame of mind than the previous evening, and no sooner had Peggy's head hit the pillow than she was out for the count.

Chapter Eighteen

The next day, which was a Wednesday morning, Peggy made sure she was up well before Jessie and Connie, as she wanted to walk them over to school on their first day of lessons. She thought they could probably find their way to the school unaided, as it wasn't too far for them to go and the Harrogate streets seemed pretty straightforward, but Peggy thought too that her niece and nephew might appreciate a little moral support from their aunt. That could never be a bad thing, surely?

Jessie and Connie were both very subdued at breakfast, though, and so Peggy felt more than a little concerned about each of them, especially as they seemed only able to answer her with a quiet yes or no, no matter how chatty her tone or how open-ended she tried to make her questions.

Mabel picked up that things weren't going too well and, obviously used to children, helpfully she made herself scarce after removing from the oven her latest batch of bread which she and Gracie made every day for needy families. Having placed the loaves to cool on a metal rack, she whisked Gracie away upstairs with her to do 'something in the airing cupboard'. Fortunately there wasn't any sign yet in the kitchen of either Roger or Tommy.

'Are you missing Mummy and Daddy?' Peggy gently asked Connie and Jessie as she sat opposite them at the kitchen table, a cup of tea before her, and plates with untouched slices of toast before the twins.

There was a poignant silence as Jessie pushed his plate away and then stared down at his lap and didn't say anything, while Connie turned towards her aunt with mournful eyes and a slightly wobbly bottom lip.

They both looked a shadow of the lively children who had been singing so loudly and dancing with such abandon only the previous evening.

'I've an idea,' said Peggy gently, breaking the silence that had started to stretch between them. 'How about I telephone Barbara at Mrs Truelove's haberdashery later this morning? Would you like that? Perhaps I can either get a message for you both from Mummy or maybe, if we are very lucky, I can make an arrangement that after school and later on this afternoon we can ring again, and you can speak to her yourselves. How does that sound?'

The words were no sooner out of her mouth than Peggy realised that she probably should have checked with Roger first that she would be allowed to use the telephone at Tall Trees in this way before promising such an extravagant treat to the children.

She really hoped he wouldn't mind; it was so damned difficult knowing what one could and couldn't do in somebody else's home without causing offence or irritation, and

Peggy was anxious not to cause umbrage as Roger and Mabel had gone out of their way to be obliging.

But Peggy thought then that her reckless gesture would probably be all right, whatever Roger's first inclination might be, as she would of course immediately offer to pay for the calls and also to make a donation to the church's collection box, as fortunately she had the money that Ted had given her to make sure the children were well provided for. And if this wasn't an example of an ideal way to spend some of what her brother-in-law had given her to take care of them, then she wasn't sure what would be.

She saw Jessie wipe under his eyelashes but drop his shoulders a notch so that they looked a little less anxious, while Connie flashed her aunt a slightly watery-looking expression of gratitude.

Peggy tried to grin back reassuringly and in a manner that let the children know that although they might be a long way away from Ted and Barbara right at that very moment, they were a wonderful niece and nephew – and daughter and son – who most surely would not have been forgotten for even a single second by their parents.

With that there was the sound of the letter box opening and then a bundle of post tumbled onto the mat inside the front door at the end of the hall at Tall Trees, close to where the muddy boots were piled haphazardly, and it wasn't too long before Mabel came in with a letter for each of the children from Barbara. For the first time that day Jessie and Connie's faces broke into what looked like genuine smiles of happiness.

There wasn't an envelope of any description for Peggy,

though, and for a moment she felt a real flash of irritation at him as surely Bill knew how much she wanted to hear from him, although experience had taught her too that for Bill, out of sight also meant out of mind, although she didn't care to probe too deeply into these murky waters.

She felt at sea for a little while, and then suddenly she experienced a real pang of homesickness too.

She *was* missing Bill and his funny ways, there was no doubt about it, she decided, and then she thought of Fishy and Fishy's loud purrs and comforting paddy-padding with her paws as Peggy tickled the puss under the chin, and the tiny terraced house they'd all shared, and the sound of their London neighbours with whom they lived cheek by jowl, and the smell of the River Thames…

She was unprepared for what she felt next, which was a moment of what she could only describe as sheer and overwhelming panic, as if all of a sudden she couldn't remember any of those deeply loved people and things very clearly at all, and then it seemed to her incontrovertibly that the old familiar Peggy was slipping away from her and what was left behind was merely a dried-out husk that approximated someone who in reality was masquerading as Peggy Delbert and who was only just a little bit like her.

Her whirl of emotions escalated, the result being that Peggy felt an overwhelming stab of fear at the thought that she or one of her loved ones or – worst of all – the forthcoming baby might not live to resume their old life back in Bermondsey.

The many casualties of the Great War, and the terrible outbreak of influenza immediately after it that had claimed just as many, had shown with unbending callousness to Peggy and all of her generation that life was tenuous and precious, and that futures most certainly couldn't be counted on.

Suddenly it seemed too terrible that they had all been reduced to this, and the very declaration of war and the unsettling process of evacuation seemed at the bottom of this feeling of terror, both being indescribably horrible and cruel, and what no ordinary person could want, whether they be British or German.

Pleasant and comfortably homely as the kitchen at Tall Trees undoubtedly was, swathed in the delicious smell of freshly baked bread, in a trice it appeared unbearably claustrophobic and much too hot.

Peggy felt as if the walls were rapidly closing in around her as if all too ready to squeeze her very life out, and she had to rise quickly and head to the scullery where she found sitting in the stone sink, a pail of chill and cleanish-looking water (goodness knows what it had been used for) into which she plunged her hands well past her wrists until she felt a little cooler.

Whatever was the matter with her? She told herself again and again in a sort of frenzied mantra that she needed to be strong, for herself and Bill and their baby, and also for Connie and Jessie too. She was so tense and shaky that she could feel her hair tremble violently about her face and her cheeks seemed to be on fire. But despite her instructions to herself, deep down she remained swamped by feelings of being terrified and utterly alone.

Try as she might to prevent them, Peggy couldn't stop the tears welling up viciously, and she held onto the rim of the pail tightly as her shoulders shook and she gave into wave after wave of desolation that coursed through every atom of her mind and body.

After a little while Gracie patted her arm and said very quietly, 'Yer go an' lie back down fer twenty minutes. I'll git t'little 'uns where they need to be. 'Ave a drink of water too. Yuill feel better, ah promise.'

Peggy hadn't heard the younger woman approach but she nodded, although she kept her eyes shut as tears began to drip desolately down her cheeks.

Then, without being able to say a word, she slipped past Gracie with her head down and shoulders hunched, and scurried away back across the yard, anxious to shut herself into the sanctuary of her and Gracie's room where she could give in to all manner of shuddering sobs.

'I bet yer each a penny to a pound that yer can't remember t'way t'school,' Gracie was saying cheerfully to Jessie and Connie, her strong Northern accent sounding a little less strange these days. That was the last thing Peggy heard as Gracie pulled the back door closed across the bit it usually stuck at, making sure not to draw the attention of the children to Peggy's swift exit.

'Where's Auntie Peggy?' Connie asked as Gracie shepherded her and Jessie down the road a little while later.

'T'Reveren' 'ad a sudden job fer 'er t'do,' Gracie said, rather surprising herself with a previously unknown propensity for stretching the truth, 'an' so I sed t'er I'd step in ter mek sure thee get t'skul.'

The children were still buoyed up by having received

the short notes from Barbara that, extravagantly, she had stamped and sent separately to each of them, and so they accepted what Gracie said without further comment or indeed much, if any, further thought.

Then Gracie distracted them further by saying that she had been a pupil at the same school in Cold Bath Road they were just about to join, and she made the children laugh when she told them about the nicknames she and her pals had given some of the teachers in their senior year there, adding that some of those teachers might well still be teaching there, and so Connie and Jessie should keep an eye out for them and report back to Gracie if they had remained appropriate nicknames. She added that on Fridays the children must remember to take a couple of pennies into school with them as there was a tuck shop, and they would be able to buy a sweetie or two, the two-for-a-penny giant gobstoppers being in the past the best value, although they wouldn't be allowed to eat them at school.

As they turned into Cold Bath Road, the tall, red-headed boy that Connie had noticed from the day before was standing on the other side of the street with an empty newspaper bag slung across his shoulder, presumably having just finished his paper round. He was holding the handlebars of an ancient boneshaker of a bicycle, and he was very obviously watching Connie intently.

Gracie looked at him and then she glanced over at the children. Jessie had clearly noticed the boy on the other side of the road as he was busy pretending to be intensely occupied looking for something in the pocket of his school shorts that meant he had to ferret around with his eyes cast down and a hand delving in first one pocket and then another.

But Connie had an unnecessarily casual, butter-wouldn't-melt expression on her face and was studiously and very palpably strolling along, swinging her pretty blue dress from side to side, also very consciously *not* looking in the direction of the boy and his bicycle. Nothing could have signalled her interest in the red-headed lad quite so clearly.

They walked a little further along the street, and then Gracie bumped Connie's shoulder softly with her arm, saying out of the side of her mouth closest to Connie, 'See you've caught t'eye o' Aiden Kell. Nobbut bt trubble, 'e be, 'as t'be sed.'

Connie found that she could understand Gracie perfectly well even though she hadn't yet been in Harrogate two full days.

She also discovered an insouciance beyond her years as she replied, 'That's as may be. Still, the cat's pyjamas, wouldn't you say?' Deliberately provocative as Connie's words were, she didn't dare to quite look up at Gracie as she said them.

'An' I were took fer bein' forward,' Gracie muttered to herself as a moment later she watched Connie march purposefully across the playground at the school, with Jessie trying to follow inconspicuously in her wake. 'Nobbut ten year ol'. T'chilren of to'day, tsk!'

Chapter Nineteen

The days passed, until it was Saturday morning.

After breakfast everybody from Bermondsey wrote letters to Ted and Barbara back in Jubilee Street.

> Dear parints,
>
> Schul is not as good as at home. Vikker and wife nice but not as good as home. I miss it. But they say yoy kan visut. Wether stil sunnie. you can sleep in the room where Jessie sleeps but he will be not there. I can call panda ~~Pettonea Pettuneya~~ Petunia.
>
> Connie

Peggy thought Connie's scribble home to be pretty feeble, but Connie always had been reluctant to do much with a pencil and paper, having driven Barbara to distraction by proving to be nothing more or less than murder to get to sit still for long enough to practise her letters as a youngster. Susanne Pinkly had said to Peggy on more than one occasion that Connie was a conundrum, as she was as bright as a button, and so it seemed so odd that she lagged far behind fellow pupils in setting anything down on paper. Helping her spell Petunia for the letter had been quite a struggle, Peggy mused, and Connie hadn't taken it at all well when Peggy had suggested that maybe the panda be named something easier to spell, such as Ann or Pandy.

Peggy hadn't said anything in admonishment, though, at the paucity of words and/or information in the letter, or tried to point out Connie's obvious mistakes, as she was still feeling so out of sorts she didn't really trust herself not to cry or to sound grumpier than she meant to be. Sometimes she thought her sharp and intense pangs of homesickness were worse than what the twins felt – or, rather, she hoped this to be the case.

Jessie's letter was longer, and Peggy hoped Barbara and Ted would be better pleased with their son's attempt.

Dear Mother and Father,

It is now saturday morning and as Miss Crab says we have worked hard this week as she asked us to do we do not have lessuns today although we mite next saturday if we dont keep up the good work. I don't like the school or the pupils in it much but the lessuns dont seem any harder than we usually do and I dont no the yorkshire lads yet. Tommy and I get on all rite tho. He is qite nortie but nobody seems to see that – he is a choir boy and has the sort of face to go with that but rilly he is up to miss chiff. Will you come and see us? What is going on at home?

Your affectionate son,
 Jessie Ross

PS Thank you for my bear. It was a nice surprise. I like the sweets. I am very pleased to have him – I have called him Neville as that is the prime minister's name. Tommy has a bear but his is brown and not nitted as he has fur and he is called Chocky as he is the same colour as chockolate.

Peggy put both of the children's letters into the envelope she had already addressed to Ted and Barbara, and stamped, and then she began to write her own, taking care to keep her writing small so that she wouldn't have to spend too much on postage.

15th September 1939

Dear Barbara and Ted,

Well, the good news is that the children seem to be settling down. In fact, you would both be very proud of them. I think they miss home, but they are being good children and are trying to make the best of a bad situation.

They loved talking to you on the telephone on Wednesday afternoon, and so please thank Mrs Truelove from me for allowing you a few moments to speak to them. It really did make all the difference to them as they had been feeling very sorry for themselves earlier in the morning.

As you'd expect, Connie seems to be finding her feet first, although she came back with a muddy dress yesterday that I had the devil of a job getting the stains out of when I came to wash it last night as there'd been a pretty brutal game of 'catch' after school.

I think Jessie is finding it harder but actually he doesn't seem too bad, or at least not as bad as I had expected. He seems to be getting on reasonably nicely with Tommy, the boy who lives here.

I think everyone is wondering how it will go once the two schools have their first lessons together on Monday and Tuesday – apparently there has been a bad atmosphere and a fair bit of animosity between the pupils from the different schools on the changeovers in the middle of the day this week, which has meant that after the first day the headmaster from Harrogate, Mr Walton, decided that morning school would have its close shifted forward to earlier in the morning so that it is now at twelve fifteen, and the afternoon school would begin at twelve forty-five, with again only the ten-minute break. The morning children have to leave the school premises immediately they are finished, and one or two of the teachers patrol the streets nearby to try 'to stop any shenanigans'.

Personally, I'm not sure all this separation is the best way to handle any prospective tiffs. If it had been left up to me, I think I'd have organised two days of games in the parks, forgoing all lessons and putting the children into teams made up of both schools in order to let them get used to one another while running about and letting off steam. But there you go, I'm not the one in charge!

To be honest, I'm feeling very out of sorts since I got here – I think the moving and closing up of the dear little house that Bill and I had, where we enjoyed such happy times (most of the while), and then the long journey took more out of me than I expected. My ankles are up and I've had some bad sickness and a bout of crying I just couldn't stop, although the children don't know this.

One good thing, though, is that I think I might have made one friend – or at least I think she will (or could) be in time – a very nice lady called June Blenkinsop, who owns a tea shop that serves a very good toasted teacake.

Do think about coming to visit. I know the train will be expensive and that you will have to change carriages at least once, and so it will undoubtedly be an effort. But Roger and Mabel say they would be very happy to have you here, and naturally the children would love it too.

I take it Bill's not written to me via yours yet? He is hopeless! I know he hates to write as he finds it difficult. I've written to give him my address but there's not been anything back, although I suppose he has only been gone just over a week, and of course he's not too good with his letters, unless – as we know – it's sorting through the runners and riders in the Racing Post!

I've been listening to the wireless every day – in fact, we all try to listen to the BBC news of an evening – and it all sounds eerily quiet in London at the moment as regards any German activity. I'm so pleased as I think of you both virtually all the time.

Everyone here has sorted out their windows with the taping, and the first people have been fined for not having got their blackout curtains or car headlights done properly. But somebody was killed by a car they didn't see coming and the driver didn't see them in the dark as the car's lights were dim and the person's clothes were dark, and so yesterday's paper said that men are advised to walk in the dark with their shirt tails dangling down behind their posteriors, which is all very well in a warm September, but goodness knows how that's going to work when the cold weather sets in!

Your affectionate sister,
   Peggy

The morning's post was about to go and so reluctantly Peggy made herself stop writing. She had actually used up a whole three sheets of her Basildon Bond writing paper, even though she had made her hand as minuscule as it could possibly go while giving Barbara a fair chance of being able to unravel her script to work out what she had been saying, as she had never written such a long letter before. The slim box of writing paper and matching envelopes had been Barbara's leaving-for-evacuation 'proper present' to Peggy (the Coty lipstick being more of a pick-me-up on a difficult day, so Barbara said), and Peggy wanted to eke out their use. But once she had started putting pen to paper she had found it extremely hard to stop, as she'd imagined Barbara sitting in front of her and consequently had found herself scribbling everything down that she would have said to her sister if they had been able to chat face to face.

Peggy folded the pages covered in her writing as tightly as she could, kissed them for good luck and then squeezed them into the envelope along with the children's missives. She stared at the fat envelope after she had licked and stuck down the back, and then with a sigh, she tore off and moistened another stamp that she placed next to the one she had already put in the top right-hand corner of the address side, as she didn't want Barbara or Ted to pay any excess in postage if she were mean with the stamps, and then she wrote the Tall Trees address on the reverse of the envelope under sender.

Chapter Twenty

After an early lunch (tinned sardines on toast) that day, Roger said he needed to clear the decks for the afternoon so that he could write his sermon for the following day, although he thought he would do something on tolerance and generosity, seeing as how many people had been evacuated to Harrogate.

Tommy said he had had an idea so that the house would be quiet for Roger to work in – he would take Jessie and Connie out to show them around Harrogate.

Roger seemed already to be lost in thought about his sermon, looking out of the window as if seeking divine inspiration and saying merely, 'Good show, good show.'

Connie hadn't said much to Tommy since she had been at Tall Trees, but now she began to chat to him about his life and what he liked to do. Once Roger has disappeared into his study, and Peggy and Mabel had gone upstairs to look at blankets, he boasted that Roger and Mabel allowed him to do whatever he wanted – which actually, Connie thought, from what she'd seen, was pretty much true

– Tommy saying that it was great and really good, and he had lots of 'schemes' going.

Connie thought that he sounded as if he had read too many adventure stories with gangsters in them.

Jessie quite liked Tommy as they had had some fun games with the soldiers, but he thought Tommy was making the benign neglect on the part of his parents sound nicer than in fact Tommy found it.

Jessie had seen how Tommy's eyes lit up if his parents wanted to spend some time with him, and he knew how troubled Tommy's sleep was if Tommy had, say, wanted Roger to read the *Dandy* with him, and then a parishioner telephoned and took Roger away. But Jessie knew better than anybody how important 'face' was, and so he didn't say anything about Tommy's exaggeration of his happy life.

Still, the twins' eyes grew round when, as they spent some time playing on the swing together, Tommy boasted further that some Harrogate children would do anything for a dare, and if Jessie and Connie proved worthy of the best top-secret dare, then he might let them know what the dare was.

Tommy's voice dropped to a sinister whisper as he said it was highly illegal and that they could be sent to prison if they were caught. There might be someone there with a shotgun who would shoot at them, and so they would have to behave as spies would.

Stealth, secrecy, speed and success were to be their watchwords if they attempted the dare: the four S's.

Even Connie was stunned into silence. This all sounded very serious, and not at all like a game.

Jessie was staring over to the chicken run, repetitively rubbing the cuff of the left arm of his flannel shirt in his right hand as if it were some sort of talisman that might bolster a feeling of safety within him. He looked as if there were just about nothing in the whole wide world he would rather do less than have anything to do with whatever it was that Tommy was speaking about.

'You need to tell us more, Tommy,' said Connie, 'and it may well be the case that me and my brother will decide not to do it, whatever it is, if it really is as dangerous as you say.'

She didn't want to say an outright no, as Tommy seemed as if he was trying to be chummy, but she didn't want to drop herself and Jessie in it either, as Barbara and Ted had been very strict in their instructions that they weren't to be caught doing anything naughty or that would give Peggy any trouble, especially as Peggy wasn't feeling quite herself just at the moment.

In addition, Connie found herself unable to feel quite sure about Tommy, and this meant that she couldn't decide if she and Jessie would be worse off or, on the other hand, better off if they agreed to go along with what he wanted.

The five days since they had met had only convinced Connie that she couldn't quite work Tommy out, and this made her suspicious as she had always prided herself on her instinctive grasp of the type of person she was speaking to.

Connie had to acknowledge that she didn't really know why she felt like this, as Tommy hadn't actually done anything obvious to make her or Jessie put their guard up, and when the grown-ups were around at least he was the absolute model son and companion. He hadn't been horrible to either of them in any way, and he seemed very willing to share his bedroom with Jessie, and even Jessie's most loyal of supporters, as Connie was, doubted that Jessie would have been quite so magnanimous should the boot have been on the other foot, with Tommy having been forced to hunker down in Jessie's own bedroom.

There was no doubt too that Tommy had a fun and charismatic side to him as well – the evening of the 'On Ilkla Moor Baht 'At' sing-along had shown them all that – and Connie could see that he had a wonderful singing voice and a good grasp of playing the piano. The way Tommy and Mabel had performed together for them showed what talent lay in the Braithwaite family.

These musical talents were both skills of which Connie was incredibly envious as unfortunately she had no aptitude for music or singing, although as she had shown all too clearly with her rendition of 'Any Ol' Iron', this lack of talent never was enough to persuade her not to have a go.

Indeed, her inability to carry a tune had been proved categorically when she and Jessie had been taken to a West End movie house to see *Snow White and the Seven Dwarfs* by their parents as a Christmas treat just before going back to school after the yule holidays at the start of the year.

It was the first time the children had been taken for an outing into the West End, and the children had both got ridiculously overexcited by the number of people milling about, the brightly lit shopfronts and the grandeur of the large cinema.

Connie had felt as if she were in a wonderful dream, and

this was a feeling she wanted to continue for the family's journey home. But unfortunately, after a bit too much loud and off-key 'Hi Ho!, Hi Ho!'ing on Connie's part on the top deck of the bus back from Leicester Square, the Ross family consensus had been that she would most definitely have failed the audition for being a singing dwarf.

Poor Connie had had to protest (not quite honestly) that she didn't care a hoot, as if she were in the film she would have wanted to be Humbert the Huntsman instead, and if she couldn't be he, then the role of the Magic Mirror would have done, as those were *wonderful* scenes.

Jessie said quickly he'd have liked to be the dwarf Happy, and then smiled broadly when nobody filled the short silence after he'd spoken by suggesting he be Bashful.

Ted claimed Doc as his alter ego, although Connie got quite shouty when she insisted that instead of the leader of the dwarfs, as Doc was, her father's ideal casting would be as Grumpy, causing Barbara to catch her daughter's eye firmly and then hold a finger in front of her lips to suggest that Connie tone her penetrating voice down a notch as possibly not everyone on the upper deck of the bus was enjoying their conversation as much as Connie was.

Then Jessie giggled when he whispered 'Dopey' at Ted, who then pretended to cuff him, causing Jessie to giggle even more wildly.

Barbara declared herself Snow White, and nobody disputed this and so presumably they agreed with her, or else thought she was better suited at the nasty Queen but were too sensible to say.

Connie looked now with concentration over at Tommy.

He appeared meek and helpful enough, but still, Connie thought she could detect a hint, a whiff of something else, a little niggle that was less bland and more conniving lurking beneath his innocent-seeming expression.

Her father had once said to her that 'you can't kid a kidder', and for the first time Connie had a glimmer of understanding of what Ted had been driving at.

There was something about Tommy that did not quite add up, Connie was more and more convinced, even though she couldn't for the moment identify what this 'something' was.

Tommy looked the part of an ordinary schoolboy admittedly, but she couldn't ignore a relentless qualm that suggested he wasn't exactly what or all he seemed. She supposed there seemed a neediness in him to be the centre of attention, and that this need sometimes got the better of him.

Connie thought about it a bit more, and then she realised that she could see this because it was a trait she recognised in herself, although it wasn't something she was very proud of and so she tried to keep it more deeply hidden than Tommy did.

The best way for her to proceed would be to go along with what Tommy suggested, to see if he would reveal what he was really up to, she felt. And if it got too hairy – whatever it was that Tommy was suggesting – then she and Jessie had better make sure that they kept their options open and have a well-thought-through plan of retreat at the ready.

'Maybe,' said Connie now, as she stuck out a leg behind

her, looking down as she scuffed the toe of her red sandal across the ground, deliberately (she hoped) putting up a show of reluctance.

If she gave in too easily to Tommy's demands, then he might become suspicious of her, she suspected, and this may well have the result that they would start pussy-footing around each other as they each tried to gauge exactly what the other was up to, and that really wouldn't help Connie get to the bottom of what made Tommy Braithwaite tick.

But if she pretended to take Tommy at face value, then perhaps in time his guard would drop and the real Tommy would be revealed.

Jessie was looking at his sister sharply with a quizzical look in his eyes, as clearly Connie's tame response wasn't the one he expected, and she had quickly to improvise by lifting her skirt to scratch very obviously her thigh just above her knee to make sure Tommy was looking at her and not Jessie as her brother's surprised gaze was definitely too easy to read.

Jessie twigged – he was good like that, Connie knew – and as per usual immediately he backed her up by echoing faintly and in an equally deliberately reluctant manner, with his words characteristically fading out, 'Um, yes, er, maybe. Later on. Or maybe tomorrow...'

'We have church on Sundays, and this means that Saturday afternoons are perfect for what we can do,' said Tommy, unable to prevent the tiniest note of dogged triumph creeping into his voice.

Tommy squared his shoulders and then spat into the palm of his hand. He rubbed them together, indicating with assertive nods at Connie and Jessie that told them that they should spit into their own hands as well.

They did so with only a little reluctance, after which Tommy indicated they should form a ring with each of them holding each other's hands.

And then Tommy raised Connie and Jessie's hands in his own, and they copied him so that they were all standing in a circle with their arms aloft as Tommy shouted, 'The four S's: Stealth, Secrecy, Speed and Success,' and then a heartbeat later the three of them yelled as loudly as they could, and as one, 'The four S's: Stealth, Secrecy, Speed and Success.'

And then for a final time: 'THE FOUR S'S. STEALTH, SECRECY, SPEED AND SUCCESS.'

It sounded terrifying. Exciting too. And for a moment, Jessie thought of a fifth S: SPECIAL. It wasn't a feeling he was particularly used to, but he recognised it was a very potent sensation.

It turned out that Tommy's idea of showing them around Harrogate seemed largely to do with pointing out things to do that grown-ups would classify as naughty.

There was ringing on doorbells and running away, calling out someone's name if you saw them in the distance but then pretending it wasn't you, trying to get an extra black jack from the sweet shop that you didn't pay for, and so on.

Keen to ingratiate himself, Jessie told Tommy about a trick he had seen older boys do in Bermondsey, but had never done himself. It involved drilling a small hole into a sixpence or a shilling – it needed to be a big enough coin that people would take it seriously – and then tying a piece of thread to it. The coin would be left as bait on the pavement, but if anyone leant down to pick it up, the thread would be yanked by its hiding owner, making the coin dance away, to the shouted chorus of 'Got you!'

'Good idea,' Tommy nodded approvingly. 'I'll get a shillin' from tomorrow's collectin' plate, an' I'm sure father'll have summat in t'shed t' make t'hole with.'

But although Tommy was sounding excited about the jape with the shilling, the truth of it was that as Jessie had been describing the trick with the coin, Tommy had been thinking of another 'S'.

An 'S' that was much less savoury.

Scrumping.

And Tommy had a plan.

Chapter Twenty-one

Connie and Jessie were unhappy. Extraordinarily unhappy.

It was the third Saturday afternoon in a row that Tommy had made them go scrumping. If there was a word they now hated the sound of, it was scrumping.

Neither of the twins could see what all the fuss was about. It was simply a field of apple trees, and Tommy would make them all climb over a very high wall.

Privately, Jessie thought it was more to do with Tommy making them bend to his will than it being anything about what they were actually doing as such, but that didn't make it any less horrid an experience for him and his sister.

The first time it had been enough that the three of them stole some apples from the trees nearest the wall.

The second time, Connie had said she and Jessie weren't going to go scrumping. She added, with her bony chest thrust forward, that scrumping was silly, and there was no point in it.

Tommy's eyes narrowed as he stared at her appraisingly.

Connie stood up straighter and looked at Tommy with

a gimlet stare. Sometimes, back in Bermondsey, that had been enough to get the bullies backing down.

There was a knock at the door, and the tension in the room evaporated a degree or two as Roger could be heard telling someone where to find the children.

After a silence, Angela poked her head round the door. She looked wary, and rather shocked to find herself at Tall Trees.

Tommy tossed his head in Angela's direction. Jessie thought it hard to tell if this gesture was inviting Angela into the room or telling her to go away.

'Yer're 'ere, an' so we can all go now,' said Tommy.

This was a surprise, thought Jessie, as he had had no idea that Tommy had even noticed Angela before.

'We're not coming,' said Connie. 'And Angela doesn't want to either.'

Angela's face looked pensive as she could feel there was something going on here that might be difficult for her to navigate.

Tommy stood stock still, and Jessie saw a muscle on the side of his face twitch, close to where the back of his teeth would be.

'Jessie and me. We're staying here. Along with Angela,' Connie reiterated.

'If yer don't, when yer aunt's babbie's here, I'll pull 'is arms off,' Tommy growled with a sneer.

'Get lost, Tommy.' Connie's tone was defiant, even though she felt anything but. To her ears, Tommy sounded very much as if he meant business.

He sidled up to her. He looked bigger and more

threatening than Connie would have given him credit for. She thought of something. 'It was you who beat up Larry, wasn't it?'

A flicker in Tommy's eye confirmed Connie's suspicion, but he didn't deign to give a response.

There was a horrible, twitchy-feeling silence.

Then, 'Yer fuckin' wan' t'test me about Peggy's babbie?'

Connie had heard swearing often before – and she could be potty-mouthed herself at times – but the shock lay in the quiet but immensely sinister way that Tommy spat these words in her direction.

She looked at Jessie, who shrugged with a defeated air.

And so she agreed that she and her brother would do Tommy's bidding.

They couldn't take the risk of going against him, not if there was the slightest chance that Aunt Peggy's longed-for baby might bear the brunt of his displeasure.

Nobody mentioned Angela, but she trotted along with them anyway, looking too shocked at what Tommy had said to risk his ire.

That day Tommy was very demanding when they were over in the orchard. He'd got some chalk and he made Jessie write rude words on the trees.

After a quantity of apples had been picked, all well past their best, Connie and Angela stood on the side edge of the field frowning at each other, as they didn't know what to do or to say, although they both hoped that eating the apples wasn't going to be part of Tommy's plan.

They turned to look at Tommy, whose attention seemed luckily to be elsewhere as he drew some obscene drawings with the chalk on a piece of tarmac that had been laid at certain points in the orchard to give access to vehicles.

Neither Connie nor Angela knew what the drawings were of – well, they could guess that one of them was of bosoms – but the other two were very rude if Jessie's shamed and tight-lipped, pale face was anything to go by.

But back at Tall Trees that evening, strangely, it was as if nothing untoward had happened earlier in the day.

Tommy laughed and joked, and played jaunty tunes on the piano when Mabel asked him, and even made sure he encouraged Connie to have the last half of the toasted teacakes, even though she had had two halves already.

The next evening Tommy behaved in the same way, and the evening after that.

Jessie and Connie talked about it, but they couldn't make out what was going on. They didn't feel able, either, to talk to Peggy, or to Roger and Mabel about their concerns: Peggy because of the threat to the baby, and Roger and Mabel because Tommy was their son and so they doubted their claims about his behaviour would be believed.

They didn't know what to do for the best, and it was an unpleasant but insidious feeling that gnawed away deep inside them every moment they were awake.

The next Saturday, Tommy jangled their nerves up and down all day, sometimes smiling at them with a guileless look in his eye, and at other times looking at them with the intensity of a pantomime baddie.

No mention was made of either the orchard or the Four S's.

This was almost worse than having to go to the orchard, Jessie said to Connie later, who could only nod; she knew exactly what her brother meant.

In his bunk bed that Saturday night, a sleepless Jessie felt his body twitch and jerk as his tense muscles slowly relaxed. Going scrumping was almost better than this, as at least something would have happened and Jessie would feel spent and worn out by the time he laid his head on his pillow with the result that he would quickly fall asleep.

Business was resumed as normal, though, the following Saturday, Tommy grabbing the top part of Connie's arm as they passed on the stairs just after breakfast. 'Do as yer told today, an' I'll call off the gangsters watching yer family's house. Disobey, an' they gets it. Unnerstan'?'

Connie understood.

Early in the afternoon Angela's tap at the door was followed by another knock. It turned out to be from Larry, and an already unbearably tense atmosphere was further loaded by Jessie and Larry finding themselves standing directly in front of one another, each furiously trying to work out the part the other was playing, and who was answerable to who. Their eyes flickered about, and they both kept putting their hands in their pockets and taking them out again.

The five of them trooped in a nervy silence over to the orchard, Connie catching sight of Aiden circling around on his bicycle in a park a way away, but perhaps close enough to take notice of them.

Jessie saw Aiden too, and felt desperate enough to tap out the Morse code signal for SOS on his trouser leg with the hand that was nearest to Aiden, not that he had any hope of Aiden seeing or understanding his message. It just felt better to be making a gesture of protest, no matter how small it was.

They got to the orchard, at which point Angela complained that she didn't feel very well. Connie didn't believe Angela for a moment, but then she rather regretted not saying something similar herself as, much to her surprise, Tommy dismissed Angela with a surly wave of his hand.

Angela didn't need asking twice and she scampered down the road back towards the town as quickly as she could without once looking over her shoulder at Connie and Jessie.

As the sound of Angela's retreating footsteps faded, Tommy indicated they should go over the wall. But when they pulled themselves to the top of the now hated wall they'd scaled so reluctantly the previous Saturdays it was to find that barbed wire had been strung around the top.

Tommy's trousers were well and truly caught, but Connie and Jessie were more frightened of Tommy than they were concerned about the wire, and so they managed to slither over it as best they could, not much caring if their flesh was nicked, and then they jumped down into the orchard.

Larry had pulled himself to the top of the wall almost right beside Tommy, but when he hesitated about untangling Tommy, Tommy leant forward and gave Larry an almighty thrust with the flat of his hand, right in the middle of Larry's chest, with a curt 'Nobody disobeys me.'

Larry's expression was one of pure surprise, and an oddly small 'oooph' escaped his mouth as the breath rushed from his lungs.

He teetered for what felt like a second stretching out into infinity, and at last crashed from the top of the wall, landing on the ground with a sickening thud; and in a shaft of weak autumn sunlight Connie saw a jewel-like shard of one of Larry's front teeth fly through the air and disappear into the grass behind her, while Jessie heard the mangled sound of the splintering on the bone in one of Larry's fingers and the sharp snap of his upper and lower teeth as they clashed together.

'Agh,' was all Larry said at first, but it sounded anguished. And then he gave a sound that could only be described as a keening, high-pitched cry.

Jessie had never heard anything like it before.

'Connie, he's hurt bad, I think,' he said.

But before anyone could decide what to do there was the sound of whistles and baying dogs.

'Larry. Larry! Get up,' somebody yelled. And then Aiden jumped neatly down from on top of the wall and pulled Larry up to a dazed standing position before Aiden moved to stand in front of Larry as the sound of the barking dogs got louder.

As a car drove at speed towards them on the tarmac path through the middle of the orchard, two dogs raced in their direction.

Jessie looked at his sister's terrified expression, and the last thing he saw before the car screeched to a halt was Tommy's anguished face as he wrenched his trousers free from the spikes of the barbed wire and hurtled himself off the wall back into the road away from them, presumably intent on trying to run away, leaving those in the orchard to their unwelcome fate.

'Got 'im!' was shouted from the other side of the wall, and then there was the sound of what sounded like a tussle, followed by Tommy's violent sobs.

There must have been a pincer movement from whomever was so irate, as they could hear that Tommy was now in the hands of somebody on the other side of the wall.

As the dogs circled them, furiously barking, the children huddled together, too terrified to speak or move.

This wasn't good by any stretch of the imagination, no, not at all.

Chapter Twenty-two

16th October 1939

Dearest Peg,

Still no envelope to you from Bill, I am afraid, and so I do hope that by the time you are reading this you will have heard from him. It must be very difficult for you if he still hasn't been in touch, as it has been quite a long time now. I do hope you are taking good care of yourself, and are getting enough rest.

You'll be pleased to know I'm becoming quite fond of Fishy as she understands the value of friendship – or at least, the value of pandering to the hand that feeds her, being very ready to sit on your lap if you are listening to the radio although, less happily, she also wants to sit on my lap if I am knitting and I have discovered to my cost that knitting and cats Do Not Mix, as cats – well, Fishy – are all too often extremely intent on playing with the wool.

The good thing is she's trying to earn her keep as,

when Ted and I were at the pictures the other night we came back to a dead woodpigeon on the doorstep that was still warm and that Fishy was sitting by very proudly – goodness knows where she had found or caught that as the only ones I have seen in London have been over Greenwich way, but I had plucked and gutted it and popped it under a pie crust by the time I had to leave for Mrs Truelove's the very next day.

The gossip in the shop is that some people are starting to bring back their children from evacuation as they can't bear to be parted from them any longer. It's been over six weeks since the children and you left us, and actually life has gone on as normal since then in that everything is still running and no bombs have been dropped. I really don't approve of those who are breaking the evacuation, but there it is.

So if the children mention to you anything about them coming home to Jubilee Street, please say back to them that you know without a shadow of a doubt that is not going to be an option for them as me and Ted still want them safe and out of harm's way. Although we miss them, I think real love can mean that sac- rifices have to be made, and how could we live with ourselves if we brought them back merely to keep us happy, and then they were hurt, or worse, if a bomb went off?

Other news is that I have blotted my copy-book rather with Mrs Truelove as I had quite a set-to with Larry's mother the day before yesterday in the shop, as she is thinking of bringing him back as he's not happy.

Even so, I told her, he is probably safer up in Harrogate than here.

She stalked out of Mrs Truelove's leaving the bias binding she'd been about to pay for on the counter, and then she (Mrs Truelove, I mean) gave me a stern talking-to, saying that I must save this sort of thing for after working hours as she 'can't have people who work for her behaving like harridans'! And then she said to me that from all accounts Larry's mother didn't have a very nice time of it at home as her husband is known for being a bit handy with his fists, which you and I know anyway.

Then the sirens went off and we had to troop out back to head down into the Andersen shelter that's been dug out (that was back-breaking work apparently as the yard had been paved over for years, Mrs Truelove was saying), although then that siren turned out to be a practice that we should have known about but which we didn't, and during it, some weasel had run into the shop and stolen some wool as Mrs Truelove had been in such a panic to vacate the premises that she'd forgotten to lock the shop door at the front. She (Mrs Truelove, not the robber!) was livid and tried to blame me for making her forget to lock it.

That evening I really wished you were here for a natter so that I could get everything off my chest! I can't remember being as short-tempered as I am these days before the war started. I think it's that feeling of being on edge all the time. It almost seems normal on the surface, but deep down we all know that life has changed and most certainly not for the better, and it's just not very easy. All I know is that I feel jittery and quick to take offence at the littlest of things.

I've posted separately the woollen gloves that I have knitted for each of the children – the talk is of clothes' rationing soon, and so I don't want the children facing the cold weather without being wrapped up properly. I know they'll be sorry at what is in their packages, but I thought an individual package, even with their new gloves in it, is going to be more exciting for them than if I sent them to you to pass on.

Hopefully we'll be seeing you all soon, and I hope you are getting enough rest, my dearest Peggy.

With deep love, Barbara

30th October 1939

Dear Barbara,

I've now talked to Bill at long last (at very l-o-o-o-n-g last, may I say!), thank goodness – he telephoned me out of the blue, although when Roger came to fetch me to the telephone I was sure it was either you or Ted calling with some sort of terrible news and so for a moment I felt as if I might be about to give birth then and there. Mabel said she was delighted that Bill had finally rung me as I'd fair worn a groove on the hall runner going to check for the mail so often.

Anyway Bill sounds like he's been living the life of Riley, being on a training camp in Norfolk on the east coast (I think it is, to judge by his hints), and getting up to lots of japes with Reece Pinkly. He couldn't say of course exactly where he is, but I think that is what he was getting at. He says they've been doing lots of training, and there's a big NAAFI and also a nice local pub nearby. He was contrite and very apologetic, but he said he'd tried to write to me several times but he hadn't known what to say – and then he felt guilty for not doing so, and then this made it even harder for him to write.

He's very likely off abroad soon, so we've agreed that every time it's a clear and starry night we'll both go outside and look at the North Star, and then we'll know that wherever we each are in the world we'll be connected, at least just a little, through the heavens – it sounds silly, I know, but oddly it's almost more comfort than if he were writing regularly to me, which I know really is most unlikely, given it's Bill I'm married to, as I know he does struggle with his letters (both in the actual writing as he had a bad time at school, and in the setting down of what he feels he should say). But while Bill is nowhere near a Wordsworth, he does have many lovely qualities otherwise – only I can't help hoping the baby takes after me a bit more than his or her daddy when it comes to reading and writing.

I'm feeling much better in general these past couple of weeks, and I've even landed myself a little job. I can't tell you how wonderful it is to feel a little useful again, even if only in the smallest of ways. June Blenkinsop, the nice lady with the tea shop, has got me in for two hours every lunchtime and I sit at a small table and tot up what people should pay and give them any change. June has been asked by the government to offer something more substantial, and to cut back on the cakes and teacakes and fancies, and they are getting busy as people are working longer hours and have less time for cooking at home.

Now for something I should have told you earlier. It's not very nice, I warn you in advance. Indeed, I was so cross about it that I couldn't tell you until I had calmed down and I forbade the children to mention it to you either when they wrote until I had told you first.

Since it happened Connie has definitely been contrite and sometimes – unusually for her, I think – verging on the tearful, asking me several times if I know whether she and Jessie will be home for Christmas, while Jessie seems now to spend most of his time holed up at Tall Trees somewhere with his nose stuck in one of Roger's books, and he doesn't have much to say about what went on at all.

The long and short of it is that Connie and Jessie and a group of other children, including Tommy and Larry, were caught stealing apples, or 'scrumping' as Tommy calls it. That doesn't sound too bad, does it?

But actually, it's much worse than it sounds – it turned out to be in an orchard that was part of an experimental government-funded research field with a special crop that was being monitored by a university with guards and all sorts – I think it's to do with working out a way to breed qualities of old fruits into easier-to-grow, newer varieties to boost food production.

The irony of course is that the garden here at Tall Trees is awash with apple trees and the fruiting has been heavy this year, with a bumper crop of round red apples, and so the children really weren't short of apples, if that was what they wanted.

It was more that they wanted to do something naughty, and was this naughty?!

The first that me, Roger and Mabel knew of it was when the three from Tall Trees got delivered home in the back of a police car, and it was parked up on the road outside in clear view of everyone, and the policeman literally led Tommy and Jessie into the garden and up to the front door by their ears, with Connie trailing behind them. (Jessie complained later that even the Bash Street Kids in the *Beano* wouldn't get treated in this way.)

For once, both Mabel and Roger were here when the Black Maria drew up and so they could speak to the policeman instead of me, as the minute I started to hear him say words like 'destroying valuable work' and 'treason' I felt woozy.

Roger proved that he is made of sterner stuff than me fortunately, and he sounded very reasonable as he spoke to the constable, and after a long talk the policeman agreed that the children could all be let off with an unofficial warning, although the school would have to be told, the policeman said. Later Roger explained to me and Mabel that the constable had been laying it on a bit thick to scare the children, although they would very probably have been charged if they were older – they'd blundered into a carefully monitored area and because of writing on the trees and climbing them they had possibly corrupted the experiments.

So, the long and short of it is that Connie and Jessie insist that the scrumping episode was all Tommy's idea: Tommy blames Larry (and your two, to some extent), and there's also been a local lad called Aiden involved somehow, although I can't quite make out what his role was – he stuck up for the London kiddies, I think, and it seems that somewhere along the way Jessie sent a panic message in Morse code that Aiden understood.

I said to Connie and Jessie, whatever were they thinking, when they knew you had forbidden them to do anything naughty? And to this they have no answer – privately, I think they were looking just to get themselves 'in' with the local kiddies, most of whom have been keeping their distance from the London children.

When it all came out into the open I was so furious with Connie and Jessie that I wanted to shake them, and so I had to go out into the garden and stand in the cold for quite a while until I had calmed down – Bucky came and sat about a yard away, and I found him more of a comfort than any of the people around me. Connie, I could believe, would perhaps have been something of a ringleader, but I was shocked that Jessie had been involved; it just felt so out of character for him to have been caught up in something like this.

I don't know, but Larry is in a pretty bad way from

all accounts as Gracie saw him the other day, and he looks as if he's really been through the wars, which is awful as on his very first day in Harrogate he got set on by local lads and given a black eye – I'm sorry, but this is another thing I didn't want to burden you with, as I thought it would only make you worry unnecessarily about Connie and Jessie been at the mercy of the local children and Connie says this was at Tommy's hands too.

There have been tears, lots of tears in fact, all round, and Tommy's been sent to Mabel's poorly mother's for a fortnight to cool off, although I think this is partly because he was shouting and swearing at his father (using the F word, can you believe? I said to Roger I'd never heard your two use it, and so it might not be from them that Tommy heard it, as Tommy immediately claimed, but you know how this sort of thing sticks), rather than for what went on with the apples.

It's all been very unpleasant and difficult, and for a couple of nights I thought Roger and Mabel would be blaming Connie and Jessie (and me too, very likely) for all that's gone wrong, and that they might expect all of us to move to a different billet, although Gracie kept saying a lad called Aiden Kell was sure to be at the bottom of it – she doesn't like him for some reason – but Connie got really angry when she heard that, and now she won't speak to Gracie.

I'm so sorry once again that I couldn't find it in myself to tell you immediately. I'm not myself these days.

Very best wishes and love,
Peggy

Within three hours of reading this letter, a tight-lipped and extremely concerned-looking Barbara was at King's Cross station, looking for the platform on which she should board the train to Yorkshire.

Chapter Twenty-three

It was too late for Barbara to speak to the children by the time she finally got to Tall Trees late that evening – they were both sound asleep when she arrived, as early nights were the order of the day since the scrumping debacle, which they didn't dare argue about – and when she peeped into their rooms they appeared angelic, with their knitted toys Petunia and Neville tucked in cosily beside them. They looked almost as if they could never be naughty.

Gracie had offered to sleep in the other bunk bed in Jessie's room so that the sisters could have some privacy, but she made sure Jessie was soundly off and away in the land of nod before she crept up the ladder and into Tommy's top bunk, as she didn't want him to wonder why she was going to bed down up there rather than in the bedroom above the stables, Gracie having to smother a bout of giggles as she heaved unceremoniously her now large belly as silently as she could – which wasn't very silently – from the wooden ladder and over into the top bunk.

Mabel and Roger were nicely welcoming to Barbara,

though, which Peggy was relieved about when she brought her sister into the warm kitchen.

Peggy had spent a very chilly twenty minutes walking up and down as she waited for the train on which her sister was travelling to arrive, her breath coming in little chill puffs as she paced along an extremely draughty autumnal Harrogate station, watching little glints of one of the first frosts of the winter form icy patterns at the edge of puddles on the tarmac of the platforms where they were exposed to the elements.

Although she hadn't eaten since a snatched and rather dry cheese sandwich she'd bought from a hole in the wall at King's Cross station at midday, Barbara was too anxious about her children to be hungry on her arrival, although she did manage a little bread and cheese, remembering to compliment Mabel fully on the quality of the bread, which was no trouble at all to do as it really was delicious, with Mabel proving herself to Barbara as an excellent baker.

Barbara gave Roger and Mabel four linen napkins from the haberdasher's, which she had embroidered prettily, as a thank you to them for allowing her to stay at Tall Trees.

Mabel seemed very touched and said that Barbara really needn't have, but Barbara insisted it was her pleasure and that she was more grateful than words could say that the reverend and his wife were providing a safe haven in these troubled times for her children and sister.

Roger held her hands and said, 'May God bless you, and them,' with a nod of his eyes upwards that Barbara assumed was towards the bedrooms upstairs where Jessie and Connie were sleeping, and then Mabel eased the atmosphere by saying she'd just got a tray of parkin out of the oven and that she very much hoped that Barbara would treat herself to a slice.

Barbara clearly had no idea what parkin was (and actually she was sporting a slightly suspicious look on her face as she was clearly remembering, Peggy could see, Roger and Mabel's fondness for tripe that Peggy had complained about in her letters not long after she had arrived in Harrogate), and so Peggy jumped in quickly to tell her sister that parkin was delicious and that Barbara would love it, as it was like a mix of ginger cake and soft, treacly oatmeal biscuits. Thus reassured, Barbara gave a weary smile of thanks.

As the sound of an ambulance's bell cut shrilly through the night air as it raced by to an emergency several streets away, Roger carried a tray with a teapot and a jug of milk and two cups and saucers, and a side plate with slices of the warm parkin, across the backyard and then up the steep stairs to the room above the stables. He had the two sisters trailing along in his wake, with Barbara carrying her travelling bag and Peggy her big tummy, and they were going to the room above the stables in order – at Mabel's kind suggestion – that the sisters could have a proper catch-up with the benefit of Peggy being able to lie in bed as they spoke.

Roger deposited the tray on the small table under one of the windows and then made sure he had turned the lamps on only after the blackout curtains were securely draped as they should be. Peggy was very touched to see that somebody – she didn't know who – had laid a small fire in the grate that Roger now knelt down to light. This was the first time there had been any heating in this room since Peggy had arrived, and it felt like luxury beyond compare.

Roger toddled off back to the main house (Mabel having been very insistent about him needing to do something with the proving mixture that she had explained to the children not long after they had arrived was a living organism, even though it looked like something disgusting and frothy – it was possible it had a not very distant relationship to tripe, Peggy had thought. It was divided carefully every day and then half of it used in the morning's batch of bread production as the raising agent).

At last Barbara could turn her attention properly to her sister for the first time since she had arrived in Harrogate, and she was more than a little shocked to see the shadows under Peggy's eyes and how under the weather she looked generally. Pregnancy really didn't seem to be agreeing with her at all.

Barbara appreciated that Peggy had been exceptionally worried about Jessie and Connie, but this was the stage of her pregnancy when she should now be looking at her best – or at least it was the period when Barbara had felt really well and full of beans, before she got just that bit too big to be able to dash about with her usual nimbleness. But Peggy seemed peaky and not at all comfortable, either when she stood or sat or lay down, although Peggy insisted this was because she'd got a bit cold while waiting in the open air at Harrogate station.

Barbara was pleased to see Peggy liven up after thirty minutes under her pink paisley-patterned feather eiderdown, and so she felt bad that Peggy had allowed herself to get so frozen at the station, when she herself would have been able to find her way to Tall Trees without too much trouble, Barbara was sure.

They talked for ages, though, Peggy absolutely refusing to admit to any feelings of drowsiness, and as they chatted they drank such a huge amount of tea that the chamber pot was well used, with the sisters teasing each other that the last time they had had to see each other spend a penny was when they were kiddies.

The sisters enjoyed reminiscing then on the japes they had got up to on the streets of Bermondsey when they had been children – which mainly consisted of knocking on doors and running away when the householder answered.

Later, they reminded themselves of the ghost stories, very tame now but simply terrifying when they were small girls, that their father had told them when they were little and sitting by the open fire grate drying off after some vigorous apple bobbing, which was a family favourite on special occasions, as they toasted marshmallows impaled on the prongs of the fork with the long handle from the set of matching brass implements for dealing with log or coal fires that Ted and Barbara's parents had been given as a wedding present, with the lamps dimmed or, thrillingly, even turned off. Their father had been very good at producing a variety of spooky voices and in doing sharp, hidden raps on the wooden floor to signify the knock of Jack O' Lantern on Halloween.

'It's probably a good thing in some ways that Connie and Jessie are in disgrace, and that Tommy is over in Leeds,' said Peggy. 'I overheard Roger and Mabel wondering whether your two would expect to go out "eening", and Roger rather hoped not as he didn't think it very Christian, and in view of the apple fiasco I don't think just at the moment we should advertise that we have any affinity for a good old pagan tradition.'

'Yes, I'm sure you're right,' said Barbara, 'although I don't suppose we do anyway.'

'I did hear Connie saying to Jessie that Aiden had told her that a group of them were going a-larking – which is what they say here for playing – for Nutcrack Night, but she said to Aiden that she and Jessie wouldn't be allowed, and just now she thought it was better if she didn't even ask if they could go.'

'Thank goodness for that,' said Barbara. 'Maybe Connie is getting a little sense in her head, after all.'

Chapter Twenty-four

The next morning everyone, including Peggy, kept out of the kitchen so that Barbara could have a good half an hour alone with the children before she walked them over to school.

'Mummy!' Connie yelled when she saw Barbara.

In excitement, Jessie almost fell down the stairs as he scurried towards the kitchen, such was his hurry to see his mother after he had heard Connie's scream of delight.

The children fairly galloped across the room to Barbara and clutched her tightly round the waist, as if they were never going to let her go, and she clasped them back just as enthusiastically.

Then she patted them and said it was time for their breakfast, and that after school she would be wanting to hear everything about the escapade to do with the orchard, but right now they were to concentrate on getting some food inside them, after which they could tell her about school and how their schoolwork was going. She added that she was very much looking forward to hearing too what they thought about Yorkshire, and all the things they had noticed that were different from their old home in Bermondsey.

'How long are you here for?' said Jessie, daring to lay voice to what he and Connie had really been thinking about from the very moment they had seen their mother.

'Is Daddy here too?' asked his sister. 'And are we going to go home with you? Back to Jubilee Street? Please, Mummy, are we? Are we?'

'Yes, Mummy, are you taking us home with you? Please say that you are. Mummy?' echoed Jessie.

For a moment, thought Barbara as she gazed down at the round cheeks and shining eyes of her beloved children, it felt quite like old times, despite the anguished-sounding appeals of her children. Happier times. Safer times, perhaps.

And for just a little while that was quite enough for all of them, surely. The world wasn't safe, and nor was it happy just now.

She didn't want for the minute to think either too closely of how much Jessie and Connie seemed to have been missing her and Ted, or how much she and Ted had been missing them in return, or how much the children yearned to be back in Bermondsey.

She didn't want to look too closely into their imploring eyes, or answer their pleas in the negative way she was steeling herself for when she would have to speak with them as to whether they would all be catching the train back to London together.

Tricky discussions on the incident to do with the apples, or Barbara leaving them behind when she caught the train back the next day, could wait for a few hours, she decided.

'Come on, you two, it's time for breakfast!' Barbara said as brightly as she could as she nodded towards the kitchen table where their breakfast was waiting.

Once the children had had their fill and Gracie had bustled in and offered to wash up the pots so that they could all get off, Peggy walked alongside Barbara and the children over to Cold Bath Road Elementary School, it being an early week for the London children.

As they got to the school at five and twenty to eight (Connie saying they had never been so early, and that they would be bound to be the first children there, which in fact they weren't by quite a long way, and so goodness knows what time *those* kiddies had had to get up, Barbara commented), it meant that she was able to take a quick peek into the classrooms and the assembly hall, the cloakroom and the lavatories.

She was shown by the twins as well the two playgrounds that were fore and aft of the main school building, not that these days the reduced timetable of lessons and teaching allowed much use by the school pupils of either spot for running around during the day to let off a bit of steam.

It was a well-equipped school, Barbara acknowledged with a nod of approval, very solid and with everything seeming to be there that one could possibly want, either from a pupil's or from a teacher's point of view.

Peggy smiled at her sister; there was a slight slant of relief about her grin, as she hated to think of what might have happened or been said had Barbara not liked anything she had seen or heard. Her sister was naturally a feisty person, even at the best of times, and it had always been easy to guess from where Connie had got her bolshy side. Right now it was a good thing that Barbara didn't want to kick up a storm about anything that she'd seen at Cold Bath Road Elementary.

Jessie and Connie were keen to show their mother where they sat in their lessons on the days when St Mark's got the proper classrooms to use as their own, as well as how, on the other days, the various class forms from London would share the assembly hall as happened when the sets of pupils from both schools came in on Mondays and Tuesdays, the Bermondsey teachers sitting in various corners of the large room and their pupils sitting cross-legged on the floor fanned out into a semi-circle in front of their teacher.

Barbara asked her children whether they found it disturbing or distracting when several different lessons were being taught simultaneously in the same space, but Jessie said nonchalantly, 'Don't worry as we're used to it now. We've been told there's going to be a prize of a day out at Christmas round here somewhere if we are all as good at the end of this term as we would have been if we were still at St Mark's.'

Connie's expression was less reassuring to Barbara. She looked like she was very probably always more interested in what one of the other forms was up to when they were grouped together in the assembly hall than in what she should have been paying attention to in her own lesson.

'Connie, I hope very much that you are doing your best too. Ted and me are wanting you to work really hard at your school books to hold up the good family name of the

Rosses, as we don't want anyone up here to think that number five Jubilee Street can only turn out nincompoops, even if we can't be with you every day to chase you up. You are a big girl now, remember, and so we have to rely on you being sensible,' her mother said seriously.

Barbara didn't expect her words to make much difference – similar conversations in the past had never had much of an effect – but she said them anyway, just in case.

Connie's expression didn't really change. And Barbara pretended not to notice.

Then Jessie and Connie wanted to show their mother how much their writing was coming on – well, how Jessie's was at least, as Barbara couldn't in all honesty detect the slightest improvement in Connie's unique and almost illegible scrawl, although she made sure she voiced plenty of encouraging words to her occasionally wayward daughter.

As they chatted, Barbara saw from the corner of her eye that Larry had slunk into the classroom behind them and slid down into a chair at the furthest edge of the back row, taking care not to catch anybody's eye and making sure he wasn't looking directly at anybody either.

Although she had had her run-ins with Larry in the past, when she had seen or even managed to catch him being unspeakably mean to Jessie, Barbara was taken aback now by how grimy and generally unkempt he appeared.

Larry's hair didn't seem to have been cut since he had arrived in Yorkshire and it was obviously filthy, while dirt appeared to be embedded into the skin of his knuckles and his knees and around his fingernails, to the point that these areas looked now to be almost elephant grey in colour and as if his underlying skin were very dry and flaky. There was a dirt-encrusted scrap of bandage splinting two fingers together.

Barbara didn't think any of Larry's clothes looked to have been washed recently either. She peered more closely, and she would have bet a pound to a penny then that his garments very probably hadn't been washed at all since he had arrived in Yorkshire, the grime was so heavily ingrained. One of his front teeth was badly chipped, she could see, and all in all he looked very neglected and, as he stretched an arm down to scratch about his ankle, extremely skinny too as his wrists poked out angularly of his threadbare shirtsleeves, and the forearm he'd extended towards his ankle was pipe-cleaner thin. If all of that wasn't bad enough, to add insult to injury there was a fetid odour wafting across the room in her direction that was most definitely emanating from poor Larry.

None of this was Larry's fault in the slightest, Barbara knew. He was only of primary school age and, as boys (and the girls too, she had to admit to herself) sometimes did need to be chivvied towards soap and hot water, the truth of it was that he should have somebody looking after him and making sure he was properly presented to the world.

She felt a rising tide of anger on Larry's behalf; this wasn't the proper way to treat a youngster.

Larry might not be an easy boy to look after, that much would be true, and he might not be a particularly likeable boy to have around either. But this looked like nothing less than an obvious case of downright neglect, and for a moment Barbara wondered if Larry's mother wouldn't after all be doing the right thing if she did decide to bring him back to London, and thus allow him to take his chances against the German bombers when they launched their aerial offensive, which they most surely would.

Barbara turned to look at her own two children, and was comforted by the welcome sight of their cleanish hair (certainly nowhere near as lacklustre as Larry's), their clear and shining eyes and their full, rosy cheeks. While Mabel and Roger might have had an issue or two in the discipline department in dealing with their evacuees on a day-to-day basis, it was obvious that Connie and Jessie were getting lots to eat and that their clothes were washed regularly, their shoes clean and their hair brushed every morning.

'I shan't be long,' Barbara told her own children, and she turned to head over to the forlorn-looking lad about whom she had once held such a shirty opinion, and as she stood before him she tried to muster a kindly tone as she said, 'Hello, Larry. I'm Mrs Ross and I saw your mother last week, and we spoke about you. Do you have a message for me to give to her if I see her when I get back to London? I can make sure she gets it, and I would be very happy to do that for you.'

Larry didn't need to know, Barbara decided, that she and his mother had been extremely prickly and tetchy with one another, almost to the point of a full-blown argument.

Once Larry realised that Barbara was addressing him directly, he leapt out of his chair with alacrity, to stand up military straight, accidentally knocking his chair out of the way with an ear-splitting scape of its wooden legs across the parquet floor of the classroom, such was the anxious manner with which he had sprung up.

He stood with his chest clearly rising and falling, and with his fists clenched and his arms, legs and neck ramrod straight, his eyes staring oddly straight ahead as they locked onto something in the middle distance in front of him.

Barbara felt a peculiar sensation of awkwardness and a feeling that was very akin to embarrassment flush right through her as she had never before had this reaction from a child to anything she had said (or indeed from anybody older), and it seemed to her a hideous parody of something that Dickens-esque paupers might have been forced to do in the cold and harshly governed boarding schools of another era.

She turned her head quickly to see where the other children were in the classroom or if anyone else had noticed Larry's reaction at her crossing the room to speak to him and thought it as odd as she did, but everyone else seemed to have their attention taken elsewhere.

Barbara thought she saw Larry smother a small but none-theless distinct flinch caused by his reaction to her sudden movement, and in an instant her heart went out to him.

She realised how much more settled and calm both Connie and Jessie looked in comparison to him, and so Barbara concluded that the problem was arising at the billet and almost definitely not at the school, as Jessie was such a sensitive and emotionally twitchy boy that if it were too strict a regime at the school, it would be bound to be very apparent in the way he looked and acted, and Barbara could see nothing untoward with her son no matter how closely she scrutinised him.

Barbara didn't want to draw further attention to how shocking she found Larry's appearance or behaviour, and especially so in front of the other children.

Larry was big for his age, and already he had a not very faint outline of a moustache forming, and therefore Barbara knew it was very important that she take extreme care not to embarrass him, in part because she was aware that as he and Jessie had had such a troubled history – she most certainly didn't want to do anything that would make *that* worse. She understood too that boys at Larry's stage of development from child (in body at least, if not in mind) to young adult were awash anyway on a tide of emotions, and so she didn't want to give Larry any hint that she was unnecessarily concerned by the state of him in case this spurred him to bravado that he might later regret, or to do anything that might convince him that he needed to be nervous of her doing something in consequence of how he looked, that might cause him to lose any all-important face in front of his classmates.

Whatever Barbara's opinion had been of him previously, and mean as Larry had most certainly shown over the previous summer that he could be in his behaviour towards smaller or weaker children, right now he was clearly having a difficult time with his evacuation hosts since his arrival in Yorkshire. A mother – well, any normal adult really – would have to have a heart of stone not to feel a tremendous lurch at the wretched sight of him, and Barbara felt at the very least she had to make him think that he wasn't utterly alone, unthought-of or uncared for.

'I know who yer are.' Larry cut across her thoughts with an attitude from which it was hard for Barbara to make out his precise feelings. 'An' I don't 'ave a message fer my ma or my pa.' His harsh-sounding words were delivered in a mechanical, one-note manner, and she found the tenor of the whole exchange very disconcerting and unsettling, especially as he was still standing preternaturally straight and rigid.

She dreaded to think what might have gone on where Larry was billeted during his time in Yorkshire.

'I understand what you are saying,' said Barbara levelly. 'But I know that your family *are* thinking about you – as I say, I was talking with your mother only last week and she was telling me a lot about you – and so I will say to her that I have seen you.'

She chose her words carefully. She didn't know who was friendly with who around here, and for all Barbara knew there could be somebody standing near to her and Larry right at that very minute who might go on to pass details of their conversation to the people he was staying with, which might not go down at all well at his billet if Barbara seemed overtly critical of his treatment at their hands or his condition.

Seeing how very downcast he looked, a mere shadow of the cocky, slightly loutish eleven-year-old of just a couple of months previously, and displaying the faintest of trembles to the muscles of his face as he looked as if he could be battling tears, she absolutely didn't want to make his life more difficult in any way.

'My sister Peggy – that's her over there in the blue coat,

215

talking to Connie; they and Jessie all live at Tall Trees as I daresay you know already, where Reverend Roger Braithwaite, Tommy's father, is the rector – anyway, Larry, Peggy can always get a message to me by telephoning me at work, or else she can telephone the Jolly, and I can pass what you say on to your mother,' Barbara said to him very quietly and seriously. She thought she saw a tense double-blink in one eye and a corresponding twitch of muscle at the outer edge of his other eye at the mention of Tommy's name as he stared off somewhere to the side of her, but she didn't know Larry well enough to be sure.

She paused, and adult and child looked at each other for a few seconds, before Barbara said levelly, 'Larry, do know that any time, day or night, Peggy would be ready to get in touch with whoever you want back in London. Her bedroom at Tall Trees is above the stables, and so if anybody wanted a word with her in private then nobody needs to go to the main house to be able to knock on her door, which is at the top of the wooden steps at the side of the building.'

She turned to go and speak to Connie – she really didn't want to make too much of this in any obvious way – but she saw from the corner of her eye Larry give her an almost imperceptible nod to show that he had taken Barbara's message on board as he turned away from her in order to slump disconsolately down once again in his chair.

Chapter Twenty-five

As she and Peggy were walking down the road a few minutes later to June's tea shop, Barbara said to her sister that even when Jessie had been at his most unhappy over the previous summer, she could never remember him appearing quite as down in the mouth as Larry was looking currently. It was just about the last thing she had expected to see in Harrogate.

'I might have thought that once,' agreed Peggy glumly. 'Now, I am not so sure. There's lots and lots of things to like here in Harrogate, I don't doubt, and the people I have spoken to have all been very kind, and of course it feels like a prosperous and grand-feeling place that's at the opposite end of the social scale to what we've all know in Bermondsey.

'But it is very hard to describe how peculiar one feels when uprooted and away from everything and everyone that is familiar – it is definitely very unsettling, and so far, not wholly pleasant in my experience. And I suspect – well, in fact, I know – it is equally as hard for those forced to offer *us* billets, and so I do have a lot of sympathy for our hosts too – we are strangers invading the sanctuary of their own homes, after all, and I think some children have been found very awkward and difficult. We are all so powerless, and this is in no way a pleasant thing to experience, is it, no matter which side of the fence you are on.'

'Some sisters too may have been a bit awkward and difficult, I expect,' said Barbara, and then the sisters laughed as they knew Barbara was making a joke. Granted, it was a very small quip, but any attempt at humour these days was very welcome, and that was really what the sisters were agreeing on. As the nights lengthened and the days drew in, with plummeting temperatures, it was hard not to feel permanently sorry for oneself.

Barbara was continuing to talk and her words ate into Peggy's thoughts. She realised her sister was speaking in a manner that was much more conciliatory in tone than the one she normally employed.

'I hope,' Peggy heard Barbara say, 'that you don't mind, but just now I told Larry that he could come to you at any time, and that he didn't have to go to the front door of the main house to do this, as I wasn't one hundred per cent sure he would come to you with a problem if he had to go through Reverend Braithwaite or Mabel, or especially Tommy, and so I explained to him where exactly you are billeted above the stables.'

Peggy agreed with Barbara, adding, 'Larry looks in a bad way, doesn't he? I did actually give him my address when he had his black eye after the first night, but he didn't get in touch, and then I meant to check up on him but somehow I never did. I feel that I've been remiss.

I was quite shocked just now actually at what I saw, the poor lad.'

Barbara asked her sister if she thought that Connie and Jessie were very homesick for London, as Peggy saw them every day and would be able to better gauge how they were feeling than she.

Peggy had to admit that she was pretty certain that they were missing their home very much indeed, and their parents too, of course. While the Braithwaites were kindly people and the house was much larger than number five Jubilee Street, with a lovely big garden for the children to charge about in as they wanted, and while Jessie very much appreciated Roger's well-stocked library of books, Tall Trees just wasn't 'home', was it?

And that was where the rub was.

Home back in Bermondsey might not be up to much in the practical sense, but in the emotional sense it was where the heart of the family lived, and not to be there made them feel vulnerable.

'It's so hard as Ted and me hate having them here too. But everything tells me that if they came back home right now, it would in all likelihood be terrible timing, even though that is a very difficult message to get over to a ten-year-old when there hasn't been any bombing, and the most obvious sign of us being at war is that usually these days it's a woman driving the buses you're going to catch,' admitted Barbara. 'This bloody war.'

The sisters had been brought up not to swear – in fact, their father had been very strict about that sort of thing, and as teenagers they knew they'd be for the high jump if ever he caught a whiff of even the slightest profanity leaving their lips – but these were days that were quite unlike those of their formative years.

They stopped walking for a moment and then turned to look at each other, Barbara with a slight but undeniably defiant air about her that Peggy was unable to match.

Then Peggy said deliberately as she drew back her shoulders full square, so that her stance looked much closer to that of her sister's, 'Blimey, Barbara. Yes, this bloody war!'

Although still terribly early as it wasn't yet eight fifteen, June Blenkinsop's tea shop was busy as increasingly people were starting to pop in after finishing a night shift.

In fact, June had confided to Peggy several days earlier that she was wondering about whether she should go to the trouble of getting a proper catering staff together so that they could start to do twenty-four-hour hot food, now that more and more people were being put by the authorities on to various kinds of shift work. It would mean thinking about the business differently and putting a lot of investment into it, June said, but she could see there was a demand for it. Peggy had told her that it was certainly something to think about seriously, and that June would be better placed to do this than some other Janey-Come-Lately.

On this first morning in November the café was simply awash with gossip, both in the tea shop proper and in an anteroom behind the kitchens at the back of the building, which June had recently had redecorated in a cheery primrose yellow and then decked out with an array of scavenged tables and chairs so that more customers could be catered for.

And the talk wasn't of very good news by any stretch of the imagination, Peggy and Barbara were to learn as June ushered them towards one of the few empty tables. They sat down to hear more about what had happened, and June pulled up a chair so that she could sit down too to join them.

Apparently one of the other evacuee children from St Mark's had had a terrible mishap while larking around out and about in the unlit streets the previous evening.

There'd been the usual pretty harmless knocking on front doors and running away, and then a more serious game had started, apparently, involving playing at spooks in a graveyard (luckily not a graveyard that had anything to do with Reverend Braithwaite's church, as undoubtedly Roger would have felt very put out if this had proved to be the case, Barbara and Peggy agreed), with what was eventually a quite large group of children gathered from both the Harrogate and Bermondsey contingents.

The children celebrated Halloween by playing at being spooks by shining the beams of light from torches upwards onto their chins to make their faces take on the characteristics of scary skeletons. The two or three torches between them were held aloft during the few minutes the children were able to dodge the wrath of the ARP wardens, who walked about every evening to make sure diligently that not even the tiniest chink of light was escaping anyone's home to break the blackout.

Needless to say, an ever-alert ARP warden had spied

what the children were up to and he had shouted at them in no uncertain terms to put out the damn light.

His admonishment hadn't been too strictly given, the children had to admit later when questioned by the police, but then the children egged one another on as to ''e's comin' t'git us', and in a matter of moments the game had degenerated into a rowdy gang of children running up and down the streets.

Overexcited and without a thought for any potential consequences, a gaggle of unchaperoned children had broken away from the others, who now were in hot pursuit, and inevitably (it seemed at least to the grown-ups discussing the matter the following day in June's café) they had run straight into the road and unfortunately slap bang into the path of an oncoming car.

The driver hadn't seen them and the children hadn't realised there was a car coming in their direction. The road was unlit and the blackout had been in full force, and the car had actually been driven with its headlights off as there had been a full moon, and so stupidly the car's owner thought he had enough light to navigate safely by.

One of Jessie's classmates – in fact, it was little Angela, who had run away down the road from the orchard on the fateful day of the dogs and the Black Maria – had taken the full force of the brunt of the collision, her small body being tossed high into the air before crashing back down to the road.

Two other children had also run into the car, but they were fortunate enough to have bounced off its huge rounded bonnet and so they had escaped with mere heavy bruising.

Aiden had been one of the children a-larking, although he'd been in the chasing group, and he had run to the nearest house to raise the alarm as the car driver, the only adult on the scene, seemed to be in shock and was incapable of doing much to help Angela.

For Angela, the outcome was much more serious than her sustaining mere cuts and bruises.

She was lying now in hospital with a fractured skull, and she hadn't shown any sign of regaining consciousness since the collision while nobody quite seemed to know what her long-term prognosis was.

She had been taken to a new hospital in Penny Pot Lane that was still under construction for use by the planned-for injured of the British forces (the memories of the Great War's field hospitals being brought into play by the authorities, with the result that preparations were being hurried along before the casualties were brought home in any great number).

It turned out that this new hospital was the only place locally to have on standby the right sort of expertise with head wounds such as Angela's, and as there was a specialist medic already there who was training up other doctors and nurses, and as Angela was a child who obviously needed expert treatment, they had made an exception that she should be dealt with there immediately rather than taken to a bigger hospital in one of the other larger towns in the county.

June Blenkinsop described what she had heard other customers say had happened.

Shaken, Peggy laid a hand on Barbara's and said, 'Connie and Jessie have been spending time with Angela, and so they will be upset.'

How strange life was, Peggy could only muse. While she and her sister had been looking forward the previous evening to the comfort of some hot tea and a sticky piece of parkin each, it was very likely that at that precise moment, and only a matter of streets away, poor Angela had been lying bleeding in the road, perhaps fighting for her life with a serious and possibly life-threatening injury. Even if she lived, perhaps it would be to face the consequences of the sort of injury that might make the rest of her life dismal. It was dreadful, and it didn't make sense. But things like this rarely did, Peggy reasoned. Although she wouldn't have said this to Roger and Mabel – they tended to steer clear of discussing much that was to do with belief and faith – it made it hard sometimes to believe that there was a God, Peggy thought. Angela was a pleasant child, and she certainly didn't deserve to be right now lying in a hospital bed far from home, that much Peggy was convinced of.

'Goodness, whatever were those children doing out at that time of night?' exclaimed Barbara meanwhile in a shocked voice. 'They would never have got away with this in London.'

Peggy didn't necessarily agree, and she didn't really think Barbara thought that either, as children in Bermondsey were often very ill behaved and out on the streets very late at night. While Ted and Barbara were strict parents, a significant proportion of their contemporaries barely seemed to notice their children, and allowed them to do pretty much whatever they wanted and when they wanted to do it, as long as they didn't ask their parents not to go out to the Jolly or for any money.

'Ah, nobutt comes out of tis reet well,' June agreed.

Peggy had already seen that Barbara hadn't been able to understand everything that June was saying as she described to them the game of spooks and what happened afterwards.

It was funny, Peggy realised, but she herself could now understand June Blenkinsop without too much difficulty, and June her, it seemed (or at any rate it was a while since they had stared at each other in incomprehension after one of them had said something), and so it showed that the accents in which they each spoke just needed a little bit of getting used to. And Barbara had already commented that morning several times about Harrogate being cold, the third time which Peggy had heard herself retaliate with one of Mabel's favourite sayings: 'There's no such thing as bad weather, only bad clothing.' It was rather as if Harrogate was having a subtle effect on her, making her quietly but indelibly a little less 'London'.

Peggy said reflectively, 'There's been increasing talk here about the evacuation, both the good and the bad. Some of the host families were horrified by the London children and how badly they behaved when they arrived – some kiddies when they got to their billets apparently seemed uncertain how to use a lavatory that flushed and thought they would drown or "die a death of cold" if they had a bath.

'There was effing and blinding, and a couple of Jewish children were put with families who tried to make them eat ham and bacon, and who got very shirty when the children refused to do so.'

In unison Barbara and June shook their heads in an identical fashion at what Peggy was saying.

'But,' she went on, 'many billets were more or less forced to take in the children. With the Air Ministry now moving up here to Yorkshire and requisitioning all the hotels, and with premium rates being paid for lodgings, as some of the banks and insurance companies are also relocating, some people think they'd be making more money, if they have to have strangers living with them, not to have the London kiddies.'

June Blenkinsop added that some locals were extremely embarrassed that a proportion of the Bermondsey school-children had been barely allowed to go to school as they were working on farms or being made to do other sorts of heavy labour, while some families had been mean and downright unkind, and others had no experience of bring-ing up children.

It was Barbara and Peggy who shook their heads in unison this time.

There was a lull in their conversation as June topped up their teacups.

'I'm sure there's been wrong, and right too, on both sides – the London and the Yorkshire. It's the government I blame most of all,' said Barbara, bringing the silence to an end. 'Really I do. And the Germans – I'm sure I speak for us all on that – as none of us would be in this position had they been content to remain in Germany, although I daresay that many of the ordinary German folk hate being at war just as much as we do. But I don't think the government thought through the intricacies of the evacuation plan anywhere near sufficiently, and nor did they do enough to tell either side quite what they should be expecting.'

The women were all quiet again.

Eventually a weary-sounding Barbara said, 'Can you show me the way to the hospital, Peg, as I'd better try and see Angela, and maybe speak to the doctor in charge. I'm sure at some point I'll have to have a word with her mother.'

Barbara and Peggy stood up and knotted their headscarves over their hair again to keep out the mardiness of the Yorkshire weather.

Peggy told June she'd be back at eleven, and then she showed Barbara the way back to Tall Trees, as she had to confess that she wasn't at all certain where the new hospital was, but she knew that either Roger or Mabel would be.

When they walked in through the back door into the kitchen it was clear that the Braithwaites had just heard about Angela's accident, and were very concerned.

Mabel said that while Roger took Barbara and Peggy over to the hospital, she would make sure that Angela's mother knew, and they could put her up at Tall Trees if she was to come to Harrogate, and in fact they could reimburse if necessary the cost of the ticket from church funds as they had an emergency fund for this sort of thing.

Roger drove Barbara and Peggy over to the hospital, and he then proved to be very effective at getting information from the doctors as to what the latest was regarding Angela's condition.

The news wasn't good – the little girl still hadn't regained consciousness, and so they were going to operate later by removing a small part of her skull as they thought there was build-up of blood that was putting her brain under pressure. It was by no means certain that she would pull through the operation, let alone regain consciousness.

Chapter Twenty-six

At lunchtime Barbara went to collect Connie and Jessie from school. She was a little early in spite of it having been quite a busy morning, what with going with Peggy to the café and then heading over to the hospital to see Angela.

If the war dragged on for a substantial time, Barbara wondered now as she waited, would Connie and Jessie get just that bit too used to all of what they were experiencing since their move to Yorkshire, such as the large houses and the sense of space? Would number five Jubilee Street seem, when they came home again, to be unbearably modest and embarrassingly hand to mouth, with the surrounding Bermondsey streets unpleasantly dirty and packed together with workers' housing, God willing, of course, that they all and their Jubilee Street house survived the war intact?

While Barbara believed with all her heart that her children were in the best place for them to be just at the moment, she thought that if the weeks stretched into months, and – a terrible thought – the months into years, it might well be the case that she and Ted would be welcoming two virtual strangers back into her home at some point.

It was a thought she'd not had before but it was one that made her feel most peculiar indeed.

She heard a school bell and she scurried back to the school gate. Connie and Jessie were amongst the first out of the building, and they skipped across the playground to Barbara, unbridled delight showing in their faces at the sight of their mother.

Barbara waved as they ran towards her. What a lucky woman she was, she acknowledged to herself, to have two such wonderful, healthy kiddies. Her heart felt an overflowing of love at the sight of them bounding happily in her direction, an overflowing that almost (but not quite) subsumed the strange thoughts she had just had as to whether her and Ted's decision to send Connie and Jessie away to another home might in fact be storing up trouble for the future.

The children each hugged her tightly. The twins had never been so demonstrative when living at Jubilee Street but Barbara supposed that this more emotionally charged behaviour was a symptom of their unsettled feelings since the evacuation.

The close clinches felt natural, though, and, it had to be said, just as nice for Barbara as for the twins as the three embraced in a little Ross family circle, with none of them caring a jot as to who saw them or who might think the children too old for such molly coddling.

Barbara then walked Connie and Jessie towards the busiest area of Harrogate, promising that in a little while they would have something nice to eat as a special treat – maybe even some ice cream too! – and then perhaps they could go to the cinema if they could find a suitable matinee.

But first they had to have The Talk, she said. The Talk about the scrumping. The children's faces shifted from a look of excitement at the promise of ice cream to something more brooding.

Their mother saw Connie and Jessie look at each other meaningfully. They had clearly known that something such as this was coming but, understandably, neither looked very enamoured of the idea.

The day wasn't too nippy now, and so at Barbara's suggestion the three of them made themselves comfortable on a slatted wooden bench in a park as they watched the occasional bird hop around on the grass.

'Right,' she began, bringing her mind back to the unwelcome task in hand, 'who out of you two is going to be the brave person who can tell me exactly what went on that got you into trouble and put your Aunt Peggy into such a tailspin that it made her feel poorly?'

Neither child said anything.

'I'm waiting,' said Barbara gently but firmly after quite a long while.

'Mummy, it's been horrible.' There was a distinct note of anguish in Connie's voice as she broke the silence. 'It was scary, and bad.'

'We didn't want to do it,' said Jessie more plaintively. 'We didn't mean to do any harm or to get into trouble.'

'Mummy, can we come home with you?' said Connie.

'Please, Mummy,' echoed Jessie.

Barbara put her arms around each of the twins' shoulders

and drew them close. Their small resigned sighs told her they realised that she was comforting them but the answer was no, they weren't going to be coming back to number five Jubilee street with her on the train – they had to stay in Harrogate and to make as good a job as they could of settling in to a new way of life while the war went on.

Barbara gave them some time to get used to the idea, and then as the children seemed reluctant still to come out and say clearly to their mother precisely what had gone on in the orchard, she patted their shoulders in encouragement, and gradually they began to open up.

Tommy, it turned out, had been the ringleader, and it had all been his idea.

He and some other lads had already been waging a war of hate on Larry, in part as Larry had been allocated the bedroom of the older brother of one of the other boys (this older brother had already been called up, but with the cruel logic of children it seemed to the younger one left behind that somehow Larry was to blame that this younger brother hadn't been promoted to the better bedroom, even though Larry hadn't said or done anything to provoke such an outcome), a feeling exacerbated when the younger brother had tried to insist within an hour of Larry's arrival that he should move into the older lad's bedroom and Larry could have his old room but his mother had put her foot down most firmly, refusing to give in to her son's pleas no matter how he framed them.

Before long these children, orchestrated by Tommy, had also taken a dislike generally to the thought of 'their turf' being invaded by the 'brats' from London.

And so not only had they beaten Larry up right after he arrived in Harrogate – this group led by Tommy had been, it was now clear, the boys who had pounced on Larry close to the compost heap he'd been sent to take the vegetable peelings to on his very first evening at his billet, and Tommy had been the first person to land a punch apparently – but on other occasions they had urinated in his bed, and they'd hidden his clothes (Barbara wondering if this had led to Larry losing the slip of paper that Peggy had given him just after he had arrived in Yorkshire).

For these misdemeanours poor Larry had been punished soundly by his host family, much to the delight of Tommy's gang, with the result that subsequently they had gone out of their way to make Larry's life a misery in every way they could think of for getting on now for two months.

Larry, much more used to being an aggressor than a patsy, had been at a complete loss to know how to handle such vile treatment by children the same age as he, and he had found himself cowed and unhappy as a result.

Somewhere along the way Tommy had told the local lads he routinely bossed around – he was well known as a bully, Aiden had confided to Connie – that he was widening the offensive to include other children from London, beginning with Jessie and Connie, and so he had hatched the plan to do with scrumping the apples in the field that the scientists had been monitoring. It had seemed a golden opportunity to get up to some mischief, for which the Bermondsey evacuees would take the blame.

'Mummy, I really don't think, though, that Tommy knew how special the field was, or what the response from the scientists was going to be, or that they would have guard dogs,' said Connie, who sounded to Barbara's ears as if she were trying very hard to be fair and grown up. 'I thought there was something wrong with the idea at the time, but I couldn't work out why. Tommy seemed friendly at first when we arrived, but I didn't trust him ever, and I thought that if Jessie and I went along with it for a little while, then he might get bored and lose interest in trying to make us do what he wanted. And if he didn't lose interest, I was certain that in that case I could beat him at his own game. But it turned out that I never got the chance.

'Tommy said that he knew where gangsters lived in Bermondsey, and if we didn't do as he wanted on this and every other day that he chose, if he felt like it, he would telephone the gangsters to send them to Jubilee Street and that it would end up that we'd never see you or Daddy again as your bodies would be thrown in the River Thames with your throats cut. I believed him as he said it just as if he really did know these gangsters, but now I feel silly for believing him. He said he was going to come with us to the apple trees and so why would we feel worried unless we were real babies, and that in any case there was nothing for us to be scared about.'

Now Connie had started talking there seemed no holding her back. 'But there was – it was awful, Mummy. Tommy kept making us go back to that orchard to climb over the wall again and again. We tried to stand up to him and then he said he'd hurt Peggy's baby when it came if we didn't keep agreeing to do everything that he told us to do. He kept making us go back, even if it were only to chalk silly marks on trees or climb them or draw rude pictures on the road that's down the middle of one of the fields. I tried then to threaten him back and it didn't work, not like it did when I stood up to the big boys in Bermondsey, as Tommy just stood and laughed at me, right to my face, telling me that Roger and Mabel wouldn't believe me if I went running to them, and that we wouldn't dare to say anything to Peggy because of what he had said about hurting the baby.

'And then I tried taking Tommy's toys for ransom and he said some very rude words back. I didn't understand the meaning of any of the words but I knew they must be very bad when he called me a troll and a tail and a shicer and a sheeny. Worse was to come when Roger then heard me yelling them back to Tommy, and he told me he was very disappointed in my language and then he made me apologise to Tommy, as he thought I was teaching those words to Tommy rather than the other way round, and so I knew just how bad they must have been.'

'Tommy looks so good, and he sings in the choir, and his parents are nice,' Jessie picked up the thread. 'At times he's been nice to me and I think he likes it that we can play together in his room, but then he just wakes up one day and he's odd for the whole day, and he'll say that terrible word beginning with F, and all the time nobody at Tall Trees seems to see it. He's horrible as well to Bucky and now Bucky won't go near him. He's a scallywag and a tearaway, and he does exactly what he wants.'

Jessie's voice made it clear he was battling tears now. 'None of us wanted to go scrumping, and of course Larry and I weren't talking so that was bad anyway, and Angela came along too after a while, which made Tommy worse as he was showing off to her. After that he made Larry be there, which Larry really didn't want to be. And I'd spent such a long time thinking how much I hated Larry and how badly I wanted him to have a horrible comeuppance, then when I saw Tommy be as mean as he was to Larry, it made me feel funny and as if I'd been thinking bad things about him, which I had, and then they were coming true.

'Then Tommy was furious on the day we got caught as he had problems climbing over the wall into the field with the apples as his trousers got caught on the barbed wire, and in a temper he pushed Larry off of the top of the wall, which is when Larry fell down – it were a long way – and he bashed his tooth and he hurt his fingers. Connie and me were already over the wall by then, and we were at the apples, and suddenly there were whistles and we could hear the dogs barking, and it was really frightening.'

Jessie was gulping for air but he couldn't stop. 'We didn't know what to do, but Tommy just got down off the wall on the other side and he tried to run away and leave us. I'd never have done that, not run away like he did, no matter what, and neither would Connie – but Tommy just didn't care what happened to any of us, and I couldn't understand that as it seemed wrong, and bad. And then this lad Aiden – he's the one Connie is setting her cap at – appeared from nowhere and he got down over the wall very quick and he helped Larry stand up, which were in the nick of time as they let the dogs out then and I think the dogs would have mauled Larry to death if he were lying down as they were that ferocious, and it was Aiden who told the policeman what had happened, and that Tommy had been there too. Aiden had been watching out for what Tommy was up to, as Tommy has a reputation and Aiden likes Connie and so he were looking out for her. Then the police dog got Larry's arm in his teeth and Larry yelled fit to burst.'

Barbara didn't like the sound of any of this in the slightest, although she was rather proud that in the midst of what undoubtedly was a very scary time, Jessie had held onto the idea that strength was to be found in sticking together. She doubted that Larry would have been badly hurt by the dogs, as surely they would have been trained to hold a robber and not to bite him, but that really wasn't the point. The point was that Jessie must have been terrified, but to try and run away in order to protect himself when other people were still left behind wasn't something that had entered his mind for a moment – indeed a cowardly reaction was abhorrent to him, it seemed, which must be an indication of a fledging bulldog spirit, his mother thought. And Connie had been brave too – she hadn't been taken in by Tommy, and she had tried to stand up to him.

Barbara drew her children close again. She was at a loss as to what to say when she thought about all the things they had just described to her. Roger and Mabel seemed so pleasant that it beggared belief that their only child, Tommy, was so ill behaved and seemed to have such a conniving and remorseless nature. He appeared to have the potential to be quite a sophisticated criminal-in-the-making.

Barbara felt in a quandary. Tommy would be coming

back from his grandmother's very soon, and then what would happen? Were Roger and Mabel simply turning something of a blind eye, or did they really have no idea as to how Tommy liked to behave? He sounded a deceitful and manipulative, cruel youngster, with a yen for pranks that were much more horrible and potentially dangerous than any ten-year-old boy should really be coming up with. But he wasn't very old and so maybe this was just a stage he was going through, and perhaps overall he wasn't as bad as Connie and Jessie patently now believed.

Parents didn't like to hear bad things about their children, Barbara knew, not least as she could acknowledge that she herself didn't care in the slightest to be told horrible news of either Connie or Jessie, and she didn't expect Roger and Mabel would prove to be any different when it came to being informed of anything less than complimentary about their own lad.

And of course the situation was made worse by Jessie and Connie being themselves caught between a rock and a hard place. The rectory was probably not the ideal billet for them long-term (although Larry's certainly sounded much, much worse), what with Tommy living under the same roof too, and there was very little chance of them finding a new billet together as the Air Ministry employees were now getting first dibs on accommodation, let alone the children managing to transfer to a billet where Peggy could also be.

Yet, if Barbara buckled and took the twins back with her to Bermondsey, that course of action was most likely to prove to be a much more dangerous and possibly life-threatening option.

'It sounds as if it has been very difficult for you both, but if anything like this ever happens again, you absolutely must tell Peggy, or else a teacher, do you both understand? Whatever it is that Tommy might say to either or both of you, or attempt to use against you in the future, even if it is something to do with the coming baby, you really must go to Peggy as your first port of call – and no arguments about that – as she is clever and wise, and very good at knowing what to do or what to say in any situation. I do want you both to remember that at all times,' Barbara said in what she hoped was a firm but calm voice.

Then she added, 'But that's enough on this subject for now. Shall we go and find ourselves some lunch? I'm so hungry my belly thinks my throat's been cut,' said Barbara with a final squeeze of the bony shoulders of her children as they nestled against her body, as a way of making the children think of happier things by using a phrase that they would remember Ted saying.

She wanted a little time to mull over these events that Connie and Jessie had told her about, and she had decided she would speak to Peggy first, and maybe she could also have a word with Aiden, before broaching a conversation about the scrumping with the Braithwaites. And meanwhile there was Angela's mother, and the condition of poor Angela to take into consideration too. What a God almighty mess she had found waiting for her in Harrogate.

Barbara thought she might need a few extra days in the town, and she wondered if that would be okay with the Braithwaites if Connie came into her bed, and Angela's mother went into Connie's. Honestly, the war was making everyone move round in larger houses as if they were playing musical chairs.

Chapter Twenty-seven

By the evening several things had been sorted.

Barbara had agreed with both Mrs Truelove when she had telephoned her at the haberdasher's, and later with a very anxious-sounding Ted (she'd been able to hear the clink of glasses and the hum of conversation at the Jolly in the background as they had talked), and then with Roger and Mabel that it was a good idea for all concerned if she extended her stay in Harrogate for a little longer.

Barbara had also talked to Ethel Kennedy, Angela's mother, who had been fetched to a vicarage near to where she lived in Bermondsey at Roger's request. The upshot was that Mrs Kennedy was going to come up by train to Harrogate the next day, with Ted standing her the cost of buying the train ticket, and Barbara taking the cost of it from the church emergency fund.

Roger and Mabel had been very obliging, saying that of course Barbara could stay a little longer, and that Ethel should definitely stay with them too. Barbara felt almost tearful at their generosity, and quite awkward too as she knew that at some point she would have to talk to them about what had gone on between Tommy and the twins. She heard herself babbling anxiously about the expensive telephone calls, saying some years went by during which she never used the telephone, not even once, but Mabel touched her on the arm to reassure her, and Barbara found herself able to stop obsessing about the cost of the calls.

Jessie and Connie, and Peggy too, were clearly thrilled she was going to be with them for a couple of days more, and so Barbara decided to concentrate for a little while on having as good a time as she could with her children and her sister.

So in the late afternoon they enjoyed a rousing game of cards, and divided into two teams for an I-Spy marathon that got everyone roaring with laughter. It seemed quite like old times at number five Jubilee Street.

'Why do you not like this Aiden Kell? Has he done something bad that you know for an absolute fact?' Barbara asked Gracie, after Peggy had volunteered to oversee the children's reading practice in the room above the stables, while Roger prepared his sermon for the coming Sunday and Mabel was out doing 'good works', which was organising something or other to do with the local Women's Institute (was it borrowing a canning machine to make sure the last of the locally grown produce from the early autumn didn't go to waste? Barbara rather thought that was what Mabel had said).

Barbara and Gracie had the kitchen to themselves and were doing the washing-up after tea, and Barbara had already broached the slightly thorny topic of Connie having sent Gracie to Coventry for a while, with Gracie laughing and saying it was all over, once Gracie had given both Connie and Jessie some chocolate that she had bought for them on the way home from the greengrocer's one day.

Earlier Peggy had reiterated Gracie's animosity towards the lad, but Connie and Jessie seemed of a different opinion as to Aiden's likeability, with Connie saying they would have been sunk without him on the final day of the scrumping, and Jessie describing him as 'all right'. Connie had obviously felt affronted by Gracie's resolute attitude against the boy as Barbara couldn't remember another instance of Connie having decided not to speak to someone, although fortunately that stand-off now sounded as if it had been neatly put to bed by Gracie.

Peggy had admitted to Barbara that she had pussyfooted hopelessly around the issue, giving Gracie several opportunities to explain her dislike of the boy, but without being quite brave enough to frame the words into a direct question and with nothing coming back in her direction as to specifically why Gracie felt so strongly. Gracie had proved a tough nut for Peggy to crack in this respect, resolutely refusing to pick up on any of the hints or opportunities Peggy kept introducing into their chat designed to encourage her to open up a little about Aiden. The most that Peggy knew was that June Blenkinsop had told her that at one point Gracie had been walking out with William, Aiden's elder brother.

Now, Barbara decided to take the bull by the horns and ask Gracie more directly about her feelings regarding Aiden Kell.

Gracie didn't seem perturbed or shocked by the question. 'I know yer Connie's keen on 'im but, pure an' simple, 'e's jus' from bad stock,' she said simply. 'In fact, t'whole Kell family's rotten t'core.'

'Jessie and Connie say that when Tommy ran away it was Aiden who help—' Barbara's words withered on her lips as unfortunately just at that moment the kitchen door from the hallway swung open abruptly.

Roger was helping one of his parishioners to hobble across the kitchen to sit by the warm range. The tottery elderly man was very chilled and more than a little drunk, to judge by the look and the smell of him, but Barbara was touched to see the gentle care with which Roger helped him towards the warmest place in the kitchen, eased him into a wooden chair, and then tenderly tucked a woollen plaid blanket around his knees before going to see if there was any tea left in the pot.

Barbara was just about to quietly bring Gracie back to Aiden Kell again when Mabel bustled in in her usual energetic albeit very slightly clumsy way, as she'd just come in from her WI canning discussions, and now wanted to sort out dividing off the yeast starter mixture from the continually multiplying master starter for the next day's bread.

With the calm of the kitchen now well and truly shattered it effectively cut short the confiding conversation that Barbara had been hoping to have with Gracie.

Barbara looked across at Gracie, who shrugged at Barbara, and then mouthed 'no good' once more in her direction.

Not much the wiser, Barbara smothered a sigh of frustration, and then she left Gracie to wipe down the surfaces as she retraced her steps back across the yard to the room above the stables to rejoin Peggy and the children.

Several hours later an overexcited and by now slightly argumentative Connie and Jessie had been persuaded that it was high time for them to go to bed, especially as they had already been reminded that they were on the early shift the next day at Cold Bath Road Elementary.

Roger had telephoned the hospital for an update on Angela – there was no change, and she would be operated on first thing in the morning – and, just like the previous evening, the sisters were sitting together in the warmth of Peggy's bed with a tray of tea and parkin balanced on their knees. They had a lot to talk about.

'Connie and Jessie finally began to talk properly to me about the scrumping when I got them from school,' said Barbara, after they had chatted about the children's school work and how thrilled the children were to have the opportunity to see their mother.

'It seems that when Tommy realised – this is my interpretation anyway – that Connie was just starting to smell a rat and perhaps not do what he wanted, then he promised he would harm your baby when it arrived, if they didn't do what he said.'

'Oh no!' exclaimed Peggy. 'What a simply dreadful thing for him to say. I had no idea.'

'I'm sorry, Peg. I wasn't going to tell you about what Tommy said about the baby as I knew it would be upsetting, but then I thought it best that everything comes out into the open,' said Barbara. 'I doubt Tommy really meant it as a proper threat. To me, it sounds like the most heinous thing he could think of that would make Connie and Jessie bend to his will. Nothing could have been further from my thoughts when I was hearing all about this, but now I wonder whether in some ways this whole sorry experience could actually become something that teaches my two a thing or two – such as not to be stupidly gullible and take things at face value, and how something can escalate very quickly into something dangerous.'

Peggy shot Barbara a questioning look.

'I think Connie was a bit too cocky in the past, as she was aware that she knew how to wrap those London bullies around her little finger, but it's been different for her here,' Barbara explained.

'With Jessie, although he went along with the scrumping, he thinks Tommy cowardly for running away, and he doesn't seem to have been left feeling particularly frightened of him or, it has to be said, Larry. Maybe I am grasping at trying to find the silver lining inside the cloud, but maybe our job – and by "our", I mean me, and you too, Peg – is to help the children all learn from what has happened in order that they don't make these mistakes again.'

The sisters ate some parkin.

'I don't think Tommy is a bad lad at heart,' said Peggy reflectively, 'as I have heard him and Jessie having what has certainly sounded like real fun playing with Tommy's soldiers, and I don't believe any ten-year-old is *that* good an actor. Certainly he's been perfectly foul and a terrible bully (nobody could deny this), but do you think that perhaps really it's mostly been about Tommy trying to get some attention from his parents?'

Barbara frowned as she thought about her sister's comments. It was an audacious thing for her to have said.

Peggy took a quick swallow of tea, and then she went on, 'Roger and Mabel seem to be truly decent people who care about those who are far less able to cope than they are. I think the generous-spirited way they have welcomed us all to Tall Trees bears full witness to that as nobody could have done more to help us settle in. But the Braithwaites are so busy with everyone else, and so it seems to me that Tommy does at times slip through the net rather.'

The sisters talked further on this for a little while, and then Barbara mentioned Aiden Kell again, saying she thought she might go to the school the next day when the afternoon session was let out, as she wondered if she might have a word with him, although she didn't want to say this to Jessie and Connie, and she was a bit worried as to how she would recognise Aiden.

'Oh, that won't be difficult in the slightest. He's a head taller than anybody else, with skinny legs and knobbly knees, and a nose covered with freckles and an absolute shock of red hair. He's impossible to miss,' said Peggy with a smile.

She added that she had never spoken with the boy but there was something about him that she rather liked the look of.

Chapter Twenty-eight

Latish the next morning, Roger and Mabel sought Barbara out as she was making a real indent into the ironing, the Braithwaites having flatly refused to accept any money for her keep while she was in Yorkshire, and so she had been trying to subdue a mountain of clean but unpressed washing that she had found stacked in a tottering and precarious pile on the scullery draining board as a helpful surprise for them.

Peggy was over at June Blenkinsop's café for her daily lunchtime stint on the till, and Roger had already telephoned the hospital to ask about Angela, but she wasn't out of the operating theatre yet. Her mother would be arriving in Harrogate on the early evening train.

'Ahem.' Barbara looked up as Roger cleared his throat rather tentatively. He paused and then Mabel, who was standing just behind her husband, gave him a fierce look, although he couldn't see this as she wasn't in his eyeline, and then what looked like a sharp prod with a finger, and so he went on more boldly, 'Mrs Ross, er, Barbara, I wonder if we might all have a word together about the incident with the apples and what our children got up to?'

'Yes, good idea. Actually, I had been going to suggest the same myself, although ideally I had wanted to have a word with Aiden Kell first,' replied Barbara, who felt a sudden lurch far down in her belly as she knew that they were about to embark on what would potentially be an extremely tricky conversation where it would be very easy for either side to take offence. And so she added, 'But before we go into any of this too deeply, I would like to say how very grateful I am to both of you for looking after Connie and Jessie so well, and my sister too of course, and so that stands no matter what we might be about to discuss or say to each other.'

The three of them looked at each other rather awkwardly, and Barbara realised that Roger and Mabel felt uncomfortable about what Tommy had done and probably therefore weren't going to be turning a blind eye to his misdemeanours with the sort of 'boys will be boys' platitudes said by them to her that some parents might have employed. She decided to take this as a positive sign.

'We're very happy to be able to help you and your family in any way that we can, as wartime does, we like to think – and Roger reiterates this in his sermon every Sunday – mean that we all need to be pulling together, and not against each other. We hardly have the words to say how very sorry we are that there has been some trouble amongst the children, not least as I think that your twins and our Tommy are still a bit too young to grasp the meaning of the sense that we are all in this together and so they must put any petty tiffs aside. I can't help but blame me and Roger for not keeping a closer eye on the children,' said Mabel.

'I think Peggy blames herself too for what happened, although I've told her she mustn't, especially as I see now that I should have taken more time to talk through what she had to look out for with the children, as although of course she knows Jessie and Connie well, she doesn't have any children of her own yet, and obviously the signs that something might be wrong might be very small at first. I'm cross with myself as well for not making sure my pair knew absolutely that they shouldn't do anything so stupid, or so bad,' said Barbara, who had nodded along in agreement with Mabel's previous comments.

'I mean, I had told them they were to be good and not get up to any mischief, but I don't think I appreciated quite as much as I should how difficult it might be for them to integrate into new surroundings and a whole group of new children of their own age. The more I think about what it must have been like for them all, the more I suppose that this sort of thing is more likely to be the norm, much more so anyway than for the children all to love meeting each other and thereafter play together as nice as pie.'

Roger gave vent to a soft harrumph that Barbara took to be a sign of approval of both his wife's and Barbara's comments.

Then Barbara said, 'In fact, and I don't know your views on this, but I was thinking that should you not bring Tommy back home right away to Tall Trees? It might be better for all if he were here, don't you think? And a good idea to make this happen while I am still here, no? After all, at your side is where he belongs, especially when he can be in such a lovely home as this rectory obviously is.'

Roger shot her such a warm look that Barbara could see how he would have built up for himself a very loyal congregation.

'I think our Tommy has been very, very naughty indeed. Extremely naughty, in fact,' said Roger, indicating with a wave of his arm that the three of them should sit down around the kitchen table. 'Hopefully Tommy will have learnt his lesson now, and if he hasn't, I shall do my very best to make sure he understands, now that everybody has cooled down a little, how he can't behave like that in the future or treat people as he did. It's not a, er, er, humane way of going about things. Hopefully, he won't dare to use that terrible language he said directly to me – if I hadn't heard it myself, I would never have believed he could be so coarse.'

Barbara thought that Roger had been going to say Christian instead of humane, but had stopped himself in an effort to broaden the meaning of what he was saying.

'I'm not saying my two were angels either. I do think they must shoulder part of the blame for things going so far,' admitted Barbara, deliberately using the word angels because of Roger's faith. She knew the more united she was with Roger and Mabel, the less opportunity there would be for the children to transgress again, not least as they would see all the adults around them being similarly firm on how they should behave.

She added, 'Both of you should know that I am going to say to my twins that they must recognise that their behaviour led to things going as far as they did. They know that Ted and me are very disappointed in them over this.'

Mabel said that she and Roger had been wondering if perhaps they themselves had been concentrating too much on pouring their energies into things going on outside Tall Trees, and not enough into being parents for their son, and that it was likely to be within the realms of possibility that Tommy, to some degree at least, had been trying to get them to think about him.

Barbara thought this was similar to what she and Peggy had been asking themselves too.

Mabel then said that if this were the case, it also very likely meant that she and Roger hadn't perhaps been paying enough attention to Connie or Jessie either, although she supposed that they had felt when the evacuees had first arrived that it would be Peggy who'd be keeping an eye out for them.

Barbara agreed that a mistake had been made in the adults not sitting down in the first day or two of them all coming together and working out the best way of doing things, but looking back, it was easy to see how this had occurred as none of them had had any experience with how evacuation worked, and so the Braithwaites and Peggy, and herself and Ted, had tried their best but, understandably, didn't really have much to go on as to what the pitfalls might be.

There were always so many people wanting Roger's and her help, Mabel elaborated, and it was very difficult to say no and to turn somebody away from their front door in their hour of need. They just hadn't got the knack of doing this, although plenty of clergy certainly had, which meant that they had even more to take care of and sort out, as often they were also dealing with people and things that came from outside Roger's parish.

But this took up a huge amount of time and was very tiring too, and there were times in the evening when she and Roger had been guilty of just wanting to put their feet up while they listened to the news on the BBC and then enjoy a little music on the radio for an hour or two, rather than having to check up in great detail as to what Tommy might have been doing during the day.

Mabel's voice dipped as she confessed that they could see now that what some people might describe as a lax attitude had been an error of judgement on their part, as Tommy was without a doubt too young not to have more guidance. This had been brought home to them very clearly by the shocking levels of animosity Tommy had shown the London evacuees, and then Roger had been very hurt in the personal sense when Tommy had stood bold as brass directly in front of his father and sworn like a navvy at him, using words that neither Roger nor she would care to repeat.

Roger reached for Mabel's hand, and she ran her thumb over the top of his hand. They looked very resolute, and as if they were going to work very hard at making sure that in the future things would be much smoother and more thought out, and that they would make their plans bend around Tommy a little.

Barbara reminded the Braithwaites of what she had said earlier. 'I suggest that Tommy comes home as soon as possible, and I stay for a couple of days after he's back, and we just watch and wait, to see how the children adjust to one another again. The first sign of trouble and we can think again and take any steps that are necessary. But it could be that everyone is a bit older and wiser now, and that somehow having gone through such a sticky patch will mean that the children can forge a better relationship with one another, and shall be able to muddle along together.'

The children weren't nearly so excited to see their mother when they saw her standing at the school gate as they had been the day before when the bell rang and they were let out for the day.

What a difference a day makes, Barbara thought, as she watched them what could only be described as amble across the playground loosely in her direction as Connie chatted to some of her friends and Jessie listened in.

Barbara felt much better following the talk with Roger and Mabel. Maybe, of course, the situation between the three children at Tall Trees had gone too far to be resolved easily. But even if it had, it didn't look like there were too many acrimonious feelings still swirling about, at least amongst the adults involved, and that was most definitely a good thing.

Once Connie and Jessie finally reached Barbara, she told them immediately as they stood in the same spot where the previous day they had been extravagantly hugging each other, that she was expecting them to be extremely grown up as it was probable that Tommy would be coming back to Tall Trees very soon.

The happy expressions on the faces of each twin tightened slightly and their shoulders lifted a little in tension.

Barbara took care to keep her voice as calm as possible. 'Listen to me closely. I'm not going to tell either of you exactly how to behave when Tommy does come home, as I think you two are old enough to work this out for yourselves, don't you?' She smiled at the children until they almost looked like they agreed with her proposition.

Then Barbara spoke more seriously, taking turns to look at them both very meaningfully. 'But you each might like to think before Tommy arrives back about the meanings of words like "sorry" or "going too far" or "new start". What, however, I will insist of the behaviour from both of you is that nothing must happen and no words be said between you children that will upset Aunt Peggy, or Angela's mother, as she is going to be arriving by train later on today, as neither of these two should have any sort of fuss around them just now as Peggy is feeling really tired and Angela's mother will be very worried about her daughter – and this means that they both need lots of peace and quiet so that they can make themselves as strong as possible. I, along with Roger and Mabel, will see how you children get on with each other, and then we will take a decision as to whether you two can stay on at Tall Trees—'

Barbara's words were interrupted by Connie and Jessie both asking excitedly if they could come back to Bermondsey with her, queries that Barbara ignored as she continued firmly, '. . . or whether I need to find you somewhere else to stay *in Harrogate*, although if I have to do that, you two will have to get used to Aunt Peggy not being with you, as it is most unlikely I can find anywhere for the three of you. And actually, if you do have to move, it might not even be possible to keep you both billeted together any longer, as I am sure that you will remember how difficult it was for the authorities to find you a place where you could all stay when you first arrived, and so you might have to get used to the idea that you could be parted if you have to move.'

Both Connie and Jessie dropped their gazes to stare down at the ground as they remembered the unpleasant selection process that had taken place in Odd Fellows Hall, and how reluctant Harrogate people had been to take into their home twins of ten years of age who weren't both of the same sex. It was obvious that the twins didn't much like the idea of not being billeted together, especially if that witchy-looking old woman still needed to find someone to billet.

Judging by the pensive look on their faces, Barbara didn't think that for the moment she needed to say anything else on this topic to the twins.

'Jessie, I hope you're feeling strong today, as I've promised Roger that you will be able to help him sort out the back bedroom where they keep all the junk, as I think they want to put up a bed in there for Angela's mother tonight, and so you nip off back to Tall Trees and have a bite to eat, and then make yourself very useful.' Barbara spoke more jauntily as she changed the subject. 'Gracie will go in the box room to sleep when Tommy comes back, and Connie, you'll come and sleep with me and Peggy above the stables.'

'All right, Mummy,' agreed Connie, as Jessie turned to

head to Tall Trees, and then Connie said more enthusiastically as something caught her eye that made her face break into a coy grin, 'There's Aiden just going into school – do you want to say hello to him?'

Chapter Twenty-nine

By the time Barbara caught up with Peggy later in the afternoon, she had lots to fill her sister in on as they sat at the table in a deserted kitchen peeling a mound of potatoes ready to boil before mashing them together with some milk and butter as the topping for a gigantic cottage pie. The meat and vegetable filling for the pie was already waiting in a large and somewhat battered metal dish that had obviously seen many years of faithful service that was white with a blue edge around the tip of the rim.

Connie had by this point also been dispatched upstairs to help Roger and Jessie with clearing out the bedroom, which was actually proving quite a mammoth task as junk and general household debris had been collecting in it for years, and there was the muffled sound of bumps and lots of things being humped about punctuating Barbara and Peggy's conversation.

Roger had taken the gramophone upstairs, though, and this meant that the tidying efforts were also accompanied by some quite loud and jaunty music that had presumably been chosen with the aim of keeping the tidiers' spirits up.

Judging by the laughs and squeals the sisters could hear, what had started as an arduous task had now evolved into one that had become much more fun, occasionally interrupted by one or other of the children running down in one ridiculous costume or another, as the church hall's dressing-up box that was used for amateur dramatics had been discovered – Roger saying upon its discovery that everyone in the church's dramatic society had been asking themselves where on earth that had got to – and now was being freely scavenged by the children.

Peggy and Barbara roared with laughter and begged, 'No more!' when the twins entered the kitchen for what had to be the fifth or sixth time, this time as the two parts of a pantomime cow costume, complete with extravagantly sized pink velvet udders for the rear of the costume. The cow's coordination wasn't as much as it could have been to judge by the stumbling sounds on the wooden stairs as she plodded back to the bedroom where Roger was.

'When Roger and Mabel came to speak to me this morning about what had gone on, I decided the softly-softly approach was best, Peg. The reality is that the three children will either find a way to deal with each other, or they won't – and if they don't, and they can't be trusted from then on not to do anything silly between them, then it's best that Connie and Jessie be moved elsewhere, I suppose,' said Barbara when they had the kitchen to themselves once more.

'I think Roger and Mabel need to work out themselves how to deal with Tommy, and whether they need to give him a bit more attention, and they need to see how he settles back in – as personally I think that them sending him off to his granny's was too much, although I suspect that course of action was taken more because Roger was so shocked at the way he swore at him. Anyway, the Braithwaites didn't need me putting my two ha'porth in as to how they should be bringing up their son.'

Peggy said that it sounded as if Barbara, and Roger and Mabel, had handled a tricky conversation very well.

Barbara described Connie doing everything she could think of to suggest to poor Aiden that he ask her out to play either after school or at the weekend, but then the bell went and he had to run inside.

Meanwhile Larry was trying to slip out of the school gates behind them without anybody noticing. 'I made sure I caught his eye so that I could ask him if he was hungry – he really is very thin and undernourished-looking at the moment – and of course he was, and he said when I pressed him that his billet didn't really make provisions for him to have anything to eat during the day, and so I took the three of us off to lunch. Connie, I am pleased to say, made a bit of an effort with him, once, that is, I'd put my foot on top of hers under the café table to let her know that she should say something,' said Barbara.

'I sent Connie off to buy some stamps, saying I'd see her back at Tall Trees later, and in the meantime she had to trot off straight back here with the stamps so that then she could go and help out Roger and Jessie with the tidying. Then I ordered a second cup of tea for me and a glass of milk and a currant bun for Larry, who polished them off in about three seconds flat. After a while he relaxed and began to speak relatively freely – he's found it very difficult in Harrogate.'

The sisters agreed that Larry must have had a completely miserable time. Not only had he had such a public humiliation at the hands of Tommy, but without any friends to spend time with, and his family far away, even if his father could possibly be a bit fist-happy as Mrs Truelove had hinted, poor Larry could only have felt very abandoned and lonely. Aside from a good bath and haircut, and all his clothes being boiled, he also needed to be taken to a dentist, Barbara thought, now she had had a close look at the tooth that had broken clean off in the fall from the top of the wall.

Later on, after everyone had eaten, Barbara and Peggy headed over to Harrogate station, leaving Mabel overseeing the twins' practice on the piano. Peggy had learnt from her last time at the station, which was when she'd been waiting for Barbara to arrive just a couple of nights earlier, that if the trains ran late, it was a perishing cold station on which to spend long standing around on a frosty November evening, and so she made them both wrap up very warmly.

Barbara actually felt a bit too warm, and so had to walk along with her coat unbuttoned and with her gloves tucked into her pocket as she had just been giving the carpet sweeper a rather vigorous outing, running it furiously backward and forward across all the upstairs floors and carpets. She had also given the now sorted-out new bedroom – which was so tidy that actually it looked verging on the spartan – a thorough dusting, and then made up the bed with freshly ironed bed linen that had previously been hidden under a positive welter of things. As a final touch Barbara had draped a clean towel over the metal bedframe at the foot of the mattress.

Roger had clearly been bitten by the tidying bug, although not in the kitchen or in the office, as he was now sorting the generously proportioned attic upstairs into some sort of order. It was where in previous generations the servants of the house would have slept, and so the two attic rooms had a good height to them, even though part of each room had a ceiling that sloped in line with the roof immediately above it.

Roger was down on his knees cramming as much as he could of the stuff he had decided was worth keeping into crawl spaces under the eaves of the roof, vaguely attempting to keep to one side the things that might be needed soonish (the box of costumes for the dramatic society, for instance) so that he could put them in last.

He'd realised that with a lick of paint and a thorough clean of the woodwork, Tall Trees could have another two bedrooms at its disposal.

Earlier Jessie had run up and down the stairs endlessly piling into a heap a selection of things that were destined to be discarded in one of the stables, Roger having said that this pile could be added to some rubbish that had been collecting in the other stable. The next day the plan was that Roger would remove any wood suitable for burning, and anything else that looked as if it could be in any way useful, as that could, with Jessie's help, then be taken over to the church hall to be stored ready for the next jumble sale.

Guy Fawkes Night was nearly there, and so although they couldn't have a bonfire at night as this would contravene the blackout, or any fireworks, they could have a blaze in the afternoon to mark the day. Sparklers indoors would be acceptable, provided the blinds were down, and one of the grown-ups could find some sparklers to buy in one of the local shops.

Jessie and Connie were very excited about this, and were looking forward to the occasion, although Barbara told them the celebrations were going to be nothing like they had seen in London, when normally they would stand in an upstairs bedroom window at number five Jubilee Street and watch fireworks that people were letting off from their gardens. Barbara also reminded the twins that there was going to be no making of a guy or hawking it around nearby houses trying to get people to give them pennies.

The sisters hadn't been standing for more than five minutes at the station after their busy day when the train hove into view, and down from it stepped just a handful of passengers, who were nearly all men. There were a couple of elderly women who got off and several factory girls who looked only to be about twenty, but there was just one woman in her thirties, which made it very easy for them to identify Angela's mother, who they knew was called Ethel Kennedy, although they didn't really know anything more about her than that.

She looked a bit lost and confused, and was clutching tightly before her a shopping basket into which she had presumably folded a few spare clothes. Her clean but slightly tatty coat and hat didn't really look up to the job of standing up to the brisk Yorkshire weather.

Barbara extended a hand for Mrs Kennedy to shake, and then took the basket from her in order that she could carry it as a gesture of welcome, as she said, 'Good evening, Mrs Kennedy. I trust your journey here wasn't too tiresome?'

Peggy, who was just behind Barbara, dug her sister in the ribs to tell her to stop trying to sound more posh than she was.

Undeterred, Barbara continued, 'I am Barbara Ross, Connie and Jessie's mother, and this is my sister, Peggy Delbert, who has been evacuated along with the children to Harrogate from Bermondsey and so is now living up here. We telephoned the hospital not long ago and Angela is sleeping; the doctor seems pleased with how the operation went, although Angela's condition will be clearer for them to assess tomorrow. We'll take you now with us back to the rectory, Tall Trees...'

Peggy couldn't resist an upwards roll of her eyes, aimed at making Barbara talk a bit more naturally. Barbara ignored her sister.

Angela's mother seemed overawed by what was happening, although she did manage to stutter out a thank you to Barbara, and say next that could everybody please just call her Ethel?

Peggy saw how rheumy Ethel's eyes looked, and she noticed that she was very thin. She didn't seem to be in the best of health, and now that Angela was so poorly, the unfortunate woman looked to be overburdened with care and concern.

Peggy understood, perhaps properly for the very first time in her life, which she felt was odd considering how much time she had spent around children either as a teacher or doing aunt-ish things with her niece and nephew, that being a loving parent could exact a terrible price.

Children could be little imps at times, and so it was easy to forget how vulnerable they could be, and how easily life could be extinguished. But one look at the dejected demeanour of a frantic mother such as Ethel Kennedy, and there could be no mistaking how grave the responsibility of being a parent was.

Barbara was adept in situations like this, though, and while Peggy found herself tongue-tied as she felt cautious as to what would be the best thing to say to Ethel, Barbara soon got her talking about home.

It wasn't a comforting picture that Ethel described, however – the Kennedys already had one disabled child, an older girl called Jill who'd had a severe case of polio when Angela had been only a few weeks old. Jill was now so crippled she couldn't walk, and in fact she could no longer attend school, and evacuation along with the other local children hadn't been appropriate for her.

Peggy thought back to little Maggie with the leg calliper, also as a result of polio, who had been standing in line with them patiently waiting to be picked for a billet, and although her heart had gone out to Maggie at the time, now she felt that Maggie was fortunate not to have had a much worse outcome.

Ethel's sister was stepping in for a couple of days to look after Jill so that Ethel could go to Angela's bedside, but Ethel didn't feel she could be up in Harrogate for too long as it was a lot to expect a relative to look after a doubly incontinent youngster.

In addition, Ethel's husband, who was quite a bit older than her, had sustained severe shell shock during the Great War and his condition had recently deteriorated to the point that now he was unable to work, and so Ethel was the sole earner for the family. The medical costs of Jill's polio and medicine for the husband's seizures had wiped out the family financially, meaning they had been reduced to now living in two tiny rooms on the ground floor of an extremely run-down rented house that was so damp as to have black mildew on the walls, and the family had to share the outside privy and the cold water tap in the garden with the two families squeezed in above them – there was no bathroom or kitchen for any of the families.

Both Barbara and Peggy looked across Ethel to each other as she spoke, and they thought how very difficult Ethel's life must be at the best of times, and what a burden it was for her that Angela had had such a horrible but unnecessary accident.

Peggy felt very queasy upon hearing of the grave extent of Ethel's hardships. She'd known money was tight for the Kennedy family, but now that seemed as if it was the least of Ethel's problems.

Peggy's head was pounding and her ankles and fingers were uncomfortable, but she felt such a charlatan to be railing against these minor complaints, compared with Ethel who was facing much more serious problems.

Peggy felt powerless as there was so little that she or Barbara could actually do to help Ethel. What Ethel needed was a clean and suitable place for her and her family to live, and a decent amount of money coming into the family's coffers each week, but that was without doubt a pie-in-the-sky pipe dream.

Luckily they had now arrived back at Tall Trees, where Mabel knew exactly how to deal with a situation like this. While Barbara showed Ethel the room she would be sleeping in and where the bathroom was, Peggy filled Mabel in as to the dire situation that Ethel was in.

By the time Ethel was back in the kitchen, her eyes glistening at the mere fact that Barbara had gone to the effort of putting ironed sheets on the bed and a clean towel out just for her own use, Mabel had made some tea and had warmed and plated up a generous portion of the leftover cottage pie and put it waiting on the table.

She said to Ethel that while of course she would be very anxious to see Angela, as any mother would be in her situation, the best thing for Ethel to do would be to refuel herself first, as 'Angela needs you to be strong, and you won't be if you don't 'ave something to eat – you might not feel like it, but make yourself finish it, love, as you're doing it for her.'

Once Ethel had started to eat, she discovered she had a bit of an appetite and it wasn't long before the plate had been emptied and then wiped clean with a thick slice of Mabel's bread.

As if on cue, Roger came into the kitchen and had a good wash at the kitchen sink. He said hello to Ethel, but didn't make too much of it, instead talking to Mabel about how he and the twins and Tommy, who was going to come back to Tall Trees tomorrow, it had been decided, were going together to whitewash both of those two attic rooms.

Peggy and Barbara agreed that was a very good idea, and the fact it was something that was useful was an added bonus.

Meanwhile, behind Ethel's back Roger had immediately sensed Ethel's reduced state, and as he washed his hands he and Mabel kept up a silent conversation of raised eyebrows, mouthed words and nods, that culminated in Roger giving a final decisive nod.

This clearly wasn't the first time that the husband-and-wife team had had to use a wordless semaphore to signal to each other the story behind somebody else's need.

'Not so green as he's cabbage-looking,' said Mabel proudly, as she passed Roger his coat and scarf, so that he could take Ethel over to the hospital, and then she whispered to Peggy and Barbara that she was sure that she and Roger would be able to think of a way of helping Ethel at least a little bit.

Chapter Thirty

On Friday afternoon Roger drove over to Mabel's mother's and collected Tommy.

Not too long after he left, everybody began to congregate in the kitchen at Tall Trees, as they knew they were having fish and chips from a chippie not too far away. The Braithwaites had never done this before, and Peggy and all the Rosses, and Gracie too, were looking forward to the meal as Gracie had been boasting how good the Harrogate chippies were.

Ethel was preoccupied and didn't seem to notice much of what was going on around her and so she sat by the range with her cardigan unbuttoned but wrapped tightly round her, and everyone let her be. There had been no change in Angela's condition, despite her having had what was deemed by her surgeon to be a successful operation.

Because there was no 'give' in Angela's skull bones, a bleed inside her head caused by the collision with the car had put the brain under undue pressure, a pressure that had needed to be urgently reduced. Now that the skull had been opened and the blood drained, it was a waiting game, but Ethel was trying to decide how much time she could be in Yorkshire for. Aside from worrying about how Jill and her husband were managing without her, she was very concerned that her job might not be held open for her, and it would be a disaster if she were to lose that, seeing as she was the only source of the family's meagre income. Mabel patted her shoulder in comfort at one point, and Ethel looked at her and tried to smile, at which Mabel patted her again and Ethel went back to staring at the range.

Although the fish and chips for everybody was Barbara's treat, as she wanted to give the twins a timely reminder of the old Friday fish suppers at number five Jubilee Street, it was going to be Roger and Tommy who would stop off at the chippie on the way home to collect what everybody was going to eat. Barbara had asked Roger to make sure that he and Tommy remembered mushy peas, as well as a selection of pickled eggs and pickled onions and, if they had any, some wallys and, most definitely, a bag of the greasy leftover little bits of batter from the fryer that she and Peggy had grown up calling scribbles but Gracie insisted were called scraps.

Roger's brow crinkled in confusion at the word wally and so Peggy explained that this was a pickled cucumber, and then she begged to ask for something for Bucky as most chippies had something they couldn't sell but that a cat would find tempting, and if everyone was having a Friday night treat, then it was only fair that Bucky had one too.

'Soft' was what Roger was heard muttering good-naturedly about Peggy's request as he left to go and get Tommy and the food.

Mabel had sliced and buttered a whole loaf, meanwhile, saying that if they were gannets and could get through all of that, then she had another loaf in the bread bin and so nobody was to leave the table hungry. The large teapot was warming on the range, ready for a brew to be made, and there was some fresh homemade lemon drink for the children, with Gracie having provided the lemons from the greengrocer's, and with Mabel having made it quite sweet, saying they'd better make hay while the sun shines as come the new year sugar would likely be in short supply.

What felt like a very long time later a frisson of excitement trembled across the room as the sound of Roger's car drawing up outside could clearly be heard, and Peggy heard both Connie and Jessie breathe in deeply and look up from the game of cards that they were playing with their aunt. They must have mixed thoughts about seeing Tommy again, Peggy thought.

Not too long after that, Roger and Tommy walked into the room carrying two large packages wrapped in newspaper, one for the hot food and the other for the pickled accompaniments.

Tommy's hair had recently been dampened down with water and neatly combed, and his clothes were pressed; he looked pale and chastened, and, Peggy could see, a far cry from the rather boisterous boy of not too long previously.

Mabel stepped forward to take the fish and chips, giving Tommy a smile and a wink, but no hug. Deliberately, she was behaving as if it was just as if he had only popped out for an hour or two, rather than almost two weeks.

'Come on, everyone,' said Roger. 'Time to—'

'Miaow!!' yelled Bucky with impeccable timing, having clearly got wind of the fish in the kitchen, making everybody laugh. Immediately the atmosphere lightened to something pleasantly convivial.

The ice broken, Tommy was told to sit between Gracie and Mabel, the women having worked this out in advance, with the twins on either side of Barbara at the far end of the table.

Although the conversation around the kitchen table was slightly mannered to start with, being just a little too often of the adults-talking-about-the-latest-war-update-from-the-BBC variety, as if that was all they were interested in, soon it loosened up and after a while the children were encouraged to join in too.

They'd all been quiet and subdued at first, and although they had looked questioningly at each other after a while, neither Connie nor Jessie had said anything directly to Tommy, nor he to them, but the adults had decided not to force things too quickly and to let the children adjust to one another at their own pace.

After a while Peggy got Connie talking about some of the lessons she had had while Tommy was away and some of the things that had gone on at school, and then Jessie described a football match in the playground with teams picked from each school, and then Mabel got Tommy telling everyone about what it had been like dealing directly with Mr Walton, who had apparently missed most of Tommy's spelling mistakes. (Despite his reputation for being a right stickler in the academic sense, Mabel's ancient mother had noticed them, despite her heart condition and the cataracts in her eyes, and then she and Tommy had looked up the correct spelling in a dictionary.)

This got Roger on to one of his pet topics of conversation, people who were supposed to be good at their jobs and weren't, and Gracie had a bit to say about this too from what she'd seen at her work at the greengrocer's.

Peggy talked about June Blenkinsop, saying that people thought running a café would be easy, but now that she herself had had first-hand experience of what went on behind the scenes, she was very much in awe of how June made everything she did look so easy and as if anyone could do it.

Then as the empty plates were being cleared, Roger pulled a rabbit from his hat. There was a surprise!

While everybody's attention had been occupied with Tommy's return, Roger had sneaked in behind their backs and placed in the scullery a huge steel bucket of ice cream that must have held about two pints in its inner container, ice and salt having been placed between that and the outer shell to keep the ice cream cool and firm, and so everyone had a pudding of thick creamy ice cream with some melted chocolate on top and a sprinkling of crushed roasted hazelnuts. Tommy had kept up the subterfuge but now he and his father smiled at each other that nobody had cottoned on to their ruse.

The Nut Sundae – or Sunday as Mabel insisted it should be spelt, bearing in mind Roger's profession – à la Tall Trees quickly proved to be a rip-roaring success, although when Peggy offered Bucky a little on the tip of her spoon he made a horrified face with his mouth wide open at the shock of the cold sensation that made everyone roar with laughter, causing Bucky to stalk away with an affronted flick of his fluffy tail at being the butt of the joke.

Ethel offered to do the washing-up but Mabel told her to get off back to the hospital, Gracie walking over with her to make sure she didn't get lost, while everyone else just piled up all the used crockery and cutlery on the draining board to be attended to later, as there was something more important to do: a sing-song around the piano.

As before, a selection of favourites both old and new were sung, and then Tommy finished off the musical part of the evening with another solo rendition of 'Danny Boy'.

Once again Peggy had a lump in her throat at the beauty of his singing. In fact, his singing was so lovely that Jessie and Connie both clapped enthusiastically at Tommy's performance without prompting from their mother or their aunt.

Later, over in the bedroom above the stables, once Connie had nodded off (she was sharing Barbara's bed, as Gracie was to have hers now that Tommy was back), Barbara and Peggy agreed that the whole evening had proved to be very enjoyable, and an excellent way of re-introducing Tommy back into the family fold.

The three children had seemed to take it in their stride and there had been no hiccups; Barbara pointed out that children could be very resilient and were often better at adapting to situations than the adults around them gave them credit for.

Peggy told Barbara that she had been heartened when she had crept upstairs to listen in at the other side of the door to the boys' bedroom to hear that they seemed to be chatting together quite naturally and with no underlying animosity as they rummaged through Tommy's collection of toy soldiers. She then heard them discuss the trials of their toy bears, Neville and Chocky, as when Jessie and Tommy had returned to their bedroom it was to discover that Connie had pinned pink satin bows to the heads of each little bear, one grey and one brown, as a joke, with Jessie saying, 'We'll have to get her back when we're doing the whitewashing of the attic tomorrow.'

It seemed that Connie had come up with a gesture that got the boys talking together very naturally, and so Peggy said to Barbara that she was very proud of her niece – Connie clearly had inherited her mother's skill at dealing with tricky situations, although when the children were whitewashing the attic rooms she was very likely to end up with a dab of paint on her nose for her troubles.

Quite early the next morning, once the children had break-fasted and were busy upstairs with the whitewashing that Mabel was supervising, as Roger had been called to the bedside of an elderly and failing parishioner, Barbara went with Ethel over to the hospital, and they sat by Angela's bed.

The little girl looked a shadow of how Barbara remembered her. She seemed to have shrunk somehow, and so she appeared very small and vulnerable lying there in a big hospital bed that could easily accommodate a man of over six feet, with her head bandaged and her cheeks sunken. Both her eyes were black and bruised, but Roger had warned Barbara about this beforehand as it was a consequence of the operation. There was a tube going into her mouth and another into her arm.

Barbara thought that somehow these tubes managed to look very basic yet also somehow highly sophisticated, and that she didn't know how she would have borne it if she were looking down at either Jessie or Connie lying there in front of her in the same way.

Ethel seemed of sterner stuff, though, as she was sitting beside her daughter with an impassive look on her face.

Roger had driven them as he could drop them off on his way over to his dying parishioner, but he made time to pop in to the hospital to see Angela. And as Barbara stood up to go and see if the doctor was available to speak to them, she heard him ask Ethel if she would like him to say a prayer at Angela's bedside. Ethel nodded, and Roger bent his head.

Personally she wasn't at all sure as to the value of prayers at a moment like this, but then she remembered how fortified she had felt when she and Ted had knelt down clumsily on the day that war had been declared, and she thought that if Ethel found comfort in what Roger was saying, then that had to be a good thing.

The doctor, who was a youngish and rather dashing man called Dr Legard – so much so, in fact, that Barbara suspected he had the pulses racing of many a young nurse – had some other people in white coats with him when she tracked him down to an empty ward where he seemed to be talking about how the hospital beds would be set out. But he was happy to have a word with Barbara, saying that he had just been discussing Angela's case with his junior staff. Barbara thought he didn't really look old enough to have junior staff, but she supposed he must be very bright if he were already the main doctor at the hospital.

Dr Legard explained that head injuries were tricky at the best of times, with some people being able to function very normally after a heinous injury where they might lose, say, even a quarter of their brain, while other people were unlucky to die after no more than a gentle bump on the head.

As far as they could tell, Angela's bleed to the brain had stopped, and so now they just had to wait to see what happened.

'Might she just slip away in her sleep?' Barbara asked, and Dr Legard admitted that that could happen, although of course he very much hoped that she wouldn't. Angela was breathing unaided and that was a good sign.

Then he added that sometimes it helped if the ill person's family and friends read to a patient in a coma, or just spent time talking to them about ordinary things.

At his last hospital he had seen some amazing recoveries, and the important thing was that everyone just had to keep strong in spirit and hope for the best. Nobody could see a brain repairing itself, but he'd witnessed enough to be damn sure that that would be exactly what Angela's would be trying to do right at this very moment.

Barbara went back to the bed and held Angela's hand as she said quietly, 'Angela, this is Barbara Ross, and I hope you know it's going to be time for you to wake up soon. My twins Connie and Jessie will be wanting to play with you, and so you had better get a move on as it will be Christmas shortly and you won't want to miss all the Christmas carols or the orange you'll have on Christmas Day, now, will you?'

Later, Ethel announced that it was time for her to go home back to Bermondsey. Much as she wanted to stay at Angela's bedside, she had Jill and her husband to think about too, and she was worried about losing her job if she didn't go in on Monday.

She left on the afternoon train, although not before Roger and Mabel had told her they had had a word with a vicar in Peckham whom Roger had trained with, and remained friendly with since. This vicar was going to visit the Kennedy household to see what might be done, and he had said it was possible that he might be able to help Ethel's family relocate to accommodation that was more suitable for them, and perhaps her husband could start helping out in one of the mobile soup or pie kitchens that were being run to service factory workers, as this would mean that the family would very likely be able to get any leftover hot food at very discounted prices, which would surely help with the family's budget.

Ethel's smile of gratitude knocked years off her, and Peggy could see that once she would have been a very attractive woman, back before a hard life and not enough money had taken their harsh toll.

Chapter Thirty-one

As she walked back to Tall Trees after seeing Ethel off at the station, Barbara had an idea.

She thought the children should go and see Angela too. It would be a salutary lesson to them about how precious life is, but it could also be useful as they could talk to Angela about school and their favourite foods, and having sparklers for Guy Fawkes tomorrow.

The minute she got in Barbara telephoned the hospital, and as she waited to be put right through to Dr Legard, she thought how incredible it would be if one day she and Ted could afford a telephone in their very own house. She felt as if she had hardly been off the telephone over the past week or two, and she was very grateful to Roger for never once having mentioned this, as she knew it would be very expensive. Just as she was considering how she could make it up to him and Mabel, there was the sound of Dr Legard picking up the receiver.

He said that Barbara's idea was unorthodox, and in fact very likely he wouldn't have allowed it in a couple of days' time as the hospital would be opening its doors proper on

Tuesday, and by the end of the week the wards would be filling up and so he wouldn't have wanted to be trying something like this for the first time then. Still, he didn't think it would do any harm, and if the children proved they could be responsibly behaved while in the hospital, perhaps they could visit Angela regularly if they wanted.

Therefore, if Barbara wanted to bring a group of children (there were to be no more than six, mind, and each time one of them spoke to Angela, they must remember to say to her which one of them it was that would be speaking to her) over at one o'clock the next day, they could have half an hour at Angela's bedside.

Barbara told Mabel what the doctor had said, and she said that Tommy should definitely go, and there'd presumably be Jessie and Connie of course, but what if – and this was a radical idea – Larry and Aiden made up the other children? Mabel would go to the hospital with Barbara, and it could be a good way of them seeing how the land lay with the children.

Barbara thought about it for a while, and then said Mabel's suggestion sounded like an excellent plan.

But should they make a bit more of the day and also ask the children back to Tall Trees afterwards for an hour or two? The bonfire was going to be lit in the middle of the afternoon anyway as it was the fifth of November, and so the children could toast marshmallows – June Blenkinsop had given Peggy some to bring home – and then light the sparklers, which Peggy had managed to buy in a shop tucked away in a back street that June had directed her to.

Barbara and Mabel embraced the idea and began to get quite carried away.

There was the sound of a telephone ringing over in Roger's study across the passageway.

After a while Roger came into the kitchen with an unusually shame-faced expression.

In a trice everyone had that clench inside that told them they might be about to hear bad news.

Roger smiled when he realised this to show that he wasn't bearing bad news, and then he said he had been speaking with the billeting officer on the telephone. The couple that Angela had been billeted with had decided that if and when Angela was released from hospital, they didn't want to have her back with them. They weren't used to children or nursing anyone who was poorly, and so they didn't feel they were the right place for Angela, assuming that the little girl would one day be well enough to be released from hospital.

They'd also been approached by the Air Ministry who had been enquiring about Angela's room for one of the administration staff from the team that were being relocated to Yorkshire from London, and so they felt that giving the room to an adult was a better way of them helping the war effort.

'Mabel, I know I should have discussed this with you first, but as me and the billeting officer were talking, I found myself offering to have Angela at Tall Trees if, God willing, she improves enough to be able to come out of hospital. And, slightly in the spirit of your favourite saying of "might as well be killed for a sheep as a lamb", then I heard myself raising the question of Larry, and it turns out his mother wanted to have him back but the father wouldn't have him, and the upshot is that after terrible shenanigans he's definitely to stay in Harrogate as long as the rest of St Mark's is here. Er... and so anyway, the result of that is there's a possibility they'll move him from where he is and send him here too,' said Roger in a contrite tone.

'Roger!' Mabel exclaimed. 'I only say "might as well be killed for a sheep as a lamb" when I'm talking myself into having a second slice of cake or a fifth biscuit, and not about something like taking not one but possibly two children in who each have a lot of problems. Really, Roger, you are the absolute giddy limit at times!'

Roger looked appropriately hang-dog, but then Peggy detected a humorous twinkle in his eye.

Clearly he knew that there was no way that Mabel would put her foot down about this when push came to shove, Peggy realised.

Immediately she thought of her own marriage. She loved Bill, of course she did, but they had never had quite that intuition about each other that Roger and Mabel clearly did, and this made Peggy feel sad. Bill's contact with her had dropped off again, and although she was cautious about getting too cross as it was possible he was in transit for foreign manoeuvres, she couldn't help but feel disappointed. If she were Bill, she knew she'd be making very sure that Peggy felt loved and supported by her husband, that was for certain. And she really couldn't say that Bill was being very loving at all just now, Peggy fretted.

Peggy realised there was a resounding silence echoing

around the kitchen as Mabel and Barbara and Gracie thought further about Roger's words, their eyes flickering between each other as they considered the implications of a very troubled boy and a very sick girl joining the household. Peggy tried to remember what Roger had been saying, but depressing thoughts to do with Bill kept intruding and so she gave up and let the silence envelop her.

'The more the merrier, eh?' Roger said at last, and then quickly made himself scarce.

Chapter Thirty-two

Connie was easily persuaded to suggest to Aiden that he might like to come to the hospital the next day with them all, and she only took a little bribing to go over to where Larry was billeted to have a word with him too, and give him the note that Barbara had written him so that Larry could be reassured when he read it after Connie had dropped it off (Barbara told her not to encourage him to open it in front of her) that it was a genuine offer, and not something bad that Tommy was instigating and that he would take the fall for.

Dear Larry,

The doctor at the new hospital says that Angela might get better more quickly if she is talked to, even though she will probably stay sound asleep while visitors are with her. You have known her a long time, and you could speak to her about St Mark's and Bermondsey. Connie and Jessie will go too, as will (I hope) Aiden. Tommy will be there too, and so will his mother. (And if there is one thing I have learnt over the years, it is that it is nearly always better to see someone you have had a problem with rather than ignoring them – it reduces the size of the problem, I promise.)

After we have been to the hospital, there is going to be a Guy Fawkes bonfire in the afternoon back at Tall Trees, with sparklers and toasted marshmallows. Connie is going to make some toffee apples this afternoon, and there will be lots of sandwiches, and so we need YOU to help the other children eat all of this up! You can tell your billet that you will home by six o'clock, and that I can be telephoned if they want to discuss the invitation.

Come to Tall Trees for 12.30 tomorrow and we can all walk over to the hospital and then back home to Tall Trees together. I hope very much that you do feel this is something you can do.

Regards,
   Barbara Ross (Mrs)
   Telephone: Harrogate 4141

In fact, Barbara wasn't certain in the slightest that Larry would feel like coming, as it would be a brave thing for him to do, but Peggy reassured her sister that it was a good letter. She added that she thought he might actually do it, the lure of the food described probably proving stronger than Larry's lingering dislike and suspicion of Tommy, especially as Barbara had cleverly made it clear that the outing was to be chaperoned and so the children wouldn't have much, if any, opportunity of being mean to Larry.

Also, agreed Barbara, if it really were the case that Larry might move over to Tall Trees to billet there at some point – a possibility that hadn't yet been mentioned to either the twins or to Tommy, or indeed to Larry – it would enable him to have a positive first experience there, as well as give the grown-ups a low-key chance to see how it might work in practice. Aiden being there too would be a good thing almost certainly, as Larry knew Aiden had tried to look out for him, and had stood at his side when the dogs were let loose, while Tommy knew that Aiden's actions had highlighted what a cowardly bully he had been that day in the experimental orchard and would most likely be quite chastened around him.

'You might have to keep an eye on Gracie for me as you know she's not a fan of Aiden, but I'm sure she won't give you any problems,' said Barbara.

Peggy rolled her eyes dramatically at her sister. 'Okay, if you insist. But I am going to have a nap in the afternoon while you are at hospital, and so don't expect me to get up until you all get back.'

Everyone was on time the next day, and Larry did decide to come, with the other children acting as if this was quite normal as they pretty much ignored him, and he them, although Barbara thought this was better than if they had made a fuss of him, as in that case he would probably have run a mile. His clothes appeared to have had a bit of a spruce-up as they didn't look quite so ratty as when Barbara had bought him lunch, although Larry himself was still just as grubby and lank-haired although, thankfully, not too ripe–smelling.

The party set off and Connie and Aiden walked side by side, with the three boys in front of them. Barbara and Mabel followed behind the children, and Barbara was gratified to see that by the time they'd reached the end of the road Jessie was making manful efforts to talk to Tommy and Larry.

She was pleased that she had made Ted string the conkers that had been hardening over the winter from the previous autumn above the mantelpiece at number five Jubilee Street, and that she had remembered to put them in her handbag.

Jessie had been really delighted when he saw them and now he was promising a proper conker knock-out challenge when they got back to Tall Trees, with Tommy and Larry soon both looking keen to take each other on in a sanctioned manner, although Jessie boasted his big sixer would beat all comers and that Tommy and Larry could have the pick of only the ones he didn't like the look of nearly as much.

At the hospital, there was quite a flurry of activity going on amongst the staff, as they were admitting a few early patients already, as well as trying hard to get the rest of the wards into tip-top shape ready for the bigger influx of patients that would begin on Tuesday. Men dressed in blue overalls were constructing bedframes and there was the occasional sound of swearing when something went wrong or a clang if a metal spanner was dropped.

Angela's bed had been moved from the ward into a small side room so that she could have some privacy, and the children fell quiet when they saw her lying stock still. They all stood in a row as they looked at her, transfixed.

A nurse came in and walked to the bed where she set about rolling Angela onto her back from where she had been propped on her side, with banks of pillows preventing her from toppling one way or another, explaining to the children that patients in a coma had to be turned over in bed regularly to prevent bed sores.

Barbara had already tried to tell the children what Angela would look like as she lay unconscious, but it was clear that the reality proved quite a shock and that it brought it home to them how very seriously she had been hurt.

When the nurse had finished Barbara went over and held Angela's hand, saying in as cheerful a way as she could, 'Hello, Angela, it's Sunday today, and it's Barbara Ross speaking to you. In fact, it's Guy Fawkes day, November the fifth, and so there's not long to go now until Christmas. I have brought Connie and Jessie to see you, and Tommy Braithwaite, and there's also Aiden Kell and Larry with us too.'

There was absolutely no response. Barbara had told the children already that this was going to be the case, but that her stillness and her silence didn't mean that Angela couldn't hear and possibly even understand what was happening around her. And so this meant they must take great care not to say anything upsetting about her or to her that they wouldn't say to her face if she were awake just like any of them were.

Jessie spoke first, telling Angela about the conkers, but then Connie interrupted, saying that that was the last thing Angela would be interested in, and if Jessie didn't shut up about his one-ers and his sixers, then Angela would decide to stay asleep forever and then who would blame her?

Mabel cut in before the conversation took a turn for the worse with, 'Angela, I'm Tommy's mother, Mabel. What about if we all tell Angela our favourite jokes? Who has got the best joke? I think it might be me as I have got a goodie: What do you call a one-eyed dinosaur?'

'Do you think 'e saw us!' called Aiden, and then he remembered that he hadn't said who was speaking, and so he added 'Aiden'.

Tommy got in next with, 'Tommy Braithwaite. What goes oh, oh, oh?' There was the obligatory dramatic pause, before Tommy gave the punchline: 'Santa walking backwards.'

That took a little working out, but then was treated with the equally obligatory groan from the other children.

'This is Jessie. I've always liked this one: why are bananas never lonely?'

'Connie. Everyone knows that one, Jessie – it's because they go around in bunches.'

More groans. And a couple of sniggers by this time.

So it went on, with the children becoming less inhibited as they tried to outdo each other, and the jokes worse.

Eventually Larry joined in. 'Larry here, Angela. Why don't ducks tell jokes when they are flying?' There was the usual pause. 'Because it would make them quack up!'

Dr Legard had crept into the room behind them, not that anybody noticed until he gave a giant guffaw behind them that made everybody jump. 'Quack up! Hello, Angela, it's Dr Legard; you and I are old friends now. I've got one – how do you ask a tyrannosaurus out to lunch?' Silence. 'Tea, Rex?'

Barbara thought the doctor's joke very funny, although as she said to him as they all trooped back to Tall Trees – the doctor having been persuaded to join them for hijinks as it was his day off and he had just popped into the hospital to see what the children were talking about with Angela – it could well have been merely the cumulative factor of the previous jokes that had tickled her funny bone so much by the time of his T-Rex joke.

'I doubt it, Mrs Ross,' he said, 'as I am naturally hilarious. Or at least I think I am as the last lady I was walking out with would say to me with regularity, although perhaps in a crosser way than ideally one would want, "Don't make me laugh…"'

Barbara gave a small exhalation of humour, and then looked at Dr Legard.

Out in the open air, he was revealed as a little older than he looked in artificial light, as she could see the odd grey in the short hair above his ears, and his twinkly eyes had the beginnings of laughter lines around them.

They arrived at Tall Trees to find Roger just about to light the bonfire, and Peggy sorting a mountain of sandwiches onto plates. Gracie was trying to unstick the toffee apples from the roasting pan in which Connie had left them to cool and harden after she had put wooden sticks into the apples and then dipped them into the hot toffee mixture.

'These'll take yer teeth oot so watch it!' Gracie said grimly, as she released the final one from the pan and placed it on a large plate with the others. 'Especially you, Larry, as you can't afford to lose another.'

Larry looked a bit shocked, but then laughed, and everyone laughed along with him.

Dr Legard – who asked everyone to call him James, if they would – said he'd give thruppence to the first person who could run twice round the perimeter of the garden, after which he would be the judge of the conker competition, and by that time the bonfire would be roaring away, he bet.

Peggy raised an eyebrow in Barbara's direction, and Barbara raised a corresponding eyebrow in reply.

The doctor's startlingly good looks hadn't gone unnoticed, clearly, and nor had his natural way with the children. And the sisters were pleased that they could still do their lifted-eyebrow trick they had perfected as teenagers to show they'd noted both of these attributes.

Meanwhile Roger looked at the bonfire. 'One can only hope,' he said, 'but I do like a challenge,' as he gave one of the lower pieces of wood a nudge with his foot to push it deeper into the pile of kindling.

Chapter Thirty-three

It was one of those rare afternoons where everything goes exactly to plan, and a very good time is had by all.

The bonfire burned without too much coaxing – well, Roger only had to light it three times – and then it gave off that lovely autumnal smell.

It even got hot enough to toast the marshmallows, which the children enjoyed. The sandwiches were soon all eaten, Larry proving to be especially hungry (which was no surprise to Barbara or Peggy).

Tommy won the running race fair and square, and the doctor's threepenny bit, and although Jessie was last, it wasn't by such a long way that he looked in any way silly or feeble.

Larry relaxed to the point that he could chat away to Aiden and Jessie, Jessie only being the slightest bit wary. Barbara thought as she kept an eye on proceedings from a discreet distance that of course her son would still remember vividly Larry's uncalled-for rough-housing of him over the summer, but that Larry no longer looked like the type of person who was going to revert easily back to that sort of behaviour. He looked older and more experienced, and as if the hard knocks life had dealt him the previous few weeks had made him think differently about things.

Larry and Tommy didn't speak to each other, but they didn't seem to be giving each other antagonistic glances, and so Barbara and Mabel agreed quietly that was a good thing, and probably about the best that could be hoped for at this stage.

Tommy disappeared for a while, and when he returned he was clutching a paper bag of gobstoppers – he told everyone that he had run down to the shop at the bottom of the road, and although it had been closed he had told the shopkeeper who lived above by shouting through the letter box that he had 'a gobstopper emergency', and so he had come back with five of the largest he could find, one for each of the children, even Larry.

Larry clearly hadn't expected this, but everyone took pains to ignore his elated grin.

Gracie was on her best behaviour too, and she unbent enough to have a word or two with Aiden, who seemed quite happy to talk with her.

As dusk started to fall, the sparklers were lit in the darkened stables, and then James said that he would walk Aiden and Larry home as they each lived roughly in the direction of the hospital.

'But before I do,' Barbara heard him say to Peggy, 'may I have a look at you in the light inside? I think you seem a bit flushed and peaky-looking.'

The next day Barbara was due to catch the early train back to King's Cross in London, after which she would jump on the number 63 bus as this would take her pretty much all the way home.

Connie and Jessie walked to the station on either side of their mother to see her off.

At breakfast they had both tried again to persuade Barbara that it was time for them to come home to number five Jubilee Street, but Barbara was steadfast in her refusal.

Connie had added, 'Mummy, I get so homesick I can't sleep or eat.'

Barbara said she was sorry about that. But actually she had been thinking that both Connie and Jessie had grown taller since they had been in Yorkshire. And she'd seen the size of the generous meals at Tall Trees they were eating, remember, and knew precisely how much Connie was eating, while furthermore she had had to be quite firm with getting each of them out of bed on more than one occasion, and so Connie was pushing it to claim sleeplessness and hunger.

Connie gave in gracefully.

'Well, it was worth a try, Connie. Wasn't it, Mummy?' said Jessie.

Barbara nodded at her children that certainly it had been.

As they waited for the train on the platform Barbara said to her children, 'I'll try to come back as soon as I can to see you, and with a bit of luck Daddy will be able to make it too. Now, remember you are both to work hard at school, and to be good. Be friendly to Tommy, but if he oversteps the mark in any way, you must tell a grown-up, ideally Peggy. Be nice to Larry too, and run as many errands as you can for Peggy. And if you can do all of that, then I shall be very proud of you both. Remember, both of you, that me and your father love you very much.'

She hugged and kissed each of her twins for a final time.

Barbara climbed up onto the train and closed the door to the carriage, and then lowered the window and said once more, 'Be good, you two!'

Jessie and Connie stood close together as they watched the train chug away, with tears obviously threatening and Barbara calling back, 'No fighting between you both, remember. And you, Connie, not too much kissing of that handsome Aiden Kell either!'

'You've kissed him!' screeched Jessie, his tears forgotten, and he punched his sister none too softly on the arm.

'No, I have not!' Connie shouted emphatically.

'Have.'

'Have not.'

'Have.'

'Have not.'

'HAVE!'

'HAVE BLOODY NOT!!'

Barbara hadn't yet got fully out of the station, and the view she had of her children was them starting to shove at each other with furious looks on their faces.

This wasn't at all what she had had in mind when she had been trying to leave them with a humorous comment for them to remember her by, when she had been anxious to divert them from being tearful or demanding they get on the train with her.

The fact that they had each shown until that moment

that they were trying to be brave and grown up had been unbearably touching, Barbara felt, and she had been very proud of them.

Until she had seen them pushing each other, that was.

The children realised this too when a toot from the train's whistle reminded them why they were in the station, and so they looked over at the train to see their mother shaking a gloved fist in their direction as a silent rebuke.

In a trice they were waving cheerily at her, butter-wouldn't-melt expressions instantly plastered across their faces.

The last thing they glimpsed of Barbara was her shaking her head in disbelief, although whether at their abrupt naughtiness or their quick transition back into good children was open to debate.

To make amends for their poor behaviour which, even by their standards, had degenerated very quickly into a skirmish, as Connie and Jessie walked home they discussed a plan to go and see Angela every day if James would allow it.

They could go either in the mornings or the afternoons, depending on whether it was an early or a late week for them at Cold Bath Road Elementary, and Larry could come with them too if he didn't have anything better to do, and maybe Aiden and/or Tommy would also come at weekends.

They thought Dr Legard might agree to their visits now that Angela was in a little room on her own.

It was agreed that they should have a word with Peggy, as she was going to be seeing the doctor over at the hospital so she could broker their request to him on their behalf.

Chapter Thirty-four

Later that day, Peggy found herself having to go through quite a thorough examination at the hands of James.

When the previous afternoon he had had a word with her inside the warmth of the kitchen at Tall Trees, and then gently manipulated her growing pregnancy bump before talking through dates with her, he said he thought Peggy should have a more thorough examination, and it should be sooner rather than later.

He could do it at the hospital, if she wanted, and as she was now, hopefully, a friend, he would do it 'off the books' so she wouldn't have to pay.

Peggy agreed, asking too whether he could also give Gracie a once-over as she was just starting to talk about finding a midwife for the birth of her baby, which she was planning would be at home at Tall Trees.

Peggy and Gracie went to the hospital the next afternoon, with Gracie knocking off work a little early in order to give themselves enough time that they didn't have to hurry. Gracie was dealt with pretty quickly, and came out beaming, saying that all was well and her baby looked like it would arrive early in January.

Peggy didn't like hospitals or going to the doctor much and, left on her own to wait in the corridor while Gracie spoke about her pregnancy to James, she felt herself getting more and more het up, and so she wished Barbara had been able to stay in Harrogate for a little longer as she really would have appreciated her sister being with her. She had an inkling there was something for her to be concerned about, although she understood that Ted and Mrs Truelove needed Barbara, too, just as much as she did.

Peggy had been fortunate enough to have had very good health as a child, but when she and Bill hadn't been able to conceive a baby very easily she had had to endure some very unpleasant examinations, that had also eaten greedily into her and Bill's 'rainy day' funds, and so she knew that to a large extent this was why she felt so anxious right at the minute.

She tried to breathe slowly and to think nice thoughts about Bill, but it didn't really work.

When Peggy went into the examination room, James was writing in a file, but he looked up from under his floppy fringe and welcomed her with a pleasant smile and offered her a glass of water. His white coat was crisply ironed and he had hung a stethoscope around his neck. He was just as friendly as he had been the day before at Tall Trees when he had been helping all the children make the most of the impromptu Guy Fawkes party, and he made it clear immediately that this was just a friendly chat for which there would be no payment required. Peggy had been feeling rather anxious on that front in case she had misunderstood him the previous afternoon, and so managed a small but tense smile of thank you back.

She was relieved to see that he had a female nurse in the room as a chaperone, as on some of her infertility examinations she had felt very awkward if she were alone with a strange man performing an intimate examination. Bill was the only man who had ever seen her naked or who had touched her, and so Peggy was wary of male doctors.

Her blood pressure was taken by the nurse – it was much too high, although Peggy already expected this as she had a low-level feeling of dizziness most of the time now – and then after she was asked by the nurse for her pre-pregnancy weight and vital statistics, she was weighed and measured, and then told she would have to give a urine sample before she left the hospital, and so she might like to have another glass of water.

When Peggy said how trim she was ordinarily the nurse said she was envious, and that Peggy would find that breastfeeding would help her regain her old figure in no time. Peggy snorted – she felt like an elephant these days, and it was hard to imagine just how lithe she had been only a year earlier.

In a matter-of-fact voice, James asked Peggy to remove her cardigan and blouse and tweed skirt, and also her stockings, indicating a screen which she could stand behind to do this. Then he made her lie on the bed in just her petty, immediately covering her up with a cotton sheet, after which the glands in her neck and under her arms were gently manipulated, and bright lights shone into her eyes and mouth. He examined Peggy's hands and her feet and ankles, here and there pushing his fingers quite hard into her bloated skin, and he asked her a lot of questions about her previous examinations when she had been trying to get pregnant, her age and usual health, what she was eating and drinking, and if her hands and feet were always swollen and when she noticed they were at their worst. He asked about her headaches and any feelings of nausea. Lastly he felt her tummy for what seemed like a long time. His touch managed to be firm but gentle at the same time, and his confident manner gradually helped Peggy to relax a little.

He asked if Peggy would mind if he got several of his junior doctors in too to have a look as he was always keen to widen their experience, but he would be with them all the time, and of course he would call a stop to proceedings immediately if Peggy got too tired or was in any way distressed. James was being very kind and so she nodded even though now she had once again a growing feeling of real unease, even though she realised that he was very important at the hospital and she was therefore lucky he was taking such an interest in her. She knew the attention he was expending on her was really because until the hospital filled up with injured servicemen he wasn't yet as busy as he surely would be, and for the moment, he had the time to think about her. It was a reassuring feeling, and Peggy almost wished he would stand still beside her for an instant and place a comforting hand on her brow.

James asked the nurse to get her a cup of tea (and one too for Gracie who was still on a seat in the hall outside as she waited for Peggy), and he added that he thought there might be some biscuits in the cupboard above the little gas ring that heated the kettle.

Left alone for a few minutes, Peggy felt unbearably exhausted despite her anxiety, and she suddenly dropped deeply asleep. She was awoken a little while later with the rattle of the nurse putting the cup and saucer containing the tea on a trolley beside her bed, and a plate with three digestive biscuits beside it.

James came back with two colleagues, who did more or less the same examination, and also quizzed Peggy closely about her dates and headaches.

At last Peggy was told she could get dressed, and when she emerged from behind the screen it was to find that everyone had now gone, other than James, who was once more writing notes at a desk that had been positioned against the wall.

'How are you feeling now? You did very well and were exceptionally brave,' he said with another smile. 'But you are bigger than you should be for this stage of your pregnancy, Mrs Delbert, and this is not a good sign as it can sometimes make the baby feel unhappy, and the mother too. I'd like you to spend the rest of your pregnancy in hospital on full bed rest so we can keep an eye on—'

'Peggy, please, Doc... er, James. I can't possibly do that, no, not at all. I just can't do that! I'm needed at Tall Trees to keep an eye on the children, and June Blenkinsop needs—'

'Peggy. Peggy! Listen to me.' The doctor's voice was kindly but firm, and there was something about it that stopped in its tracks the rising hysteria that Peggy was allowing herself to give in to. 'Peggy, that baby needs you too. I understand your concerns, but you cannot go on as you are. This is a baby you and your husband have longed for for many years, and so let's all do our best to bring it into the world happy and healthy, with you being kept in the best of health you can so that you can go on to have other babies.'

Where *was* Bill when she needed him?

Peggy felt very alone and frightened, and she realised in a depressing moment of clarity that Bill had never quite been the rock that she had hoped he would be.

He had good qualities, yes, and they knew each other so well.

But if she thought of Ted, or Roger, she knew that they would both have made sure a pregnant absent wife didn't feel quite so alone. While she didn't expect Bill to write every day, she did want his short missives to offer more support and comfort than they had done so far.

Peggy looked unhappily across at Dr Legard, who was now looking up something in a fat, wide-spined reference book. He had offered her more reassurance than Bill had done since they had been parted.

She glanced down at her distended midriff and her swollen insteps that she had only just been able to cram into her good shoes. The sight of what she could see of herself was nothing less than pitiful.

Try as she might, she couldn't prevent an avalanche of tears, and quickly James left the room – well, a man would do, wouldn't he? – while the nurse slipped in and quietly began to organise what looked like bandages and lint dressings. Peggy was grateful the nurse didn't attempt to talk to her.

Soon after that, Gracie and Roger were in the room with her, the doctor having telephoned Tall Trees in the hope that somebody was there who could come and collect Peggy and Gracie. They helped Peggy stand and then waddle unseeing out of the hospital and over to Roger's car outside, past all the nurses stocking up the medicine cabinets and the handymen putting the beds together and hanging curtains between them. In the car park Roger and Gracie gently helped her onto the red leather passenger seat as tears softly slid down her cheeks.

Peggy didn't remember anything of the drive back to Tall Trees, she was so upset.

She was helped to lie down on a sofa in the front room, with two blankets over her, and she fell asleep. When she woke it was to find that a bed had been made up for her downstairs.

Dr Legard had been very firm, apparently. Peggy was to stay in bed until the baby was born. She could do it at Tall Trees, provided Roger and Mabel felt up to it. But if James caught Peggy up and about for any reason at all, she would have to be hospitalised. James had sounded so grave that although Peggy couldn't remember much of the detail of what he had said, she knew she must do as she was told.

Over the next few weeks she wrote a barrage of notes to Bill. He sent two short cards back, saying he was missing her, but that she must rest in order to look after the baby and so he didn't want to distract her by writing too much.

25th November 1939

Dear Bill,

Thank you for the card – it sounds as if you are rather enjoying yourself. I hope that Reece Pinkly isn't leading you into bad ways! I'm really hoping too that things haven't got too hairy for you as I guess you may well be abroad by now, and that you are being sensible and are making sure you look after yourself. I miss you, but it helps if I know that you like a lot of the people you are away with. I'd hate to think of you far from everything you know, with only some nasty people around you for company.

I am still confined to bed – it's been nearly three weeks now – and I am getting used to it, and everyone is rallying round looking after me and being very kind. In fact, they are all so kind that I am not allowed to do anything for myself.

I did feel better once it was agreed that I could be looked after at Tall Trees rather than having to go into hospital, as I think that would have been more expensive than we could have afforded.

Mabel and Roger have been simply wonderful. They have moved me into a small parlour next to Roger's study and I sit up in bed like Lady Muck all day. The door is kept open during the day so that I can hear what is going on (I can see into the kitchen if the kitchen door is open, and I'm close to the downstairs cloakroom), and Roger has brought the radiogram into my room and put a huge pile of books beside my bed, so I listen to the radio a lot, or I read (I had never, to my shame, read *Middlemarch* before, but I have really enjoyed it). They all come and sit around my bed later so that we can listen to the news from the BBC together, even though from all accounts not as much seems to be happening as we expected, although I daresay more is going on behind the scenes.

June Blenkinsop, the nice woman with the café where I was taking the money at lunchtimes, comes over in the evening too when she can, and Roger has rustled up a few mothers-to-be who also come and sit with me, and we knit and drink lots of tea together, although actually I find that I am losing the taste for tea – Mabel tells me she was just the same when she was pregnant with Tommy as it tasted foul to her.

So, although I am doing very little in the physical sense, the days are passing quickly as I am actually pretty much kept on my toes what with one visitor or another.

I do feel much better with the rest, to be honest, as my ankles have gone down and my headaches are much less now, and actually I am losing a bit of weight, which seems to be a good thing as you wouldn't believe the size of me. Baby seems happy too as he or she has become much more active; I didn't realise how little he or she was moving, but now I am quite often jolted awake with what feels like a well-aimed kick. James, the doctor from the hospital who started this off, tells me I should drink a half-glass of water every hour and now I'm used to this – I find I get thirsty if I miss an hour, and sometimes I have to have a whole big glass even if I have been drinking regularly.

I didn't know, though, that it is possible to sleep as much as I do, and I am quite proud of the fact that if I want a nap then I seem able to sleep through anything, even the children playing – we have Larry here now, which brings the total up to four – or (horror!) practising their scales on the piano.

There's not much news otherwise, aside from the fact that Larry had to have three baths before Mabel thought that he was properly clean, and that food rationing is going to be starting in the new year. It all looks very frugal. Bacon, butter and sugar are definitely going to be rationed, and then later it looks like meat, tea, cheese, eggs and a host of other things will follow. Mabel is looking very down – she loves to cook. And she loves her food!

The children are going to see Angela almost every day – I thought they'd get bored of it, but they don't appear to have – but she is still unconscious, although James was telling me they think Angela is less deeply under as they seem to be getting a little response from bright lights being shone in her eyes. In fact, the news that the coma might be lifting slightly is making the children extra keen to talk to her as they feel they might be instrumental in her improvement, which actually may well be the truth.

Although poor Angela has been having a terrible time, in fact as far as the other children are concerned, she has given them something that they can pull together about, as they plan things to talk to her about. Yesterday Connie and another girl from her class were allowed to play Angela a recorder duet, although Larry told me afterwards that Jessie had said that if there were anything that was going to make Angela want to stay asleep it was going to be enforced listening to a recorder duet, but I think that was more to pay Connie back for once saying in front of the others that Angela would stay asleep if Jessie didn't stop telling her about his conkers!

Sorry that this letter is more about things that aren't happening than things that are. Everyone is trying to keep me in the middle of what is going on, but actually I don't think very much is happening these days.

All my love, darling Bill.

Peggy

PS I asked Roger to put my bed by the window as although this is chilly for me as the icy glass really does funnel the cold inside, it means that when my bedroom door is shut for the night and my light is out, I can open my curtains and stare up at the sky. I think of you a lot when I do this, hoping against hope that now and again we are both looking at that North Star at the same time.

PPS Do write soon – two lines on a card is better than nothing!

Peggy had worked hard on this letter to get the right tone, and it was much longer than she thought Bill would want to read, but it had felt very comforting to write and so she had let the words pour out of her.

It was over a week before Bill replied, and then it was only with another very short note that didn't really say anything at all or even ask once about the baby.

Chapter Thirty-five

Proper winter weather came to Yorkshire on the first day in December, making Snake Pass over the Pennines impassable for days, the snow was so deep and the road so treacherous.

Bucky took up sentry position at the end of Peggy's bed, his plump little black and white face telling everyone that it was far too cold to be outside other than for him to do the necessary, after which he would hurry back inside and straight up to his warm spot on top of the eiderdown.

Peggy begged Gracie to go around the shops to see if she could find some advent calendars. Gracie managed to find four (Larry now having been installed in the box room, with Connie in one of the attic rooms upstairs, and with no apparent problems amongst the children with this latest change), and Grace had even persuaded the shopkeeper to give her a little off as she was buying so many.

Just before the children sat down to their tea, Peggy called them in to her and gave them each an advent calendar.

With a strange seriousness they opened the little

cardboard window for the first day of December to see the festive illustration underneath, Connie saying that she thought they should each make a wish to mark the moment.

Peggy was certain that Connie and Jessie wished they could go home to Bermondsey. What Tommy wished for was harder to gauge – he didn't appear, though, Peggy was relieved to see, as if he wished for anything naughty. And Larry looked as if he was caught between wishing for a less difficult father or a mended front tooth, the dentist having told him the day before that there wasn't much that could be done right now, but that when he was grown up he could have all his top teeth taken out so that he could wear a denture to restore a normal-looking mouth.

The next day the four Tall Trees children, with Aiden in tow, crashed into the house in late afternoon and ran into Peggy's room full of excitement. They had been at the hospital, and had tried to sing some carols to Angela.

James had heard their version of 'While shepherds washed their socks at night' and he had gone in to tell them that while she wasn't yet conscious, Angela was starting to make some responsive signs.

James had insisted that they mustn't read too much into this as coma patients could show characteristics that didn't necessarily lead to consciousness, but he thought they would like to know the news.

And when Gracie went over in the evening it was to report back that Angela looked less still, and almost as if she might be about to turn over in bed of her own free will.

Peggy thought a less sceptical person might feel that the wishes made over the advent calendars might have had some influence, but she suspected good medical care and the little girl's will to recover had more to do with her seeming improvement.

Gracie had a special sparkle about her these days, Peggy noticed, and when she grilled Gracie further she admitted that she had renewed her relationship with Aiden's brother, Kelvin, even though he was away fighting. All the negative things Gracie had been quick to say about the Kell family now apparently forgotten.

Kelvin Kell had written Gracie a note that Aiden had given her at the Guy Fawkes bonfire it turned out, and already there was talk of them marrying.

Peggy quizzed Gracie over whether Kelvin was the baby's father, and while Gracie didn't exactly say he was, she laughed in a coy way and then left Peggy to draw her own conclusions.

'Gracie's not one for hanging around!' Peggy said to Mabel later.

But Mabel was more circumspect than Peggy expected. 'It's probably wise for them not to wait, don't you think? She'd feel dreadful if they did, and then he died before they could spend time together as man and wife.'

It was much too cold for the children to play outside very often, especially as none of them had long trousers, and so Peggy got into the habit of getting them into her room after school, where she could supervise activities such as Christmas-card-making, with the cards to be sold at the church's Christmas Fayre, or else making Christmas decorations that would also be sold.

Connie got the point very quickly. 'Is this your way of helping us think Christmassy things, Auntie Peggy, as we won't be getting presents?'

'More or less, Connie. I don't think anybody this year is going to be spending much on presents, if anything at all.'

To everyone's surprise, Larry proved to be quite knowledgeable about Christmas evergreens, and so Peggy made sure that she asked him lots about this as she had noticed that when Larry described his park keeper father teaching him about various trees and shrubs, it seemed to have been the one positive thing that father and son had bonded over during Larry's childhood. Larry made Jessie, Tommy and Aiden brave the arctic blast for some brief trips out together, the children returning with fingers and knees blue with cold, with armfuls of holly, spruce and ivy, and once even with some mistletoe, which they then made into Christmas door wreaths or decorations for mantelpieces, while Connie used some of her hair ribbons to twist round the mistletoe so that it could be hung in hallways for cheeky Christmas kisses.

The house took on a lovely fragrant smell, and the newly made front-door wreaths were left in the cool of the front porch so that they wouldn't dry out and spoil before the fayre.

Mabel had Tommy play the piano most evenings, and

she schooled the children in a variety of carols so that they could go carol singing in the run-up to Christmas.

As Peggy wrote to Barbara, it was a reasonably content and productive time. Everybody seemed to be pulling together, and while everyone hoped they were somewhere else or that things were different, they all got a certain satisfaction in making the best of a bad hand of cards.

The Christmas Fayre was a turning point, as all the children felt for the very first time that they were actually becoming friends.

Since the scrumping, and then Tommy's return from his grandmother's and Larry moving over to Tall Trees, they had all been on best behaviour, and had been more or less intent on going through the motions of being good children.

But without them noticing it, several weeks of acting as if they were friends and making sure nobody upset anyone else somehow tipped over into real life.

On the morning of the fayre, Roger happily watched the children setting up their trestle table, which they covered with some red crêpe paper that Gracie had managed to scavenge, and upon which they then artfully displayed their evergreen decorations and door wreaths, some of which were plain and some of which had some branches highlighted with white paint onto which silver glitter had been sprinkled before the paint had dried. Connie and Gracie had been up late the previous evening hard at work making some extra Christmas cards and these were arranged along the front of the table.

'Well done, all of you, well done – you've done us proud,' he exclaimed proudly, clapping Tommy on the back, who beamed widely at his father's pride.

Connie thought how much nicer Tommy was now that Roger and Mabel were making sure they paid him a little more attention. Roger shook Larry and Aiden's hands as a thank you, and saluted Connie, and there was something so sunny on this frosty morning about Roger's smile that all of the children couldn't help but grin back. Roger then said he had to leave them as he was going to be Santa Claus for an hour, Mabel and Tommy having made him a make-do Santa suit from the roll of crêpe paper, with some sheets of ordinary paper having been painted black for his boots, belt and buttons, and his beard being an old pale grey favourite from the amateur dramatics costume box that Mabel had whitened by giving it a thorough dousing in Cussons lily of the valley talc.

Unfortunately Bucky had been nearby at the time Mabel was wielding the talcum powder in the kitchen, and he had had a sneezing fit, prompting Gracie to say she wouldn't be giving Bucky lily of the valley cologne any time soon but she might try honeysuckle. Bucky could only stare up at her in reproach, much to Mabel's amusement.

In fact, there was a general feeling of goodwill swirling about that never really left the children that day. Therefore, when Mabel said to them as she inspected their table of wares at the fayre, 'The last one to sell something is a ninny!' they all became quite boisterous in their attempts to attract the circumspect shoppers, Harrogate being well known (according to Gracie) for having people who 'knew their onions', which eventually Connie worked out meant that they were thrifty shoppers who wanted value for money.

Connie and Jessie modelled their sales techniques on the market traders they had seen in the East End, but it was Tommy who stole the show by managing to sound more cockney than they – he really was very good at a whole range of performing skills – by yelling, 'Roll up, my lovelies! Oggie, oggie, oggie! Here's some 'olly, 'olly, olly!', and then promising any lady shoppers that if they bought some mistletoe then Santa would most certainly be asking for a kiss after his glass of sherry and mince pie.

Within half an hour every wreath and card had been sold, and a bashful Larry had even been kissed on the cheek under the mistletoe by a red-cheeked elderly woman he had sold it to, who had joked that she wanted to see if the mistletoe worked on someone as old as her, Connie being unable, despite Larry's blush, to prevent herself by saying to the woman, 'You'd better test it then!', the savvy shopper duly clasping hold of Larry and delivering a smacker to his cheek.

'Thank goodness that's the last of the mistletoe,' said Jessie to Larry a minute later, and as Larry nodded the two shared their first-ever proper smile together.

It was a contented and quite spent gaggle of children who made their way back to Tall Trees to tell Peggy all about it.

Peggy laughed when she saw how tired they looked. 'It's not yet noon! You poor old things, you.'

Several days later, on the twentieth of December, the

atmosphere at Tall Trees went from ecstasy to gloom in less than an hour.

The ecstasy began when breakfast was interrupted with Roger having to go to his office to take a telephone call. He'd walked to pick up the receiver with an expression that said of course it was time the telephone rang – he was eating, and so as often as not, that was his lot in life.

A minute later he bounded out of his study, calling, 'Lo, there is good news!'

James had rung to say that Angela had woken up, and while not yet fully conscious, the signs were good, although the children should give her a day or two before visiting, just so that she could get her bearings after such a long time in a coma.

The children jumped around in happiness, even Tommy and Larry.

The sight of it brought such a tear to Peggy's eye; so that she had to reach for a hanky.

Half an hour later, the mood in the house was much less bright.

There had been another telephone call.

Mabel's mother was desperately ill, having now been taken hospital, and she wasn't expected to make it.

Chapter Thirty-six

23rd December 1939

Dearest Barbara,

Your parcel has arrived and I've got it for safe keeping in my room, as I don't want any prying little fingers and eyes trying to work out what you and Ted have sent them for Christmas!

Mabel's mother is hanging on, and so we are all starting to miss having Mabel around as she is still over with her. Gracie's cooking is best described as 'basic' – well, actually, that would be to oversell it – and Roger doesn't know one end of a saucepan from another. June Blenkinsop is having to cook us food each day – a pie usually, or sometimes a stew – and then Gracie can just about manage to boil some cabbage (there's a glut, much to Connie's horror) and turn the oven on to heat the pie. Larry goes to the café every day to collect the food from June and to take back the washed baking tin or stewing pot, and I am paying him a shilling a week to do this. Tommy and Aiden are going for an hour every other day to help June by peeling potatoes and with some washing-up, and so this is in exchange for the food she is giving to us, and Roger is paying each of them a shilling weekly. The system seems to be working quite well because I told them that if there's just one argument between the boys, their shillings will stop.

Connie wants to earn some money too, but I said she can help me with the baby and earn a little pocket money that way, and anyway, right now how would she fit some work in seeing she and Aiden are virtually welded together? Meanwhile Mabel's bread production has had to stop, but maybe this isn't such a bad thing as it looks like flour is going to be rationed, although goodness knows what those people Mabel gives her bread away to every day are now finding to eat.

I'm still in bed, with my ankles back almost, I like to think, to what they were in my heyday. James is quite pleased with me, so he says.

From Bill's last card I think he might still be in England – he's not allowed to say, but he's using phrases like 'kicking his heels' and 'it's very jolly', which, reading between the lines, I think is saying he's still on a training camp.

Roger says we're waiting to see what the Germans do, and they are waiting to see what we are up to. Tommy had to write about the Boer War at school, and he spelt it 'Bore', so Roger says this current war will go down in history as the Bore War if it goes on like this much longer.

I hope you got my Christmas card. I would have sent presents but I've not been able to get out, but you know I wish you and Ted all Christmas greetings.

I'll stop now as I have a headache, and my fingers are so awkward I'm struggling to hold my pen, but all my love as ever,

Peggy

The next morning it would be Christmas Eve, and the previous evening Roger had told the children that after breakfast they should come with him over to the church, where, along with other children from his congregation, they could help put out the nativity scene – with its little painted wooden characters denoting Mary, Joseph, the donkey that had carried Mary, the three wise men and the shepherds, the angel Gabriel and little baby Jesus in a wooden crib, who would be watched over by a variety of farm animals in the stable – so that it would be arranged and ready for a carol service during the afternoon.

For the first time in living memory, midnight mass at Roger's church was going to be cancelled over the difficulty of blacking out the high and awkwardly shaped church windows, which Peggy thought that Roger had found an upsetting decision to make.

The children seemed happy to agree to help with organising the nativity scene, although Roger told Peggy in an aside that the previous year somebody – and he didn't think it was Tommy – had arranged two of the shepherds' sheep in a very rude position in pride of place in the nativity scene, and it was only quite a way into the Christmas Eve carols that Roger had noticed, having been alerted to the fact by some chortling amongst the younger members of the church choir. Then he had to make the choice of pretending he hadn't seen, in the hope that his congregation wouldn't notice either, or else going across to the nativity scene to remove the amorous ram to a position that was less 'frisky' and thereby drawing everyone's attention to the jape. Mabel had seen the sheep too, and had had a hard time not laughing out loud.

The children were slightly at a loose end now that school had broken up for the Christmas holidays, and aside from going to see Angela, they didn't have anything much to do, other than going over to June Blenkinsop's for the food each day.

A parishioner had given the Braithwaithes a fir tree, and the children had spent an hour draping it in tinsel, and in decorating the house with some leftover holly and spruce, with some white-painted fir cones standing out from the dark green of the boughs in pretty relief.

Peggy had decided that although Barbara had sent something for the twins, she was going to say to them that they weren't to show off about this, as Larry and Gracie wouldn't be getting anything at all, and it looked like Tommy might not get anything either as unless Mabel and Roger had been more organised than they were usually, present-buying had probably gone out of the window in the run-up to this Christmas.

Peggy thought that there was bound to be some singing around the piano to mark Christmas Day, and she had got

Gracie to bring back some oranges from the greengrocer's that had been hidden under Peggy's bed, and so Christmas Day wouldn't pass without any treats, even if the twins and Larry couldn't be with their parents. Just about everywhere was draped in paper chains as the children had had competitions to see who could make the longest one, and who the quickest paper-chain-maker was.

The twins had taken it reasonably well that they weren't going to be seeing their parents over the festive period, and Peggy thought the distractions of having Larry move in and Angela showing signs of improvement had made them realise that these were trying times, and that they had to concentrate on just getting through it all as best as they could.

Immediately the last paper chain had been strung in loops around the banisters to the stairs to the first floor, Roger and Gracie went out in the dark to take a few remaining sprigs of holly and evergreens over to the church, and soon afterwards Peggy heard a plan being hatched amongst the children.

Tommy and Jessie's bedroom was big enough, just about, to have a second set of bunk beds put in it, all the children were agreeing as they sat in the kitchen icing some gingerbread men that June Blenkinsop had sent over. Aiden was sleeping in bunks at his home, but now with Kelvin away fighting, might it be an idea if the bunks, and Aiden too, came over to Tall Trees while the evacuees were here, and then he and Larry could share the bunks that would be reconstructed on the other side of the room?

Connie was the brains behind this idea, Peggy was

certain, although she played dumb when Peggy asked her about it half an hour later when Connie brought her in some bedtime cocoa.

'You know the timing of this isn't great, don't you, Connie? Mabel's mother is poorly, and with me and Gracie having babies in the not too distant future it's going to be very busy here,' said Peggy. 'And if Angela comes back to live at Tall Trees too when she is well enough, I think Roger and Mabel will feel they've got quite enough on their plate without Aiden being here too.'

Connie didn't look defeated in the slightest. 'I know all of this, Auntie Peggy. But Roger and Mabel also think Aiden is an exceptionally good influence on the other boys, and he's quite academic, so he'd be good for all our homework as we'll work up to the level he is, rather than everyone working down to the level I am at. And it would free up space at the Kells', so they could rent to the Air Ministry, and this would mean they could pay for Aiden's keep here and still make a tidy profit.'

Connie might not be good with her books herself, thought Peggy, but she had clearly taken on board a lot of Barbara's comments about money and how the war was proving to be a welcome boost to the income of some. In fact, listening to her had been remarkably like listening to Barbara when she had set her mind on something.

'I don't disagree with you, Connie, not in the slightest,' said Peggy. 'But the truth of it is that Tall Trees is not *our* house to do with as we please, and you and the other children know that. But if you are to persist in this bunks plan, if I were you, I'd wait until Christmas is out of the way before someone mentions it to Roger and Mabel. And if I were you, I'd absolutely be telling all of my friends *right now* that it isn't at all likely that this is going to happen.'

Connie gave a demure look in her aunt's direction, and said she would go and get Peggy a gingerbread man as a parishioner had just dropped some off.

Peggy smiled to herself, thinking Connie could be a cheeky minx at times.

She heard Connie say from the passageway, 'Auntie Peggy says we are to wait until after Christmas before mentioning anything about the bunk beds. She says too that she doesn't think we are going to be allowed.'

What Connie didn't realise, however, was that she was standing in the perfect place for her reflection in the hallway mirror to be reflected back onto the mirror in Peggy's room, giving Peggy full view of Connie's thumbs up and raised brows, all of which signalled very clearly that Connie, together with the corresponding silence from the boys (who were presumably signalling back at Connie just as cheekily), thought it a done deal that Aiden and his bunks would soon be in residence upstairs at Tall Trees.

Peggy had to laugh – and suddenly she was pretty certain too that the redoubtable Connie and her chums would get their way.

Chapter Thirty-seven

Peggy's sleep was broken first thing on Christmas Eve with what turned out to be a sad telephone call long before anyone had woken up, and as the telephone was ringing in the room next to where Peggy was, and Roger didn't pound down the stairs to answer it as he usually did, she got out of bed, and with it still being pitch black outside went to answer the dratted telephone, her bare feet cold on the cool of the large grey flagstones that covered the whole of the ground floor.

It was to hear Mabel's querulous voice as she told Peggy that her mother had finally passed away, Mabel having just found her still and stiff in bed, presumably having died not long after Mabel checked on her for the night, as rigor mortis had set in already.

Peggy said how sorry she was as this must be very upsetting for Mabel.

Peggy was used to Mabel sounding capable, but now she sounded very shaken as she prattled on in a quickening tempo saying that of course the timing was dreadful, as trying to get a funeral director out on Christmas Eve, when many of the roads were closed, was likely to prove nigh on impossible and it didn't bear thinking about just leaving her mother's body lying in bed over Christmas. She had been planning on coming home anyway at lunchtime as one of Roger's parishioners had offered to go and get her, as she was determined to spend Christmas at Tall Trees, even if her mother were to slip away in her absence. She had paid a nurse to come over later in the day to look after her mother, but now she could stop that, which would save some money.

Although her words made sense, and in theory their clarity suggested all was well with Mabel – or as well as it could be when a woman has recently lost a deeply loved parent – Mabel didn't sound at all like the resourceful, rambunctious woman Peggy had become so fond of. She sounded what Peggy could only think of as diminished as a person somehow, and as if she needed some moral support, neither of which one would normally associate with the ordinarily larger-than-life Mabel.

'Let me go and fetch Roger for you, Mabel. I think he's the one you need to speak to,' said Peggy in as soothing a way as she could, given the early hour as she was feeling bleary with sleep. 'Don't go away as I can't sprint up the stairs.'

She found herself able to climb the stairs to his room only very slowly. The shock of hearing that Mabel's mother had finally died seemed to be making her feel light-headed and queasy.

Peggy tapped on Roger's door and after she'd knocked a second time, he opened it dressed in Mabel's floral dressing gown, having clearly not been able to find his woollen maroon one.

'Mabel is on the telephone, Roger – she doesn't sound very good. Her mother died during the night, and Mabel is now having a few problems as to what to do,' Peggy said in a whisper as she didn't want to wake the children or Gracie.

Roger nodded as he brushed past and went swiftly down the stairs.

He and Mabel talked for a long time, he explaining that the first thing she needed to do was to get a doctor to come and certify death, as nothing could happen until after that.

Peggy got back into bed and tried to go back to sleep. But then she heard Roger say to Mabel that he would go to help her, but he would need first for his curate to take the carol service this afternoon and to oversee the nativity.

After a while there was the ding of the bell as Roger replaced the receiver, and Peggy called to him, saying if he needed her to ring the curate for him, she could do that, as that would mean he could concentrate on getting over to see Mabel as soon as possible.

Roger came into her room and said he really couldn't do that as Peggy was supposed to be on bed rest.

'Roger, I don't think making a telephone call is going to be beyond me, I promise,' Peggy tried to reassure him. 'Mabel sounds as if she needs her husband, and I can tell Tommy what has happened when the children get up.'

'Let me make a brew and I'll think about it,' said Roger. 'I do feel I'm needed over in Leeds at the minute and so you might have hit on a good plan, even if it is Gracie who ends up doing the running around.'

Twenty minutes later Roger was in the car, attempting to navigate his way through flurries of snow so that he could be with his grieving wife.

After a while there was a strange dull thudding noise from outside, and Gracie (Roger had insisted she was up and dressed before he left, and that she was on top of what she had to do with giving breakfasts, and possibly lunches, to the hens, Bucky and Peggy, as well as everybody else) and Peggy peered out of the window next to her bedside to see the telephone pole at the end of the garden had toppled sideways, presumably having been weakened by the bad weather, wrenching the telephone line into Tall Trees off the house, so that it lay like a black snake sinewed across the white of the lawn.

Peggy thought Gracie summed up their thoughts pretty well when she lifted the now dead telephone receiver and announced, 'Well, that's a reet bugger.'

While Gracie pulled on her gum boots to go and sort out the hens, Peggy tried to decide what to do.

She needed to report the loss of the telephone connection, but she wasn't certain who to do this to. In the end she decided that the curate would have to organise this, being Roger's right-hand man at the church, and with Tall Trees being the responsibility of the church.

She wrote the curate a note explaining the situation with Mabel's mother and the broken telephone line, and gave him the telephone number of Mabel's mother's house, and asked him if he could also report the loss of the line to the telephone company and say that it was very important that Roger's telephone be established as soon as possible, as this bout of cold weather had left many of his parishioners vulnerable and people needed to be able to raise him in an emergency. Peggy then said in the letter that the curate would also have to see to getting the nativity set out from where it was stored in the crypt and then oversee the children as they put it up (she would send the Tall Trees contingent of children over to the church at eleven, she mentioned) and, finally, the curate would also have to step into Roger's shoes by taking the carol service this afternoon.

Peggy explained that she was sorry to have to ask the curate to do so much and so quickly, but Roger had had no choice but to leave first thing for Leeds. Roger planned on being back at Tall Trees to take the two church services on Christmas Day, she added as a PS.

Gracie came back in from the garden with a very pink nose and a haul of only three eggs, the hens clearly not thinking much of laying in the cold weather, and she didn't even take off her coat but just turned round and went straight out again, this time clutching Peggy's note to the curate.

Connie came downstairs for a drink of water and Peggy said could Connie drink it quickly and then nip back upstairs and fetch Tommy to her, ideally without waking Larry or Jessie, and then would Connie go back to her room and give Peggy ten minutes on her own with Tommy?

Tommy came into Peggy's room downstairs with a very pensive look on his face.

Bucky hissed at him and jumped off of the bed and onto the floor; clearly the cat could still remember Tommy's former taunting, although Peggy had been encouraging Tommy to feed him as she told him that when Bucky came to associate Tommy with food, the puss would very likely start to look forward to seeing him.

Peggy patted the bed, and told Tommy to sit on it beside her. She quickly filled him in on what had happened and that Roger had had to go to Leeds to be with Mabel.

Tommy didn't know how to react. At one moment he looked like he might cry, and then the next he looked lost, and after that quite angry.

'Whatever you feel, Tommy, is fine,' said Peggy, 'as there is no right or wrong way to behave when somebody dies. Some people find themselves very angry and others very sad. Your granny was ill and she was quite old, but you have spent a lot of time with her, and so the news of her dying will make you feel a bit strange.'

Tommy looked at her with eyes seeming to be dark, bottomless pools, a-swirl with emotion.

Without a word Peggy opened her arms, and Tommy allowed himself to be comforted.

Chapter Thirty-eight

Later in the morning the children were over at the church, after which they were going to see Angela to give her the cards they had made for her the previous evening.

Gracie had set off for the hospital already to see how Angela was, and she was going to do a little shopping before coming back. Gracie liked prattling away about this and that to the little girl, saying to Peggy one evening that she got more sense out of Angela than most of the people she was used to speaking with. And that Angela now knew just as much about Kelvin Kell as Gracie herself did.

It was very cold at Tall Trees as Roger hadn't had time to set and lay the fires, with Peggy telling him that they could manage as everyone except for her was going to be going out and so he should just leave for Leeds, and she had an extra feather eiderdown that she could put on top of the bed, and so she and Bucky could snuggle up under it as they listened to the BBC on the wireless, with Gracie lighting the fires when she got in.

And this is what they did, although Peggy discovered

with dismay that soon she was finding it very hard to make much sense, if any, of what the radio broadcasters said.

The words seemed jumbled and out of order, and she was having difficulty opening her eyes.

She lay further down in bed and tried to sleep – everyone was always telling her these days how restorative sleep could be. But it wasn't to be in this case as Peggy felt very nauseous all of a sudden.

She stumbled to the lavatory, the floor tilting this way and that as she made her way along, clutching at the walls and the furniture for support, she felt so dizzy and clumsy, but once she hung her head over the toilet bowl she found that she wasn't able to be sick.

A shooting pain in her abdomen and down in her rectum made Peggy think she was perhaps about to have violent diarrhoea, but no, that wasn't the case.

She tried to urinate, but started to panic when she couldn't squeeze even a drop out.

None of this felt right. She was hot and she was cold, both at the same time, and she looked at her left hand where once she had so proudly worn the wedding ring with which Bill had pledged his love for her, to see a drop of sweat inch across her palm, immediately followed by another and then another.

Something was very, very wrong, Peggy just knew, and she was all alone in a cold house, no fires having been lit that day and with the snow deep outside, with no telephone, and until somebody came home, which she wasn't expecting for a long time yet, totally cut off from the outside world.

She tried to make it back to her bedroom, but by now she was so disorientated and dizzy that she could only crawl along the floor, not realising she was heading in the wrong direction to her room and so was moving further away from it rather than closer.

She realised she was going to vomit but there was nothing she could do about it, having no choice other than to void her stomach as she knelt forlornly in the hall.

And with that she fell unconscious, lying half on the arctic-chill flags of the hall floor and half on a none-too-clean carpet runner that was one of three lying down the length of the hall, her flimsy cotton nightie doing nothing to keep in her body heat, and with her wedding ring on its gold chain around Peggy's neck lying on the carpet beside her face, being softly brushed by each erratic breath she struggled to take.

Nearly two hours later, the children came into Tall Trees through the kitchen door.

'Brrr, it's as cold in here as it is outside,' said Connie. 'Auntie Peggy, are you awake?' There was no answer. 'I think she's asleep, I'll close the kitchen door so that, we don't wake her.'

The children started a game of ludo but their hearts weren't in it. Tommy was very quiet anyway as he couldn't stop thinking about his granny, while the twins and Larry were feeling peckish as they had been racing each other on their way back from the hospital, but they weren't used to coming into the kitchen and there not being a grown-up on hand who would, as a matter of course, ask them if they wanted something to eat.

Jessie got up and went to the bread bin, where he tracked down half a slightly stale loaf. It was shop-brought bread, very like what he and Connie had been used to back in Bermondsey, and so it was nowhere near as tasty as Mabel's bread, even when it was fresh and slathered in butter.

Still, it was better than nothing as they were all very hungry, and then Larry found some dripping in the metal-covered meat cool box that was in a dark place on the stone floor of the large pantry, and so the children set about having some bread and dripping for their lunch.

'Listen to that cat,' said Connie, and they all stopped chewing.

Connie was right – Bucky was making an almighty racket. 'I think he must like dripping – shall we give him the bowl,' which was now more or less empty, 'to lick out?'

But when Connie went to the door to the passageway to let Bucky in for a snack, Bucky refused to come in, instead running away from her down the hall yowling furiously.

''Ow odd,' said Aiden.

'Daft 'apporth,' said Tommy.

Bucky's cries sounded more frantic.

'It sounds like he's trying to tell us something,' Jessie added cautiously.

Connie stuck her head into the hall. 'Eeuw, it smells really bad out here. Aunt Peggy, I think Bucky has been sick.'

There was no reply and so Connie crossed the passage. To her horror, there was no sign of Peggy in her bed.

Bucky's yells were now verging on screams, and all the children felt a prickle of apprehension. Something felt very ominous indeed.

Connie looked one way down the corridor, and then gave such a gasp when she looked the other way.

'AUNTIE PEGGY!' she cried, and ran towards her aunt's prostrate body, which now was looking blue with cold.

The boys charged out of the room in a tumble and the children stood in a semi-circle around Peggy, taking care not to stand in the sick.

Larry leant down and peered at her closely. 'She's breathin'.'

Jessie took control.

'Connie, get as many eiderdowns as you can to cover her up as she's freezing,' he commanded. 'Tommy, you're the quickest runner by far, so you go to the hospital and see if you can find James. Larry, you know the lady in the caff best – June, is it? – you run for her. And Aiden, you run and see if you can find Gracie – she'll be in one of the chemists looking at lipstick and stockings probably. I'll stay here with Connie, and we'll look after Peggy.'

With that the boys shrugged themselves into their coats and scarves as quickly as they could, and then raced off.

Jessie watched them go and then went to get a cushion to put under Peggy's head.

He and Connie didn't dare try to move her – she looked heavy under the eiderdowns, and they thought she had fallen down onto the cold floor too far away from either her bed or a sofa for them to be easily able to get her onto something softer.

It felt as if time was standing still, and that Connie and Jessie were watching their aunt and their baby cousin die.

It was the worst feeling they had ever had.

Instinctively the twins drew close together and held hands. Connie started to cry, and so Jessie removed his hand from hers, placing a comforting arm around her shoulder instead.

All the boys found who it was that they were looking for.

Tommy and James were back first, having run all the way, not caring if they slipped and slid on the icy pavements. The hospital only had one ambulance and it was currently on a call, but James had instructed his team that the moment it was back it was to be sent to Tall Trees.

James ran to where Peggy lay, taking her pulse and then sending the children to the kitchen so that he could check under her nightie to see if her waters had broken.

June Blenkinsop arrived next, very short of breath, as she and Larry had also been running. She took one look at Peggy, who James had now carried with extreme care to her bed where he was sponging her face clean, softly lifting her hair so that he could wipe her brow and neck, and June hurried to put the kettle on to boil while she sent the children round the house to find every hot-water bottle they could. There were always a lot of hot-water bottles in a house like Tall Trees, she insisted, and they would help warm Peggy if the ambulance took some time to arrive.

As Jessie and Larry hunted through the bedrooms on the first floor that weren't their own, Tommy having galloped over to see what he could find in the room above the stables, Jessie realised that Angela's accident, and Larry's bad time in Harrogate, and the horrible incident over the apples that had injured Larry so badly (not that he had ever uttered one word to suggest he was in pain), and Larry having run so quickly to get June, had somehow diminished Jessie's suspicions and wariness of his former enemy. Larry seemed to have changed for the better, and so Jessie thought maybe he deserved a chance.

Jessie felt he had changed too. He didn't feel scared of Larry any more – it was as simple as that. How had that happened? The more Jessie mulled things over, the more he realised that he didn't feel scared of Tommy either. He couldn't put his finger on any one thing that had happened to tip the balance in his favour with either lad, but it certainly was a good feeling not to be scared any longer.

Larry looked across the room to Jessie, laughing; he had just discovered not one, but two hot-water bottles pushed down to the bottom of Roger and Mabel's bed, and even though he was terribly worried about Peggy, Jessie found himself grinning back in return.

It was a while before Gracie got back to Tall Trees as it had taken Aiden a while to find her as she wandered from shop to shop. Immediately she set to cleaning up the hall, as she knew Peggy would be mortified if Roger and Mabel came home to an ugly pool of vomit that nobody had dealt with.

At long last the ambulance arrived and Peggy was gently positioned on a stretcher. She was still extremely cold and her teeth could be heard audibly clattering against each other as she was shivering and shaking so violently.

James's face was very grave as he climbed into the back of the ambulance with her. He didn't take his eyes off Peggy, not for a single second.

June and Gracie glanced at each other with concerned looks, but they didn't dare say anything in front of the children gathered round.

They understood that without a shadow of doubt there was a very real possibility that Peggy and her baby were both going to die.

Chapter Thirty-nine

Miracles can happen.

Peggy came to, on a darkened ward, lit by a dim light from somewhere behind her bed.

Panicked, she tried to sit up as she didn't know where she was, but she couldn't move. There was something wrong with her mid-section, she could feel it. Well, feel wasn't the right word as she realised she couldn't feel anything below her arms. But she knew all the same that there was something very wrong.

She gave a wail of anguish, and immediately James sprang awake from the chair in which he'd been dozing beside her bed, and a nurse, who must have been right outside the door to the ward, walked briskly in.

'Where am I? What's happened?' Peggy said huskily, her voice parched.

'Shh, Peggy, shh,' said James, as the nurse angled her head so that she could take a sip from a glass of water. 'You gave us all a terrible fright. But everything is all right now, I promise. I had to operate so you will be feeling the effects of the anaesthetic, and if your stomach is hurting it's because I had to perform an emergency procedure called a caesarean section to deliver your baby—'

'But it's too early.' Peggy's wails became howls, exacerbated by her inability to sit up. 'I'm only just seven months gone. The baby will be too small to survive.'

'Peggy, it's okay, trust me. You are the mother of a beautiful baby girl. We've got her in another ward just now as she is small and we are checking her over and doing some tests. But so far she looks perfect, and on the big side considering you were only seven months along.'

Peggy clasped James's hands in gratitude as she sobbed hot tears of relief.

Her grip was so strong that she quite crushed his fingers.

James found himself looking intently at Peggy's hand, and at his own within it.

Today he felt he had explored somehow the mystery of life itself, and he felt humbled. It had been a close-run thing as Peggy's pulse had dipped precariously, while the baby had been still and sluggish to breathe.

James realised that he had never operated on somebody he had known, and although he had only met Peggy twice, nonetheless this had made it a very emotional experience for him, especially as he knew that while all babies were special and precious, this was a baby that was desperately wanted as Peggy and her husband had waited so long to conceive, and that to lose her would be a tragedy of untold proportions.

James hadn't expected to come to Harrogate and to find himself emotionally touched in quite this way. He thought he would be making difficult decisions, yes, surely, and guiding his team of doctors, but he knew how to do that.

It was with the quiver of that baby girl's tiny fingers as she stiffened and clutched her fists in his direction and then – joy! – had finally taken her first breath that he felt quite undone. Just thinking about it now, he felt tears spring to his own eyes, and hurriedly he blinked them away so that Peggy wouldn't see.

Such a little thing, yet so determined to survive. And somewhere in Germany right at the same minute James was pretty certain that there would be another tiny baby trying just as hard to live and breathe as Peggy's was. It made the war seem so senseless, so futile.

But as James looked down at Peggy's tear-stained face that still smelt weakly of vomit, and her sweat-tangled hair and fingers swollen to sausage-like proportions, with her chubby legs and gargantuan feet poking out from the hospital blankets, he felt blessed somehow at having shared such an amazing experience at the hands of this woman.

'Peggy,' James said softly, 'do you think that if we help you sit up, you might be able to manage a cup of tea and some toast?'

Peggy nodded, and then the nurse added much less gently, 'And after that I'll give you a going-over with a flannel and then you'll be ready to meet your daughter. You'll want to be able to tell your husband what she looked like the very first time you held her.'

'I can't wait to meet her,' whispered Peggy, as tears pooled in her eyes.

Only now, the first time for a very long while, they were tears of happiness.

Several hours later, it was close to midnight and Peggy looked much better. She was in a clean nightie, and the nurse had indeed given her a thorough wash and brush-up.

Peggy had managed to give her daughter her first feed – this hadn't proved to be easy and she wasn't sure the baby had actually taken anything, but the nurse promised that within a day or two it would feel like second nature to Peggy.

Now mother and baby were staring into each other's eyes, the baby swaddled in a snow-white blanket. These were fathomless, very wise eyes staring up at her, Peggy thought, almost as if her little girl knew all the secrets of the world already.

Peggy offered her smallest finger, and the baby clutched it purposefully, sending a dart of pure love deep into Peggy's heart.

She peered down to look more closely at the wrinkles in the baby's face. Her daughter resembled nothing so much as a small and rather grumpy old man, but this made Peggy smile. Barbara had warned her about this, and she had promised Peggy that these gruff looks didn't last long and that very quickly that impression would be replaced with something much more pleasant. But Peggy didn't care in the slightest as she inspected her daughter's frowny face. Every eyelash was clearly visible, and she had Bill's shock of hair. Her mouth was pink and rosebud, and her fingers quite long and strong. Peggy wasn't very familiar with newborns, and so she was pleased that her baby wasn't absolutely tiny, but seemed now surprisingly hale and hearty.

Gingerly she stroked a finger across a velvety cheek and then up and across the top of the baby's head. The baby's eyes squinted and then closed dozily. Peggy continued what she was doing and then suddenly the baby felt heavier as she fell asleep, the ache in Peggy's cheeks indicating suddenly that she had been smiling for a long while now.

Bill, I will love and protect our daughter with all that I have, Peggy promised her husband. I will give my life for her if need be. There will never be a baby as loved as she is. She is perfect, just perfect.

Peggy closed her eyes and imagined a starry night sky. She thought of Bill and she hoped that he was thinking of her. Together they had managed to do something extraordinary. It felt immense and very serious.

The baby gave a snuffle and a wriggle, and Peggy opened her eyes to look at her once again.

'Care for a visitor?' said somebody in a whisper. 'Well, several visitors actually. Er, a few more than several in fact.'

Peggy looked up to see a weary-looking Mabel peeping round the screens around her bed.

She smiled. 'Come on in.'

And with that Roger and Mabel, and Connie and Jessie shuffled round the screen. Then Gracie and June came in, followed by Tommy and Larry and Aiden. It was quite a squeeze but nobody minded in the slightest.

'These useless streaks o'... er, er, nuttin' saved yer life, yer shud know,' said Gracie, clearly having been going to use a rude word but then remembering that Roger and Mabel were standing alongside her. Gracie, smiling proudly, waved a hand in the direction of the children, and Peggy got the point.

Peggy thanked each one of the children individually, and said then that she didn't have the words to say to them – what a very great thing they had done. She was very proud of them, and she would write notes to all their parents to say what clever and resourceful children they had.

'I hope this little one takes after each and every one of you,' said Peggy, 'and I really mean that. You have given to me the very best Christmas present possible.'

All the children looked as pleased as punch.

'They certainly did absolutely everything that they should have done,' added James as he squeezed round the curtains. 'In fact, they couldn't have done more.'

June and Mabel asked Peggy how she was feeling.

'Happy. And sore,' she replied, 'but I can't say any more as Gracie will be going through it for herself soon, and I don't want to worry her.'

Gracie snorted, as if to say, *As if!*

Peggy reached for Mabel's hand, saying, 'I must thank you especially for coming as it's been a quite terrible day for you.'

'Life goes on, Peggy, and so seein' you with this beautiful wee girl is the very best tonic I could possibly have,' said Mabel.

Roger put his arm around his wife and pulled her close to him, saying something about births and deaths all being part of the rich tapestry of life.

'Auntie, can I tell you something?' said Connie. 'We

went in to see Angela just now even though it's very late, as the doctor said we could as she was awake and we'd been waiting forever to see you. Do you know what Angela said? It was the first thing she's said that anyone can understand! She said to us, could she have Jessie's sixer as she's keen on a game of conkers! She must have heard Jessie show off about his sixer when we first went to see her and remembered it all this time.'

'Yes,' said Roger, '*that* little fighter looks as if she's well and truly on the mend.'

What good news, they all agreed, although Jessie chipped in to say he had told Angela no *way* could she have his sixer! Which made Peggy and her visitors laugh.

Then James positioned the lamp a little closer and everyone leant in slightly one after another so that they could have a closer peek at the baby's face.

James found himself staring at Peggy's face instead of the baby's, but she was so enraptured by her baby she didn't give him a second look, and then he heard the sound of the bell used to let the medical staff know a doctor was needed and so he had to leave them all to it.

From deep within her cosy swaddling blanket, Peggy's little girl stared up at her mother with a wise expression that seemed to say that she knew Peggy already, and that Peggy was exactly the mother she wanted to have.

Peggy looked around at everyone gathered around her hospital bed.

She had made good friends in Harrogate, she could see, and so had Connie and Jessie.

Evacuation had had its ups and its downs, but right at

this very moment, there was nowhere else in the whole wide world that she would rather be.

Peggy said, 'I'm sorry, Connie and Jessie, that you can't be at home with Barbara and Ted, and that they won't be with you here this Christmas, but hopefully having a new cousin who is going to look up to you two, and love you with all her heart, is going to mean that this is quite a special Christmas after all.'

Jessie and Connie gave a good show of making the best of a bad job.

Connie said loyally, 'If we can't be with Mummy and Daddy, then of course we want to be with you and our new cousin.'

Jessie nodded in agreement.

Tommy stood close to his parents, and Gracie put a hand on Larry's shoulder so that he wouldn't feel too alone.

There was a silence that felt rich and full of love, and nobody felt they had to rush to say anything. It was a special, significant silence, one that felt enriching and fortifying.

A peal of church bells told everyone it was midnight, and therefore was now Christmas Day.

'Merry Christmas, everyone,' said Peggy, as she looked down at the baby lying contented and peaceful in her arms, and she gave a slow smile of satisfaction.

'I've got it. The baby's name. Holly! I think she should be called Holly,' Peggy said, and everyone laughed as Holly's eyes flickered open as if she agreed wholeheartedly that this was a very good name indeed.

HQ
One Place. Many Stories

The home of bold, innovative
and empowering publishing.

Follow us online

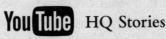 @HQStories

 @HQStories

 HQStories

 HQ Stories

 HQMusic2016